One

Monday, 30th July, 1888

By half past two the small upstairs room at the Ten Bells was full of laughter and excited chatter and the atmosphere was of unbridled goodwill. The room was furnished with chairs and tables, and a trestle at the far end was piled with plates of mutton pies and a very large fruitcake.

The July sun shone through unwashed windows but if anyone noticed, they did not care because this was a wedding party and the guests were on their best behaviour. A *real* wedding was a luxury in Whitechapel and they felt privileged to have been invited. In the opinion of all who knew her, twenty-year-old Bella Copley was marrying 'a bit of a gent' and had gone up in the world. Pretty and pert, the scrawny ginger-haired girl, who had grown up amongst them, had become 'a bit of an eyeful', as Stan put it, and had lured handsome Lloyd Massie to the altar.

Thrilled and proud, Bella surveyed the

crowded room with a heart full of joy. This, she thought, was the moment she had dreamed about since she was a small girl – a 'knees-up' to mark her wedding. Twenty minutes earlier she and Lloyd had made their vows at the altar of the nearby church, in front of all her friends and neighbours, and now they were enjoying mutton pies, ale, lemonade and gin in a familiar tavern, which had once been owned by her grandfather.

'Well, Bella, my duck,' Stan said loudly, 'you've gone and done it now! Must 'ave a kiss from the prettiest bride I ever set eyes on!'

Bella, smiling radiantly, offered her face for a bristly kiss from her neighbour, Stan Wellby. He was a coalman with a sickly wife who had stayed at home with their five children and was missing all the fun.

'Pretty, am I?' Bella fluttered her eyelashes from habit. She knew the answer to that question for she had known from childhood that she was pretty. Everyone told her so. Frizzy red curls framed her round face, big cheerful blue eyes shone above a neat nose and her pink lips were small and temptingly plump.

'Found yourself a right dandy husband, 'aven't you?' he said.

Before she could answer, Aunt Sadie waddled forward, pie in hand, and threw meaty

JACK'S SHADOW

Pamela Oldfield

Severn House Large Print

London & New York

This first large print edition published 2008
in Great Britain and the USA by
SEVERN HOUSE PUBLISHERS of
9-15 High Street, Sutton, Surrey, SM1 1DF.
First world regular print edition published 2006 by
Severn House Publishers, London and New York.

British Library Cataloguing in Publication Data

Oldfield, Pamela
  Jack's shadow. - Large print ed.
  1. Jack, the Ripper - Fiction 2. Murderers - England -
  London - Fiction 3. London (England) - Social life and
  customs - 19th century - Fiction 4. Suspense fiction
  5. Large type books
  I. Title
  823.9'14[F]

  ISBN-13: 978-0-7278-7692-8

Printed and bound in Great Britain by
MPG Books Ltd, Bodmin, Cornwall.

arms around Bella in a fierce hug. 'Trust our girl to land on her pretty little feet!' Sadie told Stan through a mouthful of pie crust. 'Always knew she'd do well for herself. Said so to her poor dead mother many a time. Afore she died, that is.' She laughed, her usual wheezy, gin-stoked laugh. 'With her looks, that girl of yourn'll go far, I told her. And now look at her. It brings tears to me eyes to see her so happy.'

If the truth were told, Sadie's tears were partly for herself because she had once been pretty and was now shapeless and unlovely. She had wasted her early promise as a dancer by a lack of discipline. Later, too many men and too much food and drink had been her undoing.

Bella preened as those closest to her obeyed her aunt and looked her over. Bella wore a dove-grey skirt and jacket which her husband had bought for her (second-hand but it fitted her very well), a choker of pearls he had given her as a wedding present, and a brand new straw hat trimmed with red and yellow daisies. She held up her hand with its slim wedding band and thought that, given the chance, she would refuse to change places with Queen Victoria herself. Not that the Queen was all that lucky, she amended, for she was getting older and still grieving for Prince Albert, but she *was* rich and lived in a sort of palace with lots of servants.

Lottie, Bella's cousin, said, 'Give us another twirl, Bella!'

Four years older than Bella, Lottie had the same blue eyes but was thinner, with wavy auburn hair and a nervous, restless manner.

'Mrs Massie to you!' Bella reminded her with a grin as she slipped from the stool and obediently spun round to show off her finery. Grains of rice flew everywhere. Laughing, she glanced up and saw her new husband watching and blew him a kiss, which provoked a ragged cheer from the guests. At the sight of Lloyd Massie, Bella felt breathless, for she loved him with all her being and had made her vows with great earnestness and a heartfelt sincerity. Lloyd – with his dark hair and moustache – was, for Bella, the dearest, most wonderful man in the whole world and she was the lucky woman who had caught his eye. She would love, honour and obey him for the rest of her life, she told herself – *and* give him plenty of beautiful children.

They could afford to have a large family because Lloyd was a wealthy man and had inherited money from various members of his family. He had an important job as a private investigator, wore a suit to work and had his own office. Bella knew she would die for him. He was good-looking with grey eyes and smooth brown hair, which he parted in the middle. At thirty he still had all his teeth and a trim, boyish figure. How, she thought, could any woman resist him? She knew how lucky she felt to have been chosen by him when he could have had any woman he wanted.

Lottie, clutching the posy Bella had carried, cried, 'More twirling, Bella! More! More!' and waited open-mouthed for a repeat performance.

Aunt Sadie tutted. Taking Lottie's arm, she gently steered her away. 'Poor Bella will be dizzy if she keeps spinning round,' she chided.

Sadie was one of three sisters. One had given birth to Lottie after a difficult birth which slightly damaged baby Lottie's brain and there had never been another child. Four years later, Bella had been born to another of the sisters but her mother, unmarried, had died in the process. Sadie, wedded to drink and a little on the wild side, had never married and felt unprepared to take on the motherless child, so Bella had been brought up with Lottie, and when Lottie's mother died, Bella remained to care for her vulnerable older cousin.

The shabby house in which they lived in White Street, Whitechapel, had been owned by Lottie's father. When he died of tuberculosis he left the house to Bella on the understanding that she would always care for her cousin. A grimy three-storey building, it had a shop at ground level, which sold second-hand clothes, and two flats above it. Lottie and Bella lived on the first floor and an elderly Hungarian couple rented the top flat. The rents were just enough for Bella and Lottie to live on.

Lottie's excitement abruptly gave way to deep anxiety as she looked at her aunt. 'I didn't mean to make her dizzy! I didn't, I didn't! Truly I didn't!'

'That's all right, Lottie, love. I know you didn't.' Sadie patted her arm soothingly. 'Now sit yourself down and have another pie, there's a good girl.'

'I don't want a pie. I want a piece of the wedding cake. I do! I really do!'

'Then you must wait for the bride and groom to cut the first slice. That's what happens at a wedding. You wait there and I'll fetch you some more lemonade.'

Sadie pushed her way through the boisterous crowd and reached the bar.

Jon, the barman, leaned towards her confidingly. ''Ere, Sadie,' he whispered. 'Who's the woman in the doorway? Nobody seems to know her.'

Sadie looked. A young woman with lank dark hair was leaning against the door, clutching the handle as though for support. Her face was very pale and her eyes appeared to be bloodshot. Her clothes were neat and of reasonable quality but she had pulled a shawl up and over her head so that it partly hid her face. She was staring round the room as if in search of someone.

Jon said, 'Friend of the groom's?'

'Not very likely. He hasn't invited anyone.'

'So who is she?'

Sadie shrugged. 'A nosy parker!' she said. 'Or maybe an "unfortunate" come up from downstairs in hopes of finding a client.'

Although poor herself, Sadie, with her single attic room in Thrawl Street, knew herself to be far superior to the many desperate women who inhabited the surrounding streets, selling their bodies for a few pence to pay for an overnight bed in one of the common lodging houses. The Ten Bells was a popular haunt for the local streetwomen who bought their gin there when they had a few pence to spare and Sadie had recommended the upstairs room as a suitable venue for the wedding 'knees-up' celebrations.

'Nah!' Jon shook his head. 'A cut above the likes of them by her clothes. And not bulky enough, if you know what I mean.'

Sadie laughed. 'You'd know, would you?'

'I'm serving 'em downstairs most nights,' he explained. 'The drabs wear all their clothes at once, poor miserable wretches.'

'All their clothes at once?' She frowned. 'What you on about, Jon?'

'Course they do. Where else do they put

them? They've got no homes, most of them. Layers and layers, they wear, even in summer. Oh yes!' He tapped the side of his nose. 'I know. All them petticoats. I can spot 'em a mile off!'

'What's it worth not to tell your missus?'

'What? Me? I wouldn't touch one of them with a barge pole, I'm telling you.' He grinned. 'My old girl's worth ten of them. Why should I waste my money on a scrabble in a back alley when I've got what it takes in me own bed!'

Sadie glanced back at the woman in the doorway. 'Well, she's not one of our lot,' she said. 'Maybe she knows the groom. I'll ask her.' Ignoring the lemonade, she pushed her way towards the door but by the time she reached it, the woman had disappeared. Still curious, Sadie glanced out of the window in time to see her hurrying away, head bent, the shawl pulled over her despite the hot July sunshine. With a shrug, Sadie collected her gin and Lottie's lemonade and rejoined her niece.

By this time people were beginning to cry 'Speech!' and Lloyd stood on a low stool to address the guests. 'Ladies and so-called gentlemen!' There was laughter from the women and groans from the men. 'I'm sorry my best man didn't turn up. The silly beggar's probably lost his way. It's a good thing I still had the ring.'

Lottie whispered, 'Doesn't he talk lovely.'

Sadie nodded. A bit of a toff, she admitted a trifle enviously. He certainly put Bella's other admirers in the shade. Put their noses out of joint too, without a doubt.

Loud laughter followed Lloyd's last comment and he continued. 'Anyway if he had been here he'd have said I'm a damned lucky man to win the hand of such a sweet and beautiful young lady but I know that already and so, I guess, do all of you.'

Stan Wellby shouted, 'Hear, hear!' and others echoed him.

Lloyd went on. 'If my parents had lived to see this happy occasion my mother would have taken to Bella at once. My father would have said, "At last!" He'd been urging me to find a wife and settle down...'

Sadie swallowed another mouthful of gin and said quietly to Lottie, 'Tragic, it was. They was crossing London Bridge – his Ma and Pa – when a horse broke free and a wagon swerved to miss the horse and ran them down. Still, at least they went together.'

'Went where?'

Sadie's forefinger jerked towards the ceiling.

Lottie stared at her. 'What d'you mean? Heaven? They was *killed*?'

'Too true they was! Died of their injuries. It broke his heart, so Bella says.'

Lloyd raised his glass. 'So let's have a toast to my lovely young wife.'

All the glasses were raised and murmurs of congratulations rang out. Unsteadily, Sadie rose to her feet. Her face was slightly flushed as she held up her glass. 'A toast to the happy couple.'

A few more cheers rang out.

Bella stood up and someone refilled her empty glass. 'I'd like to say my bit,' she told them, smiling. 'I think I must be the happiest girl in the whole world to be wed to the man I love. I'm going to enjoy being Mrs Lloyd Massie and long may we be together.' She glanced at him and put her hand lightly on his arm. 'I'd also like to say how sorry I am that not one of Lloyd's family or friends could be here today because sadly they all live in places like Australia and America. And I want to remember everyone who loved us but has passed on because I know they'd be wishing us well. So raise your glasses, ladies and gents, to absent friends!'

When the applause had died away Lottie was heard to ask again for a slice of cake and Bella decided that the time had come to satisfy her. It had been agreed by Lloyd that after his marriage to Bella, Lottie would continue to live with them. In fact his willingness to do so had impressed Bella who loved him even more for this example of his generosity of spirit.

She and Lloyd held the knife as it sliced deeply into the thick curranty mixture. The first slice was given to Lottie who, beaming broadly, immediately bit into it with gusto.

The sliced cake was handed round and the conversation gave way to cheerful munching and the noise level fell temporarily. Bella made her way towards her husband who was talking to three men who were hanging on every word.

'I'm afraid much of my work is undercover and I'm not allowed to talk about it,' he explained between mouthfuls of cake. 'I'm regularly called upon by the police who...'

Bella slipped her arm through his and smiled at his small audience. 'Isn't he a clever lad?' she asked. 'It's not every man who can claim he's helped the police. On the quiet, mind.' She looked adoringly at Lloyd. 'Tell them about the bomb plot. You know, love! Where you found that cellar...'

Embarrassed, Lloyd said, 'They don't want to hear about that. It was in all the papers. It's old news.'

'What?' asked a guest.

'Bomb plot?'

'Tell us!'

Intrigued, the men crowded closer and were joined by Stan Wellby who said, 'What's this about a bomb? Not them bloody Fenians? Blasted terrorists! I'd string 'em all up! No messing!'

Lloyd nodded. 'I stumbled on to a lead and followed it.'

'But that was in Birmingham, not London,' one of the men protested.

Bella gave him a reproachful look for interrupting her husband's story but, unruffled, Lloyd continued. 'I'm based in London, naturally, but on that occasion I'd been asked to investigate in that area. They wanted someone who wasn't known up there. I can move around freely, you see, because I'm not recognized. No uniform. Unofficial. I rented a small room up there. Once I'd found the house where they were making the bomb...'

Stan Wellby nodded knowingly. '1883, wasn't it?'

Bella said, 'Fenians? Is that who they were? You never said.'

Lloyd said, 'Of course I did, dearest.'

One of the men snorted. 'Women! No good talking to 'em about politics and suchlike.'

Bella rolled her eyes. 'Why not?'

''Cause it goes in one ear and out the other,' he said grinning.

'I did understand,' Bella insisted. 'I just didn't know the name.'

'Course you know it,' Stan said reproachfully. 'Irish revolutionaries. Keep blowing things up. They found the stuff in a kitchen. It was in all the papers.'

'I never read papers.' Bella tossed her head.

16

Lloyd nodded and continued his story. 'I had my suspicions, but I knew if I told the local police they'd descend on the place *en masse* before I...'

Bella said, 'On what?'

'*En masse*, Bella. It's French. It means...'

'Ooh! French, is it?' Bella was almost bursting with pride.

He laughed and continued. 'I was certain. I discovered the kitchen Bella mentioned – it wasn't actually a cellar – and I thought I'd better go it alone. Less chance of being rumbled.'

Bella said, 'You told me it was a cellar. I'm sure you did. Where they had the nitro ... whatever-it-was.'

He turned and put an arm round her waist and tightened it. 'It was a *kitchen*, dearest. I never said it was a cellar. You've forgotten.'

She thought he sounded rather irritated and realized she was spoiling his story. 'Have I? Sorry!' She kissed him. 'You're right. This is men's talk. I'll go find Lottie and see if she's all right.'

As she moved away she heard Stan say, 'Must be dangerous, that sort of work. I think I'll stick to heaving coal. It might be 'eavy but at least it won't blow up!'

The men laughed.

It *is* dangerous work, Bella thought proudly. My husband's not only rich and handsome, he's brave with it. No wonder the men were hanging on his every word. They had probably never met such a man. And neither had she.

That evening, with the celebrations behind them, Bella, Lottie and Lloyd sat in the tiny parlour of No 4, White Street, talking over the events of the day. The clock ticked round and the church clock struck nine.

Lloyd said, 'Time you were in bed, Lottie.'

Lottie and Bella looked at him in surprise.

Bella said, 'What you on about, love? Lottie goes to bed when she's tired.'

He smiled. 'Not tonight. She goes to bed when I say so. You and I have things to discuss, Bella. Private things.'

Lottie's face fell. 'I don't want to go to bed. I'm not tired. Really I'm not. Am I, Bella? I'm not tired.'

Bella flew to her defence. 'We can talk in front of her. She won't interfere, will you, Lottie?'

'I won't interfere. No, I won't.'

Lloyd turned to Bella. 'Let me handle this, dear, please. I do have to be master in my own home.'

'But Lloyd,' Bella persisted, 'Lottie's not a child. She's a grown woman.'

To her dismay, his expression hardened. 'Am I or am I not your husband?'

'Certainly you are but...'

'But nothing! I am master in this house

and what I say goes so please don't make me angry, Bella.'

'But it's really Lottie's house and ... and she...' Bella's voice faltered. This was her wedding night and she didn't want anything to spoil it.

He smiled thinly. 'It was left to you in your aunt's will. That's what you told me. That makes it *your* house. And I am now your husband, so in the eyes of the law, what's yours is mine. Legally I own the house. Can we agree on that?' He glanced from his wife to her cousin. The latter was staring at him, her lips quivering, tears perilously close.

Bella, dumbfounded by the speed of the threatened disaster, hesitated fatally. On any other day she would have argued with him but this was her wedding day. She was a bride for this one day only and she wanted to go on enjoying it. Perhaps it would be best for Lottie to go to bed. Lloyd had been kind enough to say she could live with them.

'You do look tired, Lottie, dear,' she said. 'Come on upstairs with me and I'll stay with you while you undress and help you say your prayers! You'd like that.'

'I'm not tired, Bella. Really I'm not!' She drew back as Bella crossed the room and held out her hand.

To Bella's surprise, Lloyd sprang from his chair and jerked Lottie to her feet. 'Do as you're told, Lottie, and go to bed. I won't give you another chance!'

Thoroughly frightened by his tone and manner, Lottie ran from the room and Bella and Lloyd listened as she scrabbled, sobbing, up the stairs.

Bella glared at her husband. 'Now you've scared her. Why did you do that? You know how...'

'Stop making excuses, Bella.' His expression was grim. This was a side of Lloyd Bella had never seen before. 'Lottie has to learn new ways. There are three of us to consider now and we all have to make changes for the better. Now go and settle her down if you must but be quick about it. Then come straight back. I need to talk to you.'

She was staring at him, shocked by his behaviour. 'Why – why are you being like this?' she asked.

For a moment he continued to glare at her and then abruptly his expression changed. 'Oh dear! My poor little love! Come here, Bella.' He held out his arms and she ran into them. While he held her close, she felt her fears evaporating. He kissed her hair and ran his hands softly up and down her back. 'I need to have you to myself sometimes,' he murmured. 'You know how much I love you and I'm not prepared to let anyone come between us or cause trouble. Lottie has to learn that I am now the most important person in your life. Things change and the sooner she realizes that the better for all of us.'

Bella clung to him, trying to convince herself that he was doing the right thing for the right reason. She had been so silly, she thought, to imagine everything would be the same. Lloyd was her dearest beloved husband and she must put his happiness first. Love, honour and obey. She *would* obey. She had vowed to do so. She would have a little talk with Lottie and explain it to her. Lottie would understand.

She eased herself from his grasp, looked up into the dear, familiar face and reached up to kiss him. 'I'll go up to her, but I'll be quick,' she promised and was rewarded with a broad smile.

'And you do forgive me, dearest girl?' he asked. 'You do understand that I have to be firm?'

'Of course I do, Lloyd. It was silly of me.'

He kissed her again and she hurried from the room and up the stairs. Lottie, her face tear-stained, was sitting on her bed and had thrown all her dolls on to the floor.

'I don't like him any more,' she cried as soon as Bella entered the room. 'He's horrible. Why did you marry him, Bella? He's not kind. He shouts ... and he hurt my wrist.' She held out her arm and Bella saw that an angry red weal marked the spot where Lloyd had taken hold of her.

21

Saying nothing, she gathered up the dolls. Confused and anxious, she tried to find something comforting to say but failed. Instead she said, 'If you don't start to undress I shan't help you with your prayers.'

Lottie began to cry and when Bella moved to comfort her, she pushed her away. 'I don't want to say my prayers. I shan't say them! I don't like him. He's a horrible man!'

Bella counted to ten. She arranged the dolls along the window seat where they usually sat and turned to Lottie. There was no time now for explanations. She would have to be firm.

'I'm going to count to ten,' she told her cousin. 'One ... two ... three...'

Fortunately this worked. Lottie began to pull off her clothes and finally struggled into her nightdress.

Bella said, '...ten! Oh you are such a clever girl, Lottie. So quick! Let's say your prayers and then I must go back downstairs.'

In the parlour, when Bella returned, Lloyd was nursing a glass of whisky. 'Would you like a small sherry?' he asked her.

Bella nodded and relaxed. This was the Lloyd she knew and loved. They settled together on the sofa and Lloyd said, 'I've got a wonderful surprise for you, Bella. We're going to move to a bigger house. A much nicer...'

'Move?' Her eyes widened in delight. 'Oh,

Lloyd. How exciting!'

'I don't want my children to be brought up in this neighbourhood, Bella. I know you grew up here and you have friends here, but it's shabby and really isn't good enough. I've spoken to my bank manager and he will lend us some money and we'll sell this house and buy something much better. How would you like that, my love?'

'It would be wonderful, Lloyd. Oh, you are clever. I didn't know you had a bank manager.'

He laughed. 'There are lots of things you don't know about me yet, dearest, but we have all our lives ahead of us. Can you imagine our children playing in a nice garden with grass and a swing? And we won't have a lodger so we'll...'

'No lodgers? But how will we pay for things? The money from the lodgers...'

'That was before you married me, Bella. Now we shall live on my earnings, which are quite sufficient. We'll be all alone, just you and me.'

Her expression changed slightly. 'But what about the lodgers here? Mr and Mrs Schwartz? What will happen to them if we sell the house? I mean, where will they go? They don't have much money and they might not be able to find anywhere else. Some people don't like Jews.'

He shrugged. 'They'll find somewhere

else, Bella. We can't be responsible for everybody. Don't fuss so!'

She frowned suddenly. 'Just you and me? But what about Lottie? She'll be there, won't she?'

Now it was Lloyd's turn to frown. 'Forget about Lottie, Bella. Do you always have to spoil things for me? I tell you this wonderful news and all you do is carp!'

'But ... But she will be with us, won't she? I mean it was her mother's house before it was left to me. We couldn't just sell it and ... and abandon Lottie.'

'Oh my poor little Bella. What a killjoy you are sometimes.' He gave an exaggerated sigh. 'But I still love you. And you still love me – and we are husband and wife now. It's up to me to look after you and our children when they come along. So you just stop worrying.' He smiled suddenly. 'And talking of children...' He rolled his eyes humorously. 'I wonder if it's *our* bedtime? What do you think, Bella? Shall *we* have an early night? Are you ready to make your husband very happy? I do hope so!' Gently he touched the bright tangle of curls which surrounded her face. 'I love your hair, Bella. I love your sweet mouth ... I want to love *all* of you.'

Bella pushed her doubts aside, threw herself into his arms and kissed him passionately. 'I am ready, dearest Lloyd,' she whispered. 'More than ready.'

As they went up the stairs, arm in arm, Bella told herself that she was the luckiest girl in Whitechapel and, despite the problems, must never forget it.

A week later, in a house not far from Bella's, Dora Hubbard was dressing slowly. She and her husband lived at No 16, Goulston Street. It was Monday and she had a lot of washing to do. She felt heavy and slightly nauseous and thought perhaps a dry biscuit might help. She was trying hard to stay calm but she glanced repeatedly at the clock and longed for the sound of her husband's key in the front door. A glimpse of herself in the mirror did nothing to reassure her. Her grey eyes were dull and unhappy, her skin pale, and her dark hair lacked the lustre it once had. She was still only half dressed because it was already close and she hated hot weather. Marriage had not been kind to her, she reflected unhappily. Now after less than two years, she felt a pale shadow of the woman she had once been. Blinking back the tears that came so easily these days, she went downstairs to start her day with the usual feeling of hopelessness.

As always, the prospect of lighting the copper in the outhouse proved frustrating. No matter how tightly she screwed the newspaper and how many sticks of wood she added, it always burned for a moment or

two, then faltered. Often it went out altogether, which meant that the water for the
wash wasn't being heated and the whole
dreary process had to be started again. Today, to her relief, the fire caught at the first
attempt. She poured cold water, soap and
soda into the copper above the fire and
stirred well with a wooden stick. Then she
added the sheets and pillowcases from their
bed and replaced the lid. Already exhausted,
she slumped on to a chair but was immediately startled by a peremptory knocking on
the front door.

'Now who on earth...?' she muttered. Pulling up garters to hold up her stockings, she
went to the window and looked down into
the street. A man stood on the doorstep.
Long dark coat, she noted – despite the fact
that it was mid summer – gloved hands and
a smart black bowler hat. Whatever was a
man like that doing on their doorstep?

She pushed up the sash window and
leaned out. 'My husband's not at home,' she
told him. 'He'll be back later.'

He took a step back and looked up at her.
'Maybe I could talk to you. That's if you are
Mrs Hubbard.'

'I am. I'll be down in a moment.' She
closed the window and put a hand to her
mouth. She shouldn't have said that, she
reflected nervously. Her husband was very
insistent that she never opened the door to

strangers. She hesitated. She had made a mistake and wouldn't go down. He'd lose interest and go away. She stood behind the curtain and watched for him to go but instead he knocked again. On the other side of the street Mrs Betts was watching from her window. Now what should she do? The neighbours would soon start gossipping if a strange man continued to stand on her doorstep, banging away on the knocker.

I'll have to go down! she decided

Quickly she finished dressing, brushed her hair and rubbed a damp flannel over her face.

She opened the door as narrowly as possible. 'What do you want with me?'

'Just a few questions if you're willing. I shan't take up much of your time.' He smiled and she liked the look of him. Nice face, good manners, well-dressed with a pleasant voice.

'I can't ask you in,' she told him. 'My husband would be furious. He says strangers in the house always spell trouble.'

'I'm thinking of you, Mrs Hubbard. That is your name, isn't it?' She nodded and he went on. 'Some of the questions are rather ... are of a personal nature. Would it be all right if we just talked in the hall and didn't go into any of the rooms?'

Dora came to an abrupt decision. Anything was better than a talk on the doorstep in full view of Mrs Betts. She had also become curious and vaguely flattered by his need to question her. She opened the door and he stepped inside and took off his hat.

'May I?' He indicated towards the hall-stand and, receiving a nod, hung up his bowler. He had nice fair hair and blue eyes. Then he took a small notebook from his pocket, put on a pair of spectacles, and flipped over the pages as though refreshing his memory.

'Mrs Hubbard, what is your full name?'

'Maude Alice Hubbard but everyone calls me Dora.'

'And your husband's full name?'

'John Bernard Hubbard.'

'And his occupation?'

'He's a doctor at the London Hospital. He works different shifts, mostly at night but not always. That's why he isn't here. He's on the night shift.' She shrugged. 'I'm never sure when to expect him.'

'I may have met him there,' the visitor said. 'The name rings a bell, as they say. I occasionally have to attend the hospital. Dark hair, moustache ... Is that him?'

'Why yes! That would be John.'

'Thank you...' He scribbled something. 'How long have you lived here, Mrs Hubbard?'

'About eighteen months.'

'And before that?'

'I lived at home with my parents in Spital-fields. Until I got married and then we came here. What's this all about, Mr ... What is your name?'

'Undershot. Mr Undershot. I'm a debt collector. The previous tenant owed a lot of money and we're trying to trace him.'

'What's that got to do with my husband?'

'I wanted to make sure that he hadn't changed his name and to ask if your husband has any details about his whereabouts. Did the previous tenant leave a forwarding address, for instance?'

'Not that I know of.'

He wrote again. 'So your husband's a doctor.' He regarded her closely and she suddenly wished she had taken more care with her appearance. 'If you don't mind me saying so, you look rather unwell. Also rather worried, Mrs Hubbard. Is there anything you want to tell me?'

'I've not been well,' she said at once, defending her appearance. 'I'm not sleeping at the moment and I get bad headaches.' She was torn between resentment at his presumption and pleasure at his apparent concern. Her husband tended to reject her complaints, insisting that she exaggerated her ailments out of a desire for sympathy. Mr Undershot was standing very close to her in the narrow hallway and she looked down at her hands to avoid eye contact.

'But your husband is a doctor.'

His voice was kind, she thought.

'Can't he help you?'

'I wish he would.' She gave him a quick glance but his expression was hard to read. It was his voice that encouraged her confidence. 'He doesn't take me seriously, Mr Undershot. My health, that is. He does give me a pick-me-up once or twice a week. A tonic mixture he makes up himself. Something he learned from his mother, God rest her soul. I never met her. But he can't give me any proper medicine, if that's what you mean. He gets that from the chemist. John's not that sort of doctor. He ... He examines dead people.'

'I see. So he's a pathologist who works varying shifts.' He made another note in his book. 'Why didn't you say so?'

'It's not a very nice subject, is it? That's what my husband says. People don't understand the work but someone has to do it.'

'Do you know where your husband lived before he came here with you?'

'No, I don't. He doesn't talk about the past because people died and it was all very tragic and it upsets him. Are there any more questions?'

'Just a couple. I'm sure you're busy but you've been very helpful.'

'I do have some work to do. It's wash day.' She rolled her eyes.

'It won't take long. How long did you know your husband before you married him?'

Her face brightened a little. 'Oh, not long at all! It was a whirlwind romance.' Her face lit up. 'That's what my friend said. A love match. We were married a month after we met.'

He closed the notebook and put it away. 'Thank you for your help, Mrs Hubbard. I needn't trouble you any further.'

'Right. I hope you find him.'

'Find who?' He reached for his bowler and settled it on his head.

'The man you're looking for ... that owes the money.'

'Oh yes. Him. Oh, we'll catch him, don't you worry.'

A minute later she was closing the door behind him and rather regretting that the conversation hadn't lasted longer.

Ten minutes later when her husband came home, she said nothing about the visitor. He would be sure to disapprove, she thought, and there was no harm done. She had enough questions of her own to put to him when the time was right. A week earlier he had told her he was going to a funeral and he wouldn't take her because it would depress her. She had followed him. Instead of the funeral she had found him enjoying a wedding.

On Monday morning, the 6th of August, Sadie arrived at No 4, White Street, where Bella and Lottie were breakfasting on porridge and toast.

Lottie beamed. 'Bella's trying to fatten me up!' she cried. 'Do you want some porridge, Aunt Sadie?'

'No thanks, love. I'm fat enough already.' She patted her bulging stomach before settling herself on a chair. 'But I'd die for a cuppa.'

Bella reached for the teapot.

Lottie said, 'We're going to live in a new house, Aunt Sadie, because Bella and Lloyd are married now and he has to be the master.'

'The master, eh!' Sadie laughed. 'Men! Don't they just love it, pushing us women around. But moving house? Why, Bella? What's wrong with this house? Your aunt wanted you both to be safe here for the rest of your lives. This isn't a bad little house and you've got a bit of rent coming in. Not a very nice neighbourhood maybe but you've kept the house neat all these years.'

Bella explained the thinking behind her husband's decision and reluctantly Sadie nodded. 'Well, you can see it from his point of view, I suppose. A man like him's bound to have aspirations.' She caught Lottie's puzzled look and said, 'Aspirations. Big ideas, Lottie.' She blew on her tea to cool it. 'Jon at the Ten Bells was saying the police have been in there asking questions. Seems like they're still looking for a man who they think murdered his father!'

'His own father?' cried Bella. 'That's terrible, that is! How'd he do it?'

'They think he poisoned him – if he did it!' Sadie rolled her eyes. 'It might have been some sort of accidental poisoning. Or even suicide. I don't know what the world's coming to! Really I don't.' She shook her head. 'Seems these days there's more bad people than good.'

'I'm good,' Lottie told her earnestly. She stopped scraping the last of the porridge from the bowl and licked the spoon. 'You ask Bella. I go to bed every night when it's my bedtime. Nine o'clock on the dot. That's what Lloyd says and off I go. Don't I, Bella? I'm one of the good people.'

Sadie stared at her. 'Nine o'clock? What you on about, Lottie?'

Bella said, 'It's Lloyd's idea.' She was flustered. 'He wants us to have a bit of time to ourselves. Him and me. You can't blame him.'

'But ... I mean ... Nine o'clock! Lottie's not a child.'

Bella felt her face redden. She hated being put on the defensive where Lloyd was concerned. 'He's very kind to her. He's going to buy her a very special doll for her collection.'

Lottie's face lit up. 'Very, very special! I like dolls. I really do.'

Bella decided to change the subject. 'So this man – haven't they found him yet? This murderer?'

'Seems not. Not enough manpower. That's what they're saying. They were following him a few weeks back and then he gave them the slip again. It's not that they don't know who he is. At least they think they do.'

Bella brightened suddenly. 'I bet they'll be asking Lloyd to help them investigate. Like they did with the Fenian bombers. He could follow them. He's used to following. Tracking, he calls it. Finding clues, following and observing the suspect – that's what he has to do. Any time of the day or night ... Oh! And making deductions. It sounds like fun.'

'Maybe Lloyd's already tracking him. He wouldn't be able to tell you, would he?'

Sadie looked interested and Bella felt relieved that her aunt had been distracted from Lottie's bedtime.

'Maybe he is,' said Bella. 'He wouldn't tell me because he knows I'd worry about him. Being a private investigator is risky work. It's not like the police. If they get themselves into a scrape they just call out all their colleagues. A private investigator can't do that. He's got no one watching his back. That's how Lloyd put it.'

Lottie said, 'Nine o'clock on the dot!'

Bella cursed inwardly.

Her aunt, however, was already off in another direction and appeared not to have noticed. 'D'you two remember that woman that turned up at your wedding do? Standing in the doorway with that shawl over her head?'

'What woman?' Bella stared at her. 'I didn't see any woman.'

'Well, she saw you. She had a good look at everyone. I went over to speak to her but she slipped away. Sickly-looking woman. But nicely dressed. Stan noticed her. Trust him! Only I saw her again yesterday at the market. I cottoned on to her right away but she spotted me looking at her and hurried away again.'

'Perhaps Lloyd knows her. He might have invited her to the wedding.'

'He said he didn't invite anyone. If he saw her, he didn't speak to her.' Sadie shrugged. 'She didn't speak to anyone as far as I saw. Just hung about in the doorway. Maybe she's the shy sort. Some people don't mix well with strangers.'

Lottie spread dripping on her toast. 'Do I mix well with strangers? Do I?'

Bella said, 'Course you do, love.'

Sadie sipped her tea and settled back in the chair. 'So, Bella, how's married life?'

Bella felt herself blushing. 'No complaints

so far!'

Her aunt laughed. 'I suppose the next thing is you'll be talking about "a happy event"!'

'Who knows?' Bella felt embarrassed to be talking like this to an aunt who had never married. How could Sadie advise her about babies? Not that much had been happening between the sheets, for Lloyd had been at work, late home four evenings out of the seven they had been married. Bella was a deep sleeper and hadn't even heard him come in some nights. In fact, for a newly married man, he hadn't been around much at all.

Two

Later the same morning Detective Sergeant Douglas Unwin was sitting at the kitchen table, in No 7, Philpot Street, eating bread and jam and reading through his report. It was written in ink in a careful hand without any blots and DS Unwin was proud of his efforts. He sat at the kitchen table in the house he shared with his widowed mother and listened for signs that she was getting up. Douglas liked to speak to her for a few minutes before leaving for work but this morning he was anxious to get round to the police station and so far she hadn't stirred. Still asleep, he presumed. Getting up from the table he closed and opened the kitchen door in the hope that the noise would disturb her sleep and she would think she had woken naturally. She hated being roused, always protesting that he had ruined a perfectly good dream. Sounds of bed springs reassured him that she was stirring and he returned to his report.

Monday the 6th of August 1888: I proceeded to the suspect's home at No 16, Goulston Street, Whitechapel, arriving there at quarter past eight in the morning. I introduced myself as Mr Undershot, a debt collector, who was trying to trace a previous tenant with a view to collecting the money owed. I had hoped to speak directly with the man originally known to us as Gerald Cummings but his wife answered the door. This was a Dora Hubbard who was married to John Hubbard so it would appear that our suspect has yet again changed his name. She claims that he never speaks of the past because it's too tragic and upsets him. She also claims he is a doctor who examines 'dead people' – presumably he uses this as a convenient cover for his activities and to explain any absences from home. He works very late hours and sometimes works through the night. The 'wife' herself seems to be in poor health and I gathered that her husband is unsympathetic to her complaints. She appears nervous and suspicious and claims that our suspect forbids her to allow strangers into the house because they 'cause trouble'. She appears gullible and would no doubt reveal much more if pressure was put upon her but I was careful not to arouse her suspicions for fear she alerted our suspect by her account of our meeting and the direction of my questions.

He glanced up as shuffling footsteps sounded in the hall and his mother appeared in the kitchen. Annie Unwin was small and wiry, her hair prematurely grey. She had worked long hours as a shop assistant to keep their home together after her husband died. Now Douglas was making a good career in the police, he was pleased that she could take life a little easier.

'Toast?' he asked.

'Yes please, dear.'

He poured her a cup of tea, cut a thick slice of bread from the loaf, pushed it on to the toasting fork and held it close to the red coals in the stove.

His mother indicated the report. 'Is that what kept you up late?'

He nodded.

She studied it for a moment. 'You always did write well, even at school. Your teachers always said so.' She looked at her good-looking son with satisfaction. She'd always wanted a daughter but the only girl born to her had died a few weeks later like the little boy before her. Annie sighed at the memories. Her three children had, inexplicably, been frail little souls and she had felt herself very lucky that Douglas survived. So much like his father. Same fair hair and short-sighted blue eyes. He wore similar spectacles for close work and in some lights she was so struck by the likeness that it made her catch her breath. Young women found him attractive but he scarcely noticed them. Too wrapped up in his work to even think of marriage and that pleased her. He was only twenty-seven and there was plenty of time for a wife and children. She would miss him dreadfully when he eventually left home. The spectre of a lonely old age haunted her but she would never try to stop him marrying.

'We're getting closer to him, Ma,' he said, blissfully unaware of the direction of her thoughts. 'I'm looking forward to the day we nail him. I want to see the wretch behind bars.'

'So did you actually speak to him?'

'No. He was out. But I spoke to his wife. Poor soul. She doesn't suspect a thing.

Thinks it was a love match. I ask you!'

'Wicked,' she muttered. 'Fancy killing your own flesh and blood. Makes me go all cold at the thought of it. I hope he dangles on the end of a rope. Nothing's too bad for him. And it'll be all thanks to you when they hang him. You've been after him for so long, even when nobody else believed it was murder. If it wasn't for you, he'd have got away with it.'

'I shall have to be in court to give evidence.' He grinned. 'That will be a special day, I can tell you. You'll have to come in and watch me.'

'What come into court? Never!'

'Not even if I buy you a new coat ... with an astrakhan collar?'

'New coat? Well, that's different, that is. I'll have to think about that.' She smiled at him.

He turned the bread over and toasted the other side. 'There you are.' He put the toast on her plate and pushed the butter dish towards her.

'I fancy dripping,' she told him.

She scraped some on to the knife, spread it on the toast and added pepper and salt. 'Aren't you going to do me another slice?'

'No time, Ma. Sorry. Got to get to work and hand this in. Can't wait to see the guvnor's face when he reads it.'

Twenty minutes later Douglas arrived at the station to find it an unwelcome hive of activity with people running about in all directions. His immediate superior, he was told, was 'out on the case'. A great sense of frustration swept through him as he thought of the report which would now languish on a desk, its importance overshadowed by whatever 'the case' turned out to be.

Dammit! he thought, his good mood evaporating.

The cause of the excitement turned out to be a particularly unpleasant murder. A prostitute had been found dead. Such deaths were not unusual in the area where hundreds of the poorest citizens huddled in deprived conditions and struggled to earn enough money to survive one day at a time. Women who regularly sold their bodies to any man who would give them a few pence sometimes died untimely deaths, but these were mainly from sickness or accident. A few were the result of beatings. This particular woman had been stabbed more than thirty times. The police were describing it as a 'violent and sadistic attack'.

'Get over to George Yard Buildings,' Douglas was told, 'and take PC Riggs with you. And Riggs, put that pipe away. Pipes are for relaxation, lad. You know I don't favour them while on duty. We're going to need every man we've got if we're going to apprehend the perpetrator.'

He turned back to Douglas. 'Go! Get out

41

of here! You're needed! I want to see results and the sooner the better or my head will be on a platter.'

Douglas and the young constable set off at a brisk walk to George Yard, a turning off Whitechapel Road. On the way Riggs eagerly filled in the details for his Detective Sergeant.

'A bloody murder, and I do mean bloody! Dozens of stab wounds. Poor cow! I don't hold no brief for the likes of her but what a terrible way to die. And why? What did she have worth pinching? Nothing! And if he had some kind of gripe with her, one or two stabs would have been enough to snuff her out. I mean, why hang about all that time when he might have been seen by someone?'

Douglas glanced at him and groaned inwardly. Riggs, in his opinion, was hardly police material but the force took who they could. The recruits frequently came from poor backgrounds and looked upon the police force as a respectable career. One step up the social ladder, so to speak. Riggs was no worse than many but he fancied himself as a prankster and tried hard to be popular.

'So she was a prostitute?' Douglas asked. He couldn't see the constable earning a promotion in the foreseeable future.

'So they reckon. They found her stretched out on a landing in George Yard Buildings just before five this morning. Killed sometime during the night. Course, they don't know exactly when. Found by a man called Reeves on his way to work. What a shock for the poor bloke. Enough to give him a heart attack!' He laughed.

Although inspired by his superior's air of urgency and the familiar thrill of the chase, Douglas was disappointed at this turn of events. He'd been looking forward to delivering the report and receiving congratulations for his perseverance. Now it looked as though he would have to wait. A current murder obviously took top priority. The population would expect it and there would be pressure brought to bear by the newspapers. But as soon as they had solved the crime, Douglas would make sure that the findings in his own report were read and acted upon.

'Does the victim have a name yet?' he asked, preparing to concentrate his energy on the case in hand.

'Not for sure although someone thinks it might be a woman called Martha. So it'll be knocking on doors for the likes of us for the next few days. Or maybe not for you, you being a detective.'

They reached George Yard where senior policemen huddled together in urgent conversation. Douglas and PC Riggs stepped forward and were at once swept into the investigation.

That evening the mood in the Ten Bells was unusually subdued if not exactly fearful. The women talked in low tones, glancing around them from time to time as though expecting to be attacked at any moment. The occasional arrival of a strange man was greeted with suspicion and he was quickly driven out again by hostile mutterings. A few of the women thought they might have known the dead woman and they could imagine her state of mind as her attacker struck at her repeatedly. 'Frenzied' was the word the police were using and that struck terror into all their hearts.

'Frenzied! That's what they say.'

'But do they really give a toss, Mae, about the likes of us?'

Making a living on the streets of Whitechapel was hard enough at the best of times and many of the women had suffered at the hands of brutal, mean-spirited men.

Mae Dunnley shrugged. 'When that drunken sot split my lip and knocked me tooth out they wasn't too interested. Never done nothing to him so far as I know. I gave them a description but they said it would be my word against his. "Look at my bleeding mouth", I told them. That's evidence, that is.'

From behind the bar, Jon glanced over. 'When was that then?'

'April, I suppose – round about Easter.'

Millie said, 'Nice Easter present!' Her raucous laugh rang out.

Someone said hopefully, 'Maybe they've caught him by now.'

'And maybe pigs can fly!'

'A penny to a pound he's still out there.'

For a moment they fell silent, remembering their own past troubles. Many had been battered by drunken thugs in a dark alley in the late hours of the night when no one was near to hear their cries for help. The police seemed little interested in these attacks and, because of this, most went unreported. Tonight, aware how little interest the murder would arouse among more fortunate members of society, they drew closer to their friends. They nursed their meagre drinks and put off the evil moment when they would have to go back on the streets to earn a few pence to pay for a bed overnight in one of the common lodging houses. For most of them there was no viable alternative. To earn a 'respectable' living they could stay home and make matchboxes for which they would be paid a pittance, but for that kind of 'home work' you needed a home and most of the women had nowhere to live.

One by one, as the evening wore on, they abandoned their empty glasses and moved reluctantly out of the security of the gaslit pub and on to the gloomy pavement. Wisps of fog drifted through narrow streets and clung to dilapidated buildings, the walls of which were blackened by years of soot and grime. With falsely cheerful cries, they separated, wending their solitary ways in search of customers. Always aware of the threat of violence, the latest victim's dreadful death had now made this a distinct possibility.

Eight days passed and the murdered woman was officially identified as Martha Tabram, but she had already been forgotten by people who felt removed from such dangers. Bella was one of these people. Marriage to a private investigator had given her a sense of security and she gave herself up to the delights of being a married woman and the new status this gave her. As she hurried about on her daily errands she carried a brand new shopping basket and took great pleasure at the sight of herself in shop windows. How lucky she was to be Mrs Lloyd Massie, she thought – and how lucky he was to have her for his wife. With new confidence she argued with shopkeepers, haggled over prices and repeatedly referred to her husband.

'My husband prefers beef sausages,' she told the butcher and felt that the rest of the women in the queue envied her.

'I'd like to buy this scarf,' she said, 'but can I bring it back if my husband doesn't care for it? He likes to come shopping with me but he's a private investigator and works awkward hours.'

She cleaned the house more diligently than before, made new curtains for the kitchen and took pains with her cooking. The extra housekeeping money excited her and she turned her hand to ambitious pies and unusual puddings which she had never attempted before. Some were a success, others a dismal failure, but Lloyd made encouraging noises and ignored the burnt pie crust and the gooey, partly cooked desserts. Bella, her confidence undented, smiled and laughed through both triumphs and disasters and ploughed on with undiminished enthusiasm.

Only Lottie caused her disquiet. Her cousin had taken a dislike to Lloyd – who had conveniently forgotten her doll – and while Bella sympathized she was determined to remain loyal to her husband. She mustn't take Lottie's side against his, she decided. She wanted to be the perfect wife. She took to giving Lottie long lectures about their new circumstances and the changes Lloyd expected them to make. These were received by Lottie with a sullen expression, and the easy friendship which had always existed between them was becoming strained.

On the 14th of August Bella came home to Lottie in a state of intense excitement to tell her the latest news.

'Remember that dead woman they found in George Yard? The one that was stabbed? The butcher says the police have found her husband and he's identified her and her name was Martha Tabram but she left him ages ago.'

'Did he kill her?'

'No. They reckon it was a soldier what killed her because she was seen walking with a soldier but they can't find him. They should ask Lloyd. He'd track him down in no time.'

'Lloyd's going to buy me a doll, isn't he Bella?'

'Give him time, Lottie. He's busy investigating. But this poor woman – they counted the stabs he gave her and it was *thirty-nine*!'

'That's a lot, isn't it?'

'It certainly is!'

'Is he still out there then, the murderer?'

''Fraid so, Lottie, but don't fret yourself. You're quite safe here. He's only dangerous if you go out after dark and you never do.' She took off her jacket, hung it on the peg behind the door, then carried the shopping out into the kitchen. She gave a scream. 'Lottie! What's all this? My lovely new curtains!'

The orange gingham curtains of which she was so proud, now hung in tatters, the ragged strips fluttering in the breeze which came in through the open window.

Lottie followed her out. 'He said I could! Lloyd did. He said I could cut up the curtains ... so I did.'

Bella stared at her in shock. 'Lloyd told you to cut up the curtains? Don't tell such wicked lies, Lottie. Of course he didn't. Why would he do such a thing?' She covered her face with her hands. 'My lovely new curtains.'

Lottie blinked nervously. 'But he said I could. Do it, he said. It will be fun! So after he'd gone I did. Are you cross, Bella?' Her mouth trembled.

Bella closed her eyes and tried to think sensibly. Why on earth was Lottie telling such a bald-faced lie? She must know that Lloyd would never, *never* say such a thing and that he would deny it. And why had she done such a thing? Fun? Where had she got that idea from? She had never been destructive in the past. Was it because she didn't like Lloyd? Was it because of the doll that he kept forgetting? Was this ridiculous accusation by way of a protest? Did that make any sense?

'Please, Lottie,' she begged, uncovering her face, 'tell me the truth and I'll forgive you. I promise I won't be angry. I don't want you to blame it on Lloyd.'

'But he told me to! He really did!'

Anger bubbled within her. 'When exactly did he tell you this?' she demanded, grim faced.

'When he came home. After you went shopping he came home. He did. He came home because he forgot something ... and he said I could have some fun.'

Bella turned towards the ruined curtains. Whatever would Lloyd say when he saw them? And what would he do if he knew about Lottie's lies? She would have to tell him. How else could she explain what had happened to them? She sat down heavily.

Lottie said, 'Lloyd doesn't like me, Bella. He doesn't. He really doesn't. And I don't like him!'

'Well don't let him know that, you silly girl!' she cried, exasperated. 'Do you want him to send you away?'

'No. No, I don't. I really don't.' She stared at Bella. 'Send me away! Where?'

'Never mind.'

With trembling fingers, Bella began to take down the curtains, which were strung on tape between two hooks, one on either side of the window. She threw them into the waste bucket under the sink, frowning as she did so. An idea was forming in her brain. She would go back to the drapers and buy some more gingham. She would make new curtains and re-hang them before her husband came home. That way he need never know what Lottie had done. She would have to find many economies to make the housekeeping balance but she could do it.

'Put on your things, Lottie,' she said. 'We're going out to buy some more material and we *must* be quick!'

As they rushed to the drapers, Bella did her best to impress on her cousin the need for secrecy.

'You must not say a word to Lloyd about the curtains,' she insisted as she steered Lottie along the crowded pavements. 'Not a single word. Do you understand?'

Lottie nodded vigorously. 'Cross my heart and hope to die!'

Bella rolled her eyes. 'That's a bit drastic.'

Inside the shop they were lucky to find more of the same gingham remaining on the bale; within half an hour they were back home and Bella was busy with the sewing machine. An hour later the new curtains fluttered at the kitchen window and Bella let out a sigh of relief. She had averted a major disaster, she thought, but her small triumph left her feeling uneasy. Suppose Lottie did something else. Had she perhaps treated it too lightly? Was Lottie going to be reassured because she hadn't been punished in any way for her transgression? What would Bella's mother have done in the circumstances? She was still troubled by the questions when Lloyd came home, earlier than usual and in a very cheerful mood.

He gave Bella a kiss and smiled. 'How are

my two favourite girls?' he asked and winked at Lottie.

'We're very well,' Bella assured him.

'Did anything exciting happen while I was away?'

Lottie said, 'We didn't do anything, did we, Bella?'

Bella shrugged lightly. 'We went shopping and did some housework. Not very exciting.'

'We didn't do anything wrong.' Lottie glanced anxiously at her cousin.

Lloyd turned towards her. 'You didn't?'

'No!' Bella gave Lottie a warning look. 'Why should you think we did?' She was hoping that Lottie would leave the talking to her.

Was it her imagination or did her husband look surprised at their insistence?

He held his hands up in mock surrender. 'I only asked! Just a joke!'

Lottie frowned, looking down at her hands which were clasped tightly in front of her chest.

Bella said brightly, 'You're home early today. Does that mean your work is going well?'

'Well enough.' He wandered towards the kitchen, opened the door and took a quick glance round.

Lottie said, 'I didn't do anything. Really I didn't!'

Lloyd beckoned Bella into the kitchen then

closed the door. He leaned back against it and spoke in a low voice. 'I had to come back for some notes earlier and Lottie was behaving very strangely. Said she was going to cut up the curtains ... for fun! I tried to talk her out of it and I see that I was successful.'

Bella tried to hide her shock. 'She said *what*?'

He repeated it. 'I thought it very odd. Obviously she thought better of it. You must keep a close eye on her, dear. I believe that since you and I married she has become a little strange. Stranger than usual, I mean. It's rather worrying.'

Bella hesitated, wondering whether to tell him the truth, but that meant revealing her own intention to deceive him. Better perhaps to say nothing.

'I think it has upset her a little but I'm sure she'll settle down.'

'Let's hope so. I don't like the idea of her becoming ... well, dangerous. Unpredictable. We must be able to trust her if she's to stay in this house.'

'But Lloyd, this is her home. Where would she go?'

'If she's mad, Bella, or becoming mad...'

'Mad? Oh no! A little slow, that's all.'

'There are places for the mad, Bella. Asylums where she could be cared for. I'm only saying *if*. If Lottie becomes unstable and we can no longer trust her, it would be my duty, as your husband, to take whatever measures I saw fit to protect you, Bella.'

At that moment, Lottie tried the door handle but Lloyd was leaning against it, holding it shut. 'Go away, Lottie. You can't come in. We're talking!'

Bella said, 'I could never do that to her. Never!'

'I know that, dearest Bella, but *I* could. So do keep an eye on her and let me know if she does anything else – or threatens to do anything. I shall be very unhappy if you disobey me on this. Who knows what is going on in that mind of hers? She might suddenly snap and do something ... Suppose for instance we were asleep and she came into our room with scissors or a poker. She could hurt us while we slept!'

Bella stared at him, open-mouthed. 'Hurt us? Oh, how could you say such a dreadful thing? Lottie loves us. She would never...'

'She might love *you* but she doesn't love *me*. We both know she resents me being here. Oh, don't try and deny it, Bella. And don't start to cry. I'm saying this for your own good. She is your cousin and we do our best for her but we must be prepared. She may get worse. Now that is all I want to say on the subject.' He held up his hand to silence her protest. 'We'll say no more. We'll watch and wait.'

With a heavy heart Bella watched him

open the door. Lottie glared at them.

'What are you saying, Bella?'

Bella pulled herself together with effort and held out her arms. Hugging her cousin, she said, 'It was private, Lottie dear. Nothing about you.' She drew back and regarded her cousin intently. She was sure Lloyd was over-reacting – but suppose he was right? Was she, Bella, wrong to hide the truth from her husband? The awful image of Lottie in their bedroom brandishing a poker and attacking Lloyd made her heart race with anxiety. Sighing, she set about preparing a meal for them while Lottie laid the table and Lloyd settled down with *The Times*. If only her mother were still alive. She would know what to do.

As she whisked eggs for the omelette, she wondered how it was possible to be married to someone you love and still feel lonely.

On the morning of Friday, the 31st of August, Sadie made her way unsteadily along Buck's Row. It was just after six and she had spent the best part of the night drinking with friends in Brady Street and ended up too drunk to find her way home. Reluctantly they had allowed her to stay the night. She had slept on the floor with her head propped on a pillow and on waking had been horribly sick in the fireplace. Making good her escape before her friends awoke, she set out for home with a head that ached abominably and a stiff neck. The thought of her own cheerless attic room depressed her and she abruptly decided to make her way to Bella's house instead, where she could be sure of a welcome and maybe a glass of milk to settle her stomach.

She walked through the early morning fog, thankful for the tall walls on either side of the street which kept the daylight from her eyes. Her stomach rumbled and she muttered, 'Give over, damn you!' and then came to a halt.

A sour-faced police constable was barring her way, his arms folded. 'Sorry, missus. This is a crime scene. You can't come past.'

She regarded him dispassionately. He looked about sixteen with his faint blond moustache struggling to establish itself below a thin nose. 'A crime scene? Where's the crime?'

'It was just there!' He pointed to the pavement near the entrance to a stable yard. 'The body's been removed. We have to investigate every inch of the vicinity for clues. Where you headed?'

Behind him she could see a group of people talking earnestly. Most of them were in uniform. A crime scene? She blinked in an effort to clear her head. 'What sort of crime? You mean ... like another murder?'

''Fraid so. So where are you going?'

Where was she going? Sadie had forgotten. She tried to concentrate. 'To my niece in White Street...' she said at last. 'It's not the same man, is it, what done the other poor woman? Martha something-or-other.' With a hand to her thumping head, she peered past him. Curiosity overcoming her squeamishness, and despite his comment about the removal of the body, she rather hoped to see the woman lying in a pool of blood. She was disappointed. All she saw were chalk marks on the pavement and a dark stain in the road. Uniformed men knelt on the pavement in silence, presumably searching for clues, but there was no sign of the victim.

'We don't know, do we?' the policeman said irritably. 'Maybe it is. Maybe it isn't. Christ! The body's hardly cold and you think we should have cracked it already? What d'you take us for – geniuses?' He seemed exasperated by her, but she was too ill to feel resentful.

He went on. 'Go back, turn to your right and make your way down Whitechapel Road then cut back along Osborn Street.'

Sadie wasn't listening. She had grown up among these streets and knew every inch of them. She didn't need a copper to tell her how to get to Bella's place. She said, 'Stabbed, was she? Or strangled?'

'Never you mind – but it was very nasty. Very nasty indeed. Some kind of madman, if you ask me. A raving lunatic! Still, what can you expect? These miserable wretches wander round these dark streets in the middle of the night. Asking to be done in.'

Sadie felt vaguely argumentative. 'Some of them have got no homes. Where else can they go?'

'They could get a job.'

'What would you know?' She sniffed disparagingly. 'They do what they can. That's all they know.'

He shrugged. 'Well, he's put this one out of her misery and no mistake. But you get along or I'll have my sergeant breathing down my neck.'

'So who is she? Got a name, has she?'

'Gawd only knows – now hop it, will you!'

Sadie stood her ground. It irked her to be ordered about by this pipsqueak constable. 'I might know her.'

He gave a mirthless laugh. 'You'd better hope you don't know her. Poor soul was cut to...' He stopped himself in time. 'Not allowed to give information to the public, so you get along.'

Sadie burped loudly and patted her chest. 'It's a free country.'

'Fine. You stay there then – and I'll arrest you for loitering!'

An elderly man arrived with a small terrier on a lead and the policeman switched his attention to the dog, who had started to bark hysterically. Sadie admitted defeat and turned back. She stumbled along Whitechapel Road, was sick in the gutter, and was eventually banging on Bella's door.

Bella came downstairs, still in her nightclothes, and eyed her aunt with despair. 'You been on the gin again?' she asked, closing the door behind them and making her way back up again.

'What if I have? Got a cuppa, lovey, or some milk? My throat's that dry.'

While Bella made tea, Lottie joined them and the two young women listened enthralled while her account of the new murder was described. Faced with a sympathetic audience, Sadie had rallied. She was a natural story-teller and added a wonderful variety of details to the few facts she had gleaned from the policeman.

'I bet the police don't do nothing,' she reflected. 'She was only a streetwoman. No one cares a jot about them.'

Three

A few days later, on September the 6th, when Dora's husband returned from work he was surprised by the enthusiasm of her greeting. As soon as she had closed the front door behind him, she threw her arms round his neck and clung to him.

He freed himself and stepped back to look at her. 'What's all this about, Dora?'

'The funeral,' she said, following him into the kitchen. 'I saw her funeral. That woman that was all cut up. Polly Nichols. It was so sad, John. Two of her children were there. Can you imagine that? It made me feel frightened. That could have been me, I thought. It could be me, lying dead in my coffin!'

'In your coffin? Not yet, surely dear. You're a young woman still.'

'But *she* was young ... Well, middle-aged. There were crowds of people there all along the pavements. Lots of women. Some quite poor. You know, John, *those* sort of women. Lots of them were crying.' She paused for breath and went on. 'The police were there, keeping people away from the hearse. One woman shouted that if they'd done their job they'd have caught the killer by now. Another woman spat at them.'

'This is the woman found in Buck's Yard? Mary Nichols known as Polly?'

She nodded. 'That's her!'

'Save your pity, Dora. The world is better off without them.'

She went on as though she hadn't heard him. 'I was on my way to collect your shoes from the cobbler – they're under your side of the bed, by the way – and I saw all these people in Barker's Row following a hearse and a woman said it was the murdered woman and a man said it was the second woman he'd killed so he's a serial killer and that it was very serious. A man from Scotland Yard is being brought in to be in charge of the investigation.' Breathless, she sat down on the nearest chair, a hand on her heart. Her hair was unwashed, there were dark circles under her eyes and her face was the colour of putty.

Her husband looked at her with distaste. 'Did you get any sleep last night?'

'Not much. I had those dreadful stomach pains again. Suppose I'm ill, John. Suppose I die. I could end up in my coffin without being murdered. I think I should go and see Doctor Rivers and...'

'I've already told you that *I* will decide if and when you go to the doctor, Dora. It costs money and there's nothing wrong with you. A bit of indigestion, that's all. You're always malingering. Stir yourself, Dora. Do more housework and do it faster. Go out shopping and *hurry* yourself.' His voice rose reproachfully. 'You sit around reading those foolish magazines and mope about. No wonder you're sluggish and can't do anything.' He gave an exasperated sigh. 'Is my breakfast ready?'

'It's only porridge. It won't take long.' She stood up unsteadily.

'I've been out all night working and you offer me porridge! Day after day! I want a proper breakfast. I'll have some fried bread and an egg and some bacon – and get a move on.' He had taken off his jacket and now handed it to her.

In silence she hung it on its hook and turned to face him. 'John, I should go to the doctor ... for another reason. I think ... but I'm not sure ... I may be having a baby.' Her expression was a mix of hope and fear. 'I mean, you did say you wanted lots of children ... What's the matter, John? You don't look very...' Her voice trailed away.

He turned quickly away and when he spoke his voice was quietly controlled. 'That's splendid news, dear. A baby. Our first child. Then we must get you fit and well.

I'll give you another pick-me-up this evening, before you go to bed.' He turned back, a strange smile on his face. 'A baby! Goodness me! We certainly are blessed, Dora.'

She smiled tentatively. 'So you are pleased, dear? I did wonder. You seem so distant lately. To tell you the truth...' She swallowed hard. 'I began to wonder if you had fallen for someone else. I thought perhaps you had fallen out of love with me.'

His smile broadened. 'Oh, my poor little Dora. What a worrier you are. I still love you and there has been no one else in my life since the first day I set eyes on you. You will be my dearest wife until the day you die.'

'Oh, don't speak of dying!'

'It's just an expression.' He kissed her. 'There now. Have I set your fears at rest?

Nodding, she once more threw herself into his arms and held him close and a wave of relief and happy anticipation swept through her. John loved her and she was going to have his child.

The following evening, Friday, the 7th of September, only a few streets away, Lloyd announced that he was tired and would go up to bed early.

Smiling as he smothered a yawn, he said, 'There's no need for you to accompany me this early, Bella. You and Lottie can carry on with the jigsaw puzzle for another hour. I see you've nearly finished it.' He leaned over the table on which they were working on a picture of the Houses of Parliament, which he had bought to keep Lottie quiet.

Lottie beamed. 'I can do jigsaws. Really I can. And Bella says I'm patriotic because it's the Houses of Parliament and I can do it.'

To Bella's surprise, Lloyd reached out and patted her shoulder. Such affectionate gestures were almost unknown and Bella was ridiculously grateful. If only he could convince Lottie that he liked her, she reflected, her cousin might end her illogical dislike of him.

He was studying the pieces of jigsaw and suddenly reached out, picked one up and pressed it into place in one of the windows.

Lottie squealed with excitement. 'Oh, Lloyd. How clever you are!'

He winked at Bella. 'I'm off to bed.' She turned her head for a kiss and he again patted Lottie's shoulder as he made his goodnights.

When he had left the room, Lottie grinned. 'He is clever, isn't he, Bella?'

'Yes he is. And he likes you, Lottie.'

'Yes he does. He really does.' She picked up a green piece that was obviously grass and studied it with exaggerated concentration.

'You like him, don't you, Lottie?'

'I like him. Yes.' She tried to press the piece into a tree. 'Go *in*!' she muttered and her mood at once changed.

Quickly Bella took it from her and placed it in the grassy area. 'You must be patient, Lottie,' she said, with a shake of her head.

Lottie frowned. 'Some of the pieces are the wrong shape!'

'No, they're not. They can't be, Lottie, because they make a picture and then cut it up into small pieces. You are simply trying to put them in the wrong place.'

She was silently composing a few more kind phrases to use about her husband when they heard him clattering back down the stairs. The door flew open and Lloyd glared at Lottie. To Bella he said, 'You'd better come and see this!'

Bella felt a rush of dismay. Now, what had happened? She rose to her feet, glancing at Lottie, who looked as surprised as she was herself.

'What is it?'

Lottie also rose but Lloyd pointed an accusing finger at her. 'Not you! You stay where you are!'

'But I want to come with Bella.'

Bella shook her head. 'You wait here, Lottie. Do as Lloyd tells you.'

Inwardly quaking, Bella followed her husband up the stairs and into their bedroom. The bedclothes had been pulled roughly back. She took a few short steps forward and then gasped. 'Oh no!'

The mattress was soaked with what appeared to be water and the water jug from their washing table was on its side below the window.

'Oh no! Not Lottie? How are we going to sleep there tonight?'

His face was stony. 'Who else? I didn't do it and I don't imagine you did it!'

'But ... why would she?'

'To punish me for marrying you. You can see how hard I try to be nice to her but she throws my kindness back in my face. I did warn you she was getting rather strange. I do sincerely fear for her sanity, Bella.'

Bella's throat was dry. There was no way she could save Lottie from her husband's wrath. And she mustn't seem to take Lottie's side against him. She straightened up. 'Please leave this to me, Lloyd. I shall...'

'No. I shall deal with her myself. Please fetch her, Bella. If she is not going to slide into madness, we must be firm with her. Fetch her, I say!'

When Bella still hesitated, he pushed past her to the door and shouted down the stairs. 'Lottie! Come up here at once!'

To Bella's surprise Lottie came up willingly and stood in the doorway looking at them expectantly.

Lloyd pointed to the bed. 'Why did you do

this, you wicked girl?'

Lottie blinked, then stepped closer to the bed. Seeing that the mattress was soaked, she gave a shriek. 'I didn't do it. I didn't. Really I didn't.'

She looks genuinely shocked, thought Bella, surprised. Had she forgotten what she had done? Was her memory suddenly failing? Perhaps Lloyd was right and she *was* getting worse.

Lloyd grabbed Lottie and threw her on to the wet bed. She screamed and tried to get up but he held her down.

Bella cried, 'Don't hurt her, Lloyd! Please don't hurt her.'

Lottie was struggling to get up but he pressed her further into the wet mattress. 'I'm going to make you sorry for this,' he told her. '*You* are going to sleep in this nasty wet bed and Bella and I will sleep in *your* bed.'

Bella watched in horror as they struggled together. Tears of fright poured down Lottie's face and Bella could see how terrified she was. No one had ever tried to hurt Lottie. Bella could stand it no longer. She dashed forward and tried to pull Lloyd away from the bed. He turned, pushed her fiercely then turned back to Lottie. Caught off balance, Bella tottered, struggled to regain her balance, then fell backwards. For a moment she was winded and lay still, dazed by the speed of events.

She heard Lloyd say, 'Stay there, Lottie. If you move from that bed I shall beat you.'

He turned to Bella and knelt beside her. 'Bella, dearest. I'm so sorry. I lost my temper. It's Lottie's fault. I'm so sorry, my dearest. It will never happen again. Are you hurt?'

Dazed, she whispered, 'I don't think so.'

He helped her up and she stole a look at Lottie who was curled up on the bed, with her hands around her head. She looked small and helpless.

Lloyd steered Bella outside on to the landing. In a low voice he said, 'I shall say no more to her. But she must learn her lesson. Every time she does something like this she will be punished.'

'You said such cruel things, Lloyd.' Bella stared at him. 'You said you would *beat* her!'

'Of course I shall do no such thing. You know me better than that, Bella. It was a threat, nothing more. Now you go back down downstairs and continue with your jigsaw while I see that Lottie goes to bed. In *our* bed! I shall bring my nightshirt and your nightdress and we will sleep in Lottie's room. The bed is narrower but we shall snuggle closer.' He smiled and kissed the top of her head.

'I don't want to work on the jigsaw,' Bella told him, her voice shaky. 'I'll come to bed now with you ... But Lottie ... She might catch a cold, sleeping in a wet bed.'

'Serve her right if she does. That way she will learn the dangers of such foolish tricks. Do you want her to be put away in an asylum? Would she like that? If not, we have to stop this madness from developing by any means we can devise. It's in her own best interests, Bella. You must surely understand that.'

Bella was torn by the enormity of the decision to be taken. Lottie would die if she were sent to an asylum. 'Let me think about it,' she suggested.

Lloyd's mouth twisted impatiently. 'Think as long as you like, Bella dear, but you will not change my mind.' He lowered his voice. 'Face the fact that she might become a danger to us. Suppose she set fire to the curtains in the middle of the night. We could die in our beds.'

'She never would!'

'Did you think she would ever pour water over our mattress?'

Bella shook her head.

'Suppose she harms herself. Suppose she leaves the house in the middle of the night. Is that want you want – to take such risks?'

Bella shook her head. For some reason, she felt she was being trapped by his line of questioning. Left to her own devices, she thought, she would probably see it all differently. Suddenly she came to a decision – but one she would keep to herself. She would confide in Aunt Sadie.

Without another word she went downstairs. She locked the doors and windows, lit a candle and turned out the gaslights. When she went back upstairs all was quiet in their bedroom and Lloyd was fast asleep in the bed in Lottie's room. Undressing quietly, she felt a pang of remorse, and before she blew out the candle, she made her way to where her cousin was sleeping in the ruined bed. To her surprise she discovered that the door was locked and the key missing. At first she was alarmed, but then she told herself that Lloyd must have had Lottie's safety in mind. She might otherwise have sneaked downstairs and, in her present state, might even have run away. The thought of her cousin wandering alone through the dark streets while the mad killer was still at large was intolerable. But she would speak to him about it in the morning. She went back to the narrow bed and slid into the remaining space. She didn't want to talk to her husband. She wanted time to think.

She lay in bed, staring up at the pattern made on the ceiling by the moonlight, remembering her own father. He had been a weak, stupid man who had earned a limited living working, when he felt like it, for his brother, who ran a greengrocer's shop. When he died, Bella had been glad to see him go. He had spent most of the money he earned on gambling – horses were his downfall.

Bella wondered what sort of father Lloyd would turn out to be. At least he had a decent job and was respected. A smile spread over her face, chasing away the dark thoughts. Lloyd would be a wonderful father – the kind of father she would have liked when she was a child. He would be kind but firm and would take an interest in them as they grew up. The boys would look up to him and the girls would adore him. Finally, her cheerful spirit won over the doubts and she fell asleep with a smile on her face.

When Bella awoke early next morning she found that Lloyd had already left for work and that Lottie's room had been unlocked. She found Lottie sitting on the edge of the bed, her eyes red-rimmed, her expression dark and brooding. She was already dressed but had not washed or combed her hair.

'I hate him,' she said when she saw Bella. 'I hate him! Hate him.'

Bella folded her arms. Lloyd was right. They had to be firm. It was for Lottie's own good.

'It serves you right,' she said. 'It was a silly thing to do. Lloyd was cross with you and so...'

'I didn't do it.'

'Lottie! You must have done it. There was nobody else here. Just you, me and Lloyd. And I didn't do it. Neither did Lloyd. Why should we want to spoil our bed? We had to squash together in your bed.'

Lottie giggled and Bella's patience evaporated. 'It's not funny,' she shouted. 'You silly girl! You don't see how much trouble you are in and I am doing the best I can for you. Now go downstairs with your flannel and soap and wash in the kitchen sink. We're going round to Aunt Sadie's and...'

Lottie turned to look at the clock. 'But it's only just gone seven.'

'I don't care. We're going now. You're driving me up the wall with your tricks and I need her advice.'

'But I didn't do it. I really, really didn't!'

Bella hardened her heart. 'Don't argue, Lottie. I want you downstairs in five minutes.'

Half an hour later they were being welcomed into Sadie's poky room. It was not only small, but dark and looked out over grimy rooftops. The window was never opened but fresh air came in through a hole in one corner of one pane. The room smelled stale and unloved. Sadie's small income, earned from ironing other people's laundry, went on the rent and gin. Their aunt was still in her nightgown but pulled on a faded dressing

72

gown and tied it round her ample waist.

She took one look at Bella's face and sensed trouble.

'Lottie, dear,' she said. 'I want you to go round to the baker's for me and fetch a large loaf. You can buy yourself a penny bun with what's left of the money.'

Lottie had sat down but now she sprang joyfully to her feet. 'Can I have a gingerbread man?' she asked eagerly. 'With currants for his eyes and a bit of red for his mouth...'

'Certainly you can, lovey.' She smiled. 'And take your time. There's no hurry. Me and Bella will just sit here and chat.'

When she had gone Bella launched into her sad story and Sadie listened appalled.

'And I do believe he will send her away if she goes on like this,' Bella told her, wide-eyed.

'Send her away? What right has he got to send her anywhere? Who does he think he is – Lord Muck?'

Bella felt obliged to defend her husband. 'You can see his point – about the danger,' she said. 'If she did set fire to the house...'

Sadie clapped her hands over her ears. 'I'm not hearing this!' she cried. 'I've known Lottie from the day she was born and she wouldn't hurt a fly.'

'But why did she cut up the curtains? And why soak our bed? I wonder if she's jealous because I have to give Lloyd a lot of my attention. She does seem to be changing, Aunt Sadie.' She hesitated. 'I woke up this morning and thought – if she gets this difficult over Lloyd what will she be like when ... if I have a baby?' Seeing the sudden gleam in her aunt's eyes she said quickly, 'Not that I am just yet but when I do...' She sighed.

Perplexed, Sadie bit her lip. 'It's a right poser,' she admitted. 'You just try to carry on same as always and I'll think about it. We'll find a way round it, don't you fret, Bella. You're married now to this lovely bloke and you deserve to be happy.' She smiled gently. 'If the truth be told, I wouldn't mind a bit of that myself! I always have fancied men with moustaches. Lloyd certainly is a handsome devil.' Noticing Bella's shocked face, she quickly changed the subject. 'But about Lottie. This telling lies and stuff might pass. Maybe he's right. Lottie may have learned her lesson. You know. Spare the rod and spoil the child. Give her a bit more time.' She grinned suddenly. 'What d'you reckon Lottie'll bring back?'

Bella laughed. 'Last time it was muffins. It's never the loaf, is it? I don't know if she forgets or she just fancies something else.'

Sadie found a small tumbler and a quarter inch of gin in a bottle hidden under the sink and settled herself with a sigh of contentment. She sipped slowly to make it last and they talked about the funeral of Mary

Nichols until they heard Lottie returning.

★ ★ ★

Around this time, a few hundred yards away in Goulston Street, Emily Trott was opening her front door. Goulston Street was no better and no worse than any of the other streets in the area. What made one house different from its neighbours was the attention paid to it by the tenants. No 18 was one of the fortunate houses. Emily Trott, a widow of fifty-five, worked at home. True, she had a very menial job making matchboxes for Bryant & May but she considered herself fortunate that she no longer had to work in the factory at Bow where she had spent several years as a young woman. Although the home work was tedious and poorly paid, she no longer had to mix with rowdy women who used coarse language and sometimes fought each other. Now she could make time to polish the front-door knocker even though the landlord refused to repaint the door itself. She also regularly whited the step. Unlike many servants employed in bigger houses elsewhere, she was not ashamed to be seen on her knees every morning scrubbing away. For others it might be proof of their lowly status. For Emily it was proof that she was a good housewife and one step above most of her neighbours. She despised the other inhabitants of Goulston Street who spent too little time in their homes and too much in the pubs and taverns. Emily was one of the few people who attended church on Sundays and she had only to look out of the back window across their neighbours' yards, to see how little washing they hung out on a Monday.

Since the death of her husband she had scraped together an existence by working at home for Mr Pearson. He paid her to make matchboxes, which he collected each evening. Emily rose at five each morning in summer and six in winter so that she could spend nine hours on her work. The rest of each day was her own. Today she had been woken by the birds at dawn and, unable to return to sleep, had got out of bed at ten past four to make an early start. Just after seven o'clock the previous night she had finally finished the amount of matchboxes required to earn her day's money. Then she had hurried into her tiny parlour and diligently scattered tea-leaves on to the almost threadbare carpet so that she could brush the dust into the pan without it flying up and settling on the few cheap ornaments.

Now she tidied her greying hair, pressed her thin lips together to encourage a little colour in them, and opened her front door to whoever was knocking. She found a goodlooking man outside, and felt the familiar relief that her newly whitened step had not been found wanting. Mind you, there was a mountain of matchboxes on the kitchen table and she was glad he couldn't see them, and glad she had had the sense to snatch off her apron.

He said, 'I'm Mr Undershot from the...'

She frowned. 'You're a bit early, aren't you? It's not nine o'clock yet.'

'I am, yes. I'm sorry but I have a lot to get through today. I'm from a debt collection agency in Bow. I wonder if I could come in for a moment and talk to you – ' he leaned forward and lowered his voice – 'about your neighbour at number sixteen.'

Guilessly, she welcomed him in. It didn't enter her head for a moment that she might be doing anything rash. It was just so good to have someone to talk to. Someone who had polished his boots and had clean fingernails. Her husband had been a poor but fastidious man.

Mr Undershot explained that he was trying to trace a debtor named Cummings who had probably changed his name.

Emily's eyes widened with excitement. 'Come into my front parlour,' she suggested. 'I expect you'd like a drink.' Without giving him time to refuse she almost pushed him on to a chair. 'I'll bring you a glass of my own lemonade.'

Three minutes later she was telling him all she knew about Mr and Mrs Hubbard.

'The man works most nights. I hear him

going off. I think he works at the London. You know – the London Hospital in Whitechapel Road.'

'He's a doctor, then?' He produced a notebook.

'So Mrs Betts says. She lives opposite them. Very nosy woman. Into everything. I don't care to associate myself with the likes of her, Mr Undershot, if you know what I mean. This isn't a very salubrious area but I do my best to rise above it. Most of the people in this street are ... Well, let's just say there are more undesirables in this street than I care to shake a stick at.'

'Could you describe him to me?'

'Who?'

'Your neighbour. The husband.'

She frowned. 'Dark hair, middling height. Large moustache...'

'And beard?'

'No beard.' She studied the ceiling, trying to conjure up his image. 'Rather dark eyes. What you might call piercing.' She smiled at him as he scribbled in his notebook. 'Not that I don't like dark eyes. My husband had dark eyes. Very dark brown ... Not that I don't like blue eyes either, Mr Undershot,' she added quickly. 'I do but...'

'Do you talk to the wife at all?'

Emily shook her head. 'I try not to. She's a miserable sort of woman. Whenever I do bump into her she moans about her health.

78

Headaches, stomach pains, can't sleep, feels sick...'

He looked up sharply. 'Feels sick? You don't mean...' He raised his eyebrows.

She stared at him. Fancy a man speaking of such things. For a moment she was taken aback but quickly recovered. 'Morning sickness? Ooh ... I never thought about that.'

'Is she the right age?'

She looked at him in surprise then smiled knowingly. 'Aha! You're obviously not married, Mr Undershot, or you'd know these things. Yes. She is the right age. At least I think she's between twenty and thirty although she could be older. She just looks so ... so *sickly* all the time. Doesn't bother with her looks. D'you know what I mean? If I were her husband I'd tell her to pull herself together. But then if she's in the family way ... It does take some women like that.'

He was frowning, writing furiously. He glanced at her. 'Could she be ill, do you think? Seriously ill?'

'I've no idea.' His manner had changed, she thought. More earnest, somehow. 'I could pop round, I suppose. See if she's all right.'

'I'm sure she'd appreciate a friendly word or two.'

She regarded him eagerly. 'What will you do when you find this man? Does he owe a lot of money?' Her mind began working overtime. 'It's not Mr Hubbard who owes all the money, is it? I mean, how can it be him if his name's not Cummings?'

'No, no! Not at all. It's just that we have information from a previous address where he owes the rent. The man did a moonlight flit. You know the phrase?'

'Did he really? Ooh yes! I know it. You mean he disappeared in the night!'

'Exactly. Someone where he used to live thinks he moved to this area. To Goulston Street but nobody that I've spoken to so far goes by the same name. So he may have changed it.'

She sat back in the chair, hiding her disappointment. How wonderfully exciting it would have been to find out she was living next door to a man who was wanted by a debt collector.

He wrote again then looked up. 'So the wife appears to be ill. Poor soul. But if her husband's a doctor...'

'Oh, Mr Undershot! You're right. He should be helping her. Treating her – or is that illegal? Can a man be his own wife's doctor?'

He snapped the notebook shut and jumped-ed to his feet. 'I've wasted too much of your time, Mrs Trott. Forgive me. I must get about my business. I'll start some enquiries in Wentworth Street. I may have better luck there.'

She followed him to the door and opened it reluctantly. 'I wish I could have been more help, Mr Undershot.'

'You've helped me a lot ... to get things clear. And thank you for the lemonade.'

She watched him walk down the street, long coat flapping, and sighed. Nothing to do now but have some breakfast, fill the sack with yesterday's matchboxes and wait for Mr Pearson to collect them. She went into the kitchen and buttered a slice of bread and wondered for the first time about Mr Hubbard.

Later that day Douglas Unwin went home to write up his report. A report which he feared would not be read by his superiors until the man behind the current Whitechapel murders was caught. It was now generally accepted that the same man had killed twice and seemed to be targeting the unfortunate streetwomen. Douglas could not quarrel with the fact that finding their killer was priority but he had been tracking a killer for months and now he felt he was close, the new murderer was taking priority and causing *his* case to be set aside.

'It's so frustrating, Ma,' he complained as they settled down to a later than usual breakfast. 'I'm so close to Cummings or whatever his real name is. I can *feel* it in my bones. The woman I've just been talking to – a Mrs

Trott who lives next door to the suspect – says the wife is in very poor health. They said the same about poor old Edmund Cummings. Poisoned by his own son who called himself Alfred then. It must have been his real name because his father was Edmund Cummings. Now he's John Hubbard and married to Dora *and* he's Lloyd Massie and married to Bella.'

She looked up from her cheese and pickles. 'You *think* so, Douglas. You don't know for sure. You will be careful, won't you, dear? If you're wrong about him...' She shook her head.

He leant forward. 'Old Edmund Cummings's neighbour told me he was perfectly healthy until his son came home from the army. Nobody knows why. Rumour has it he was cashiered. You know what that means, Ma. He did something dishonest.'

'But the army didn't say what it was, did they? They didn't say he'd poisoned someone.'

'The army likes to keep its secrets, Ma. They've always been the same. They have their own court martials and they deal with misconduct in their own way. He may not have poisoned someone but he must have been accused of something serious for him to be thrown out. Came home penniless and very bitter, according to a neighbour. And what happened next?'

She finished her mouthful before answering the familiar question with the well-worn answer. 'The healthy father took to his bed, sick to his stomach and died soon after.'

'*Very* soon after. Dead and buried and only forty-eight years old! And who got all his savings? The son. I'm going to get that exhumation order, Ma, if it's the last thing I do. It may not prove anything but we have to try it.'

'Why didn't you ask for one when the father died?'

'I did, Ma. Twice! And each time they turned me down. Not enough evidence. They insisted it could have been self-inflicted. The son said his father had been severely depressed and they took that into account. It's very serious, an exhumation and I understand that. You can't go round digging up bodies without a very good reason. But I have a reason and I'm not giving up yet.'

She shrugged. 'Still, you shouldn't have to do it in your spare time, son. If your father were still alive he'd have something to say about the way you carry on. You're working yourself to death. You'll have a heart attack.'

'Course I won't, Ma. I get tired, yes, but not that tired. There's nothing wrong with my heart – and I won't give up! I want this man to *know* that I'm closing on him. I want him to be looking over his shoulder the whole time. What I'd like to do is call on them when he's there, but that would alert him.'

'It would give him a fright, though!'

'He'd disappear and I might never find him again.'

For a moment they ate in silence.

His mother sighed. 'They don't seem any closer to catching this new chap that kills those poor women.'

'They shouldn't be on the streets. They're asking for trouble. They know he's about and now it looks as if he'll go on killing until they catch him ... And we *will* catch him, Ma. Scotland Yard have sent three of their top men to help us. Abberline, Moore and Andrews. All high-ranking men. Oh, we'll get him, Ma.'

Much as the local force outwardly resented the suggestion that they could not run this case with their own resources, they were secretly rather impressed by the fact that such a notorious killer was operating in their area and that the 'grisly murders' were making headlines in the national newspapers. Douglas knew that the words 'serial killer' were being bandied around and if that were so they would certainly need help from above. The men seconded from Scotland Yard had impressive records. Chief Inspector Moore specialized in murder cases and had made several high-profile arrests. Inspector Abberline was very experienced and knew the East End and the criminals it harboured. The third man, Inspector Andrews, was highly respected by his colleagues and feared by all wrongdoers. Although Douglas was still obsessed with Cummings he nevertheless felt proud to be working alongside such important men on such a significant case.

His mother said, 'I reckon it's a butcher because he uses those long knives. Or else it's that Leather Apron man. I don't know why the police didn't keep him in prison. He might have done it even though he says he didn't.'

'He had an alibi, Ma. He's been vouched for by several people. It wasn't him. Remember, anybody can get hold of a long knife – you've got some in the kitchen drawer! We can't arrest every butcher. Even if we did they're not likely to admit it unless we have some proof. Then we could challenge them. The thing is, Ma, that if we charge the wrong man, the real villain goes free. He'd be laughing at us. And he'd be killing another woman before long, just to prove we'd made a mistake.'

'Well, I think it's dreadful. Cutting people up like that! Ugh! It ought to be against the law.'

He grinned. 'Ma, it *is* against the law.'

'You can laugh but you're not a woman. It's women he kills. Cowardly, I call it.'

'You'd be happier if he killed a few men,

would you?'

An exaggerated sigh was all the answer he received, but after some thought she said, 'They should put you on the case.'

'I'm already *on* it. Why d'you think I can't spend so much time on Cummings?' He felt the usual wave of exasperation. He had explained this to her before but it seemed to go in one ear and out of the other. 'Because we're all being thrown into this case and we have to get him. I accept that. He's a very vicious man. Frenzied is the word they're using in the newspapers and it's true. As to only killing women of a certain sort – we're warning them all to stay home at night but they *have* no homes, many of them. They can only sleep in a common lodging house and for that they need a few pence and they have to earn it by ... by doing what they do.'

Annie sniffed. 'They could take in washing or ironing. That's respectable.'

'Where would they *do* this washing and ironing if they have no homes?' he demanded. 'You don't think things through, Ma.'

For a moment or two his mother frowned down at her plate and Douglas waited for the reprimand that usually followed an argument, however slight. She was beginning to show signs of forgetfulness, he thought, but of course she was getting older. If he ever married, she would have to live with him and his wife, but his mother would hate that. She was a very independent person. He pushed the thought to the back of his mind. Worry about that when the time comes, he told himself.

She glanced up. 'What do you think of my home-made pickle, Douglas? I got hold of some cheap apples in the market. Apple, onions and sultanas with a bit of ginger.'

Surprised and relieved, he said, 'Very good, Ma. Tasty.'

Outside, the church clock struck the quarter. 'What time are you supposed to be back on duty?'

'Ten o'clock.'

'You'd best get a move on then or you'll be late.'

Four

On the evening of the same day, Bella and Lottie were on their way home from the shops just before six when they came across a group of excited women standing on the corner of Hanbury Street. One of the women turned to them, her eyes wide with fear. 'Have you heard? He's done it again. The murderer. He's killed another one. Ripped her up just like before!'

'He never has!' cried Bella and Lottie began to whimper. 'Lottie, love, you don't have to be scared...' Bella began.

The women shouted her down. 'Course she should be scared with a monster like that on the loose. I'm bloody scared and I don't mind admitting it.'

'In this very street,' one of them told her, pointing down Hanbury Street.

'Do they know who it is?' Bella asked, putting her arm round Lottie's trembling shoulders.

'Not yet, but they will. They're asking at all the lodging houses. Funny, but they all seem to be married women who've left their husbands...'

'Or he's left them.' Bella shrugged. 'I suppose that's why they're out and about late at night while we married women are tucked up in our beds.'

Lottie said, 'Bella got married five weeks ago but I don't like him now. I really don't!' She gave Bella a challenging look.

'Ooh ... a newly-wed,' one of the women mocked and Bella felt her face flush.

A second woman returned to the main item of conversation. 'Swarming with policemen this road was, first thing. Uniforms everywhere and a few of those men wearing their own clothes. Detectives, they were. I was on my way to see my mother and they were everywhere. Never saw the poor soul what copped it, though. Lying in the back yard of number twenty-nine, she was. Poor old chap what lived there found her and was scared out of his wits. They say she was still warm when he found her!'

A small plump woman with a pock-marked face pushed forward. 'And it was *daylight* when he done it. Must have been, they reckon. He's not skulking around in the dark any more. He's getting a mite too saucy for my liking.'

There was a loud chorus of agreement.

The women gathered round them, all talking at once, and Lottie and Bella listened with increasing horror as the story unfolded. Like the last victim, the murdered woman had had her throat cut and some of her internal organs had been removed from her body.

Lottie began to cry and Bella did her best to comfort her but as the women continued she decided she would have to take her home. Her cousin was in enough trouble already now that her behaviour had worsened. Hearing about the murders might alarm her and make her even worse.

Reluctantly, Bella tugged her away from the group and they continued homeward in a subdued state of mind. This was the third murder in less than two months – and all had taken place less than a mile from White

Street where she, Lloyd and Lottie lived. So far he had restricted his victims to prostitutes, but who would be next? He was getting bolder, they said, and it was true. Suppose he took to climbing in through the windows of respectable people's homes ... or murdering women in the middle of the day. Bella shuddered. She would talk to Lloyd and see if their house locks were good enough. She would warn the Schwartzes upstairs to be on their guard. Perhaps, even though it was still summer, they should all sleep with the windows closed until the killer was caught and safely behind bars.

The next day Lottie stood at the kitchen sink peeling potatoes while Bella did the ironing which she should have done Tuesday. That morning Lloyd had complained about the fact that he could not find a clean shirt and Bella had apologized, explaining that with one thing and another – she didn't want to mention Lottie – she had fallen behind with her housework. Lloyd had been distant and had gone off about his business without giving her a goodbye kiss. This oversight had upset her more than she would admit. How would she feel if he was somehow killed during the course of his work and she hadn't kissed him goodbye? Bella tried hard to forget this but deep down the awful thought nagged – that maybe Lloyd had deliberately left the house without kissing her as a punishment for the missing shirt. Recently she had become rather worried about the nature of marriage. Was it supposed to be like this? Was there no romance after the wedding day? Because she loved Lloyd so desperately, she couldn't bear the thought that he now thought of her as a less than dutiful housewife and not as a desirable sweetheart.

For her part she went through the rest of the day counting the hours until he was due home. He was a little later than usual and she worried about his safety. Was he in any danger? she wondered. As the minutes passed she became irritable with poor Lottie. When she heard the front door open she broke into a radiant smile and flew down the narrow hallway to greet him.

As soon as their embrace ended, Lloyd drew her into the parlour with his finger on his lips. He closed the door and sat her down.

'I just want you to know that I have made an appointment for Lottie to see the doctor. Or rather, for him to see her. I have explained to him that her mind is in a fragile state and...'

'Oh Lloyd! She will be terribly frightened. You know she will!' She stood up but he pushed her down again.

'Hear me out, Bella!' he said sternly.

'But Lloyd, I don't think a visit to the doctor is necessary. She really is...'

His face darkened. 'Bella! I haven't asked you for your opinion. When I want it, I'll ask for it. This matter is decided. You can make up any excuse you like, but get her to the doctor's surgery tomorrow at nine o'clock sharp. If you do not promise to do this, *I* shall take her myself and I can assure you, she would not like that very much. She is your cousin and I have been very patient.'

'But Lloyd, what is the doctor going to say? How will he examine her? I don't understand what is going to happen to her.'

'He will do some tests. Ask her some questions. That's all. There's nothing much to it. The point is that if she deteriorates further we shall take her for further tests and then the doctor will be able to compare the results.'

He was already looking at her coldly, but abruptly he took a few steps towards the window and, thrusting his hands into his pockets, he stared out, his back rigid and unapproachable.

Bella turned his words over in her mind, unsure what to make of the proposal. It sounded reasonable and Lottie had been behaving very strangely ... but suppose the doctor wasn't pleased with the answers to his test. Then what would happen? She tried to think of an excuse that she could give to

Lottie. She would feel such a traitor, luring her to the surgery on false pretences – but she agreed that it was better they go together. She dreaded to think how Lottie would behave with Lloyd as her escort.

At last she said, 'And if he says she's all right, then ... then she needn't go again ... I suppose.'

Lloyd turned abruptly on his heel. 'I've also asked Doctor Hague to give her a draught, Bella.' His voice had changed and he looked at her kindly. 'Something to take to keep her calm ... and happy. A spoonful first thing on waking or last thing at night. Something she can easily remember. She'll get into a routine and be quite her old self again. You can't object to that, surely, dear?'

'A draught? Why no!' She felt weak with relief. This proved that her husband was as sweet and caring as she had always imagined him to be. 'That sounds like a wonderful idea. How thoughtful of you, Lloyd. That's just what she needs. Something to soothe her. I'll tell her that. And maybe I'll say that there is a nasty sickness going round Whitechapel and you want us both to see the doctor – to make sure we have no symptoms. That will do nicely.'

Smiling, he held out his arms and she rushed forward, pressing her face into the cloth of his jacket. She was instantly happy again.

Doctor Hague was a middle-aged man, thick set and inclined to be surly whenever his digestion was playing up. He drank a little too often and it was rumoured that he had private money but nobody wanted to know more. In Whitechapel, people only went to the doctor as a last resort because it was expensive by their standards. Consequently there was no one else in the waiting room when Lottie and Bella arrived Monday morning at nine o'clock.

The doctor came to the door of his surgery and said, 'Well, come on in then. I haven't got all day.'

Bella stood up but Lottie remained in her seat.

She said, 'I really don't want to! I really don't.'

Bella reached for her hand but she shrank back, eyeing the doctor suspiciously.

He said, 'Well, you'll miss the sweet then. What a shame!' and turned back into the room.

Lottie stood up.

'A sweet, Lottie. I wonder if he'll give me one.' As she spoke, Bella was leading the way, deliberately not looking back. Fortunately, Lottie decided she wanted a sweet and did *not* want to be left alone in the waiting room. She hurried after Bella and was offered a toffee from a large jar, which the doctor then returned to the shelf behind him.

I shall have to come to this man, thought Bella, when I'm having my baby. I shall have to ask him to give me the name of a midwife. She smiled. 'Lottie's going to answer all your questions, aren't you, Lottie?'

Lottie nodded, busy with the toffee wrapper.

Doctor Hague looked at her. 'Would you like your cousin to stay with you while you answer the questions?'

Lottie nodded again, pushing the toffee into her mouth. Bella was delighted that the session was going so well.

He opened a drawer and pulled out a folder inside of which there were a few papers. One was obviously a list of questions, but another was a printed picture. He pushed this across the desk to Lottie and asked her to explain what was happening in the picture. Bella peered over Lottie's shoulder. A dog was running away with a string of sausages. An angry man was running after the dog and a woman and a child were watching with tears running down their faces. Bella studied it with interest. Her interpretation was that the dog had stolen their dinner. The mother and child were crying because they were hungry and the man was trying to catch the dog and rescue the dinner.

Lottie stared at the picture then looked at

Bella for a clue. Bella said nothing. The doctor said, 'What's happening in the picture?'

Lottie fiddled with the toffee paper, screwed it into a ball and put it in the pocket of her jacket. 'He's a nasty man. He looks cross. He made the woman cry and he made the little boy cry and now he's chasing the poor little dog.' She narrowed her eyes. 'He's nasty and he tells lies!'

Bella gasped. Please, Lottie, she begged silently, don't start that again. Dragging Lloyd into the conversation will only convince the doctor that she was indeed a threat. Bella had worked hard to explain to Lottie how she should reply to the questions. She had warned her not to mention Lloyd or the wet bed or the ruined curtains. Had she forgotten so soon?

The doctor steepled his hands and surveyed Lottie over the top of them. 'I see.'

Lottie beamed at him and flashed Bella a triumphant glance.

To her relief he didn't follow up on the last comment but instead dipped his pen in the ink and wrote on the questionnaire in a slow, careful hand.

He said, 'What day is it today, Lottie?'

She chewed the toffee thoughtfully. 'Is it my birthday?'

'I don't know. Is it?'

'Because I do have a birthday. Once a year.

96

I really do.'

'I mean, which day of the week is it? You know the days of the week, don't you?'

'Monday, Tuesday, Wednesday...'

'But which day is it today?'

Bella was willing her cousin to answer correctly. Lottie knew it was Monday, didn't she? It was hard to tell if Lottie was being deliberately vague or genuinely understood less than Bella had thought.

'Can you tell me the name of the Prime Minister, Lottie?'

'No. I don't want to. I don't like him. He tells lies.'

The doctor rolled his eyes and glanced at Bella. He seemed rather amused but refrained from comment. A difficult question, Bella thought, guiltily aware that she herself had no idea who the Prime Minister was. Women weren't expected to know such things. Politics and voting were for the men to worry about.

Seemingly reading her mind, he said, 'Let's make it easier, Lottie. Do we have a king or a queen? And who is it?'

'Queen Victoria. Hurrah!' Lottie clapped her hands.

'Indeed.' He wrote again.

How was her cousin doing? Bella wondered anxiously.

He pushed a list of words towards his patient and asked her to read them. Bella relaxed because she knew Lottie could read reasonably well. She crossed her fingers.

Lottie glanced down the list and then said, 'Yes.'

'Yes what?'

'I've read them.'

'I meant you to read them *aloud*, Lottie.'

Lottie went through the list of two, three and four-syllable words with only a few errors.

'Well done!' he said.

Bella allowed herself a smile. It was going to be all right. Lottie was co-operating and the doctor was impressed. At least she hoped he was. After all, she reassured herself, hundreds of people couldn't read or write so Lottie was doing very well.

'Can you add up, Lottie? What do five and five make?'

'Ten!' Lottie glanced at her hands as if for reassurance.

'And ten and seven?'

After a slight hesitation Lottie said, 'Seventeen.'

'And six and four and ten?'

'Yes.'

'Can you add them up for me?'

She stared at him. 'Lloyd tells lies. He tells big lies. He...'

Bella cried, 'Lottie! Stop that at once!' She had jumped to her feet and now shook Lottie's arm. Her heart was racing with fright.

Lottie was going to ruin everything.

Bella turned to the doctor. 'She's very tired. She's done well. I must take her home now.'

He regarded her sharply. His careworn manner had vanished. 'Sit down, please, Mrs Massie. I will tell you when I'm through with this test.'

She sat down. 'But...'

'No buts, please. Compose yourself. This may be the problem your husband was describing – some kind of persecution mania. That's exactly how he described it.' He turned back to Lottie, who was now watching them with a worried frown on her face.

She said, 'Can I have another toffee ... please?'

Bella closed her eyes and prayed. Please God, don't let her say anything too awful.

'You may have a toffee to take home, Lottie,' the doctor said. 'Just tell me what you mean about your brother-in-law, Lloyd Massie. You say he tells lies?'

Lottie leaned forward. 'He tells lies and he hates me and he said I should cut up the curtains and then he said I made the bed all wet and I didn't and ... and I hate him. I really do.'

'Oh dear, Lottie.' He leaned forward. 'You sound very upset about poor Mr Massie. Would you do anything to hurt him?'

Bella cried, 'Of course she wouldn't! She

does get mixed up sometimes and ... and my husband has to speak sharply to her but ... No, of course she wouldn't hurt him. She wouldn't hurt anyone!'

Lottie said, 'Yes I would. I would hurt him. He hurt me. He slapped me. He locked me in the bedroom and tied me to the bed and it was all wet. He hates me and I hate him! I do, Bella! '

Her lips were quivering and Bella panicked. This was all going wrong. Whatever would Doctor Hague write in his report? She stood up, grabbed Lottie's arm and jerked her roughly to her feet. 'You've said quite enough, Lottie,' she warned. To the doctor she said, 'You've upset my cousin and we're leaving. You can write whatever you like but I know that my cousin is not dangerous in any way. She couldn't hurt a fly.'

She urged her cousin towards the door and opened it. The doctor had risen to his feet and was protesting, but she ignored him. As she propelled Lottie along the passage and out of the front door, she knew she had a taken a big risk.

Lottie stumbled along beside her. 'But Bella, where's the nice medicine he was going to give me?'

'Which nice medicine?'

'The soothing medicine to make me feel happy.'

'He forgot it. We'll fetch it another day.'

'And have we got the nasty sickness?'

Bella marched on, her head held high, her heart thumping. 'What sickness?'

'You said there was nasty sickness in Whitechapel and...'

'Oh that! No, we haven't got it. Don't worry, Lottie. Everything's going to be fine.'

But it wouldn't be, would it? There was a lump in Bella's throat. Already, Bella was regretting their hasty departure. Whatever would Lloyd say now? One thing was certain. He would be very, *very* angry.

On Tuesday, the third day after the murder of Annie Chapman, Douglas Unwin made his way to the London Hospital. He had spent the day, like most of his fellow officers, conducting general inquiries in the neighbourhood of Whitechapel. Dozens of police, constables and detectives alike, knocked on dozens of doors asking the same questions again and again: 'How many men live in this house?' 'What are their names?' 'Have you been approached by anyone suspicious?' 'Did you see anything out of the ordinary happening on the night of the latest murder?'

They noted the replies, always longing for a clue but expecting to be disappointed. 'Do you know anyone who is always out at nights?' 'Is anyone in your street behaving in a suspicious manner?' 'Have you seen a foreign-looking man with piercing dark eyes, a large moustache and dark hair?'

They also stopped people in the street with the same questions. Occasionally there would be a hopeful lead, which, on further examination, led nowhere. The policemen grew weary and frustrated by their many failures. Women who lived in the area grew more resentful, claiming with great bitterness that the authorities cared nothing for the deaths of unfortunates, and would make more effort if the victims had been wealthy women or the wives of powerful men. Douglas suffered the same frustrations but he also felt oppressed by the sights and smells of so much poverty. In Whitechapel and Spitalfields many of the worst slums were found and the inhabitants, inevitably dragged down by circumstances, touched Douglas's kindly heart. This apart, he also resented the fact that his own long-standing case was now given no priority whatsoever and he was forced to continue his investigation unofficially and in his own limited time.

Once in Whitechapel Road, he walked swiftly along to the hospital entrance and made his way through the gate and inside the imposing brick building. It had a frontage of five hundred feet and was five storeys high. Douglas was immediately struck by the distinctive smell all hospitals have: a stifling mix of floor polish, cold tiled walls, disinfectant; and the presence of many sick and wounded human beings crushed into one large self-contained area. His nostrils flared as he turned right into a small area known as the receiving room, but he forgot the smell as he concentrated on the task in hand.

An attractive woman, in a white high-necked blouse, was seated behind the desk. A few chairs lined one wall and a variety of prospective patients sat on these. Douglas presumed they were waiting for their names to be called. A woman with an apron over her shabby dress and a shawl round her shoulders darted nervous glances in all directions. A man with a bandage round his head regarded the receptionist with narrowed eyes as if she were 'the enemy'. An elderly man in badly worn boots huddled on his chair, obviously terrified to find himself in such a vast and intimidating place. Douglas felt for them all. Having a strong constitution, he had never been inside a hospital except when doing his duty as a policeman. He sincerely hoped he never would.

As Douglas approached the desk the young woman glanced up from behind it. She had a bored expression on her face but brightened when she saw a good-looking young man waiting to speak to her.

'Yes, sir?'

'I'm looking for a man named Hubbard. He's a doctor here – or so I'm told. I'd like a word with him if that's possible.'

She frowned. 'Hubbard, you say? I don't recognize the name. In what department is he?' As Douglas hesitated she said, 'Eyes nose and throat? Infectious diseases? Respiratory?' She had brown hair drawn back into a bun.

'I'm afraid I don't know his speciality but perhaps you have a list somewhere. We might track him down that way.'

Further along the corridor, to the right, a man in a white coat appeared through a doorway and called, 'Wragg. Thomas Wragg.'

All heads turned and a young man, perhaps in his early twenties, rose slowly to his feet, clutching a grimy cap in his hands. He moved towards the man who had called his name, his reluctance showing in every movement of his body.

The man in the white coat said irritably, 'Do hurry along, Mr Wragg!'

'I'm not sure...' he began. 'That is, I'm feeling a lot better and...'

'Mr Wragg, you are not at all well. We can help you. Now do come along.'

The man increased his speed marginally.

Douglas turned back to the desk where the young woman had found a list and was reading quickly through it. 'No, sorry,' she told Douglas. 'There is no Doctor Hubbard at this hospital.'

'He may be on another list. He works

nights, I'm told. Maybe in the mortuary.'

'The mortuary's closed most nights.'

Douglas was aware of an increase in his pulse rate. So Massie, alias Hubbard, had been lying. If he didn't work nights in the hospital then what did he do if he was away all night?

Young Mr Wragg had disappeared and a nurse was now standing in the corridor, calling for a Miss Baines. This elderly woman hurried towards her, grumbling about the long wait and vanished through another door.

Douglas said, 'Maybe you have some temporary staff. Or doctors who work part-time. Is that possible?'

'Not to my knowledge. Are you a prospective patient, Mr ... er...'

'No, no! A private matter. I'm unable to disclose the purpose of the visit.' He lowered his voice. 'Police work. Confidential.'

She was clearly impressed. Lowering her own voice she leaned forward. 'Are you a policeman?'

He nodded. Then, unable to resist it, he added, 'Detective Sergeant.'

She leaned even further forward. 'You're looking for *him*, aren't you? The killer! The maniac who killed Annie Chapman – and the other two!'

Douglas shook his head. 'There are other cases under investigation.'

She smiled, shaking her head. 'You're looking for the Whitechapel murderer! Why pretend?'

'I'm not pretending. There's no shortage of crime round here. I'm on the trail of a poisoner.' Even as he uttered the words he regretted them. It was not discreet to discuss on-going cases with perfect strangers, but on this occasion vanity had led him astray. Stop it, Douglas, he told himself. You don't have to impress every pretty girl who comes your way. Not that many do, at the moment. He realized with a sudden pang that he had no life outside his work. His mother nagged him about it. Perhaps she was right.

'There are other hospitals,' she was saying. 'Maybe this is the wrong one ... I think there's one somewhere between Plaistow and ... Let me think ... Yes. Canning Town. Not a big hospital like this one but a hospital just the same. He might be there, your Doctor Hubbard.'

'Don't worry. I'll find him if it's the last thing I do. Thank you for your help.'

He retraced his steps with a light heart. He was getting somewhere at last.

'Hubbard or Massie? Whatever you call yourself now,' he muttered, 'I'm on to you and getting closer each day.'

When the doorbell rang the following day, Dora hurried to open it in case it was her husband come home unexpectedly. She was trying to give the impression of being brisk and efficient around the house. That's how he wanted his wife to be.

It wasn't John and she felt relieved. Mrs Trott from next door stood there, a covered dish in her hands.

'Yes?' Dora took in the details of her neighbour's appearance. She wore a clean cotton apron over a shabby brown skirt, and a small dark bonnet covered her hair.

'I know you've been poorly...' the woman began.

'Who says I'm poorly?'

Mrs Trott looked apologetic. 'I'm afraid the walls are rather thin and ... and I've heard you groaning. I thought perhaps it was your stomach. I used to suffer with mine and I...'

Suddenly Dora longed for some sympathy and interrupted her. 'Come in, Mrs Trott.' Hopefully John would never know she had asked the woman in. They went into the shabby but clean parlour and sat down.

Mrs Trott held out the dish. 'It's a custard,' she said. 'I always used to find it very comforting if my stomach was bad. It's just for you. An invalid diet!' She smiled to show that she was partly joking.

Dora was surprised. Mrs Trott unveiled the custard and Dora stared at it. It was pale lemon in colour and the top had a soft attractive glaze. It looked wonderful. Dora was touched by her kind gesture and for a moment she had to blink back tears of self-pity. It had been a long time since anyone had been truly sympathetic.

Mrs Trott went on. 'It's easily digested, you see. If it helps you I could give you the recipe.'

'How very kind.' She would make one for John and impress him. 'I'll have some of it for my dinner. I'll just put it in the larder to keep cool.' In fact she would eat it all before John came home and would hide the dish until she got a chance to return it. She didn't want him to accuse her of wasting time hobnobbing with the neighbours when she should be busy!

In the kitchen she tried to adjust her opinion of Mrs Trott. She had always considered her neighbours a nosy lot but today Mrs Trott had surprised her and she was prepared to give her the benefit of the doubt. It was true that the walls were too thin for privacy. She had often heard raised voices from the other side but not a sound from Mrs Trott. She wondered how much Mrs Trott knew about her circumstances. If all she had overheard were a few groans, it didn't matter.

Mrs Trott settled herself in the chair. For a few minutes she listened patiently to Dora's description of her various aches and pains.

'What does the doctor say?' she asked.

'I haven't seen one. Mr Hubbard brings me medicine from the chemist. It doesn't seem to help, but he says it's indigestion and that his father suffered from the same thing. But he's dead. He collapsed and died quite suddenly.' She shrugged. 'My husband says it was his heart. He was broken-hearted, poor man. He gets so easily upset and he adored his father. Still, he left him all his money, his father did. Mr Hubbard told me he had promised him a nice little windfall. And it wasn't so little.'

'So ... he didn't have any debts?'

'Debts? Who, his father? Of course he had debts. Everybody has debts, don't they? But my husband paid them all off and we moved here when we married. It's not where we'd choose to live but it's only for a short while. One of my grandmothers was comfortably off. She lived in Chiswick, which is very nice. She didn't approve of her son marrying my mother because she was inferior, if you know what I mean. At least, she thought she wasn't good enough although he was only a labour-er at the docks but he'd worked his way up to foreman.' She sighed at the memory. 'Grandmama was a terrible snob, but I never told her that to her face. How could I? I hardly ever set eyes on her. Sometimes I wish I had.'

'Didn't she visit you?'

'Never. But we went to visit her once a year on her birthday. She lived in a very posh flat with a little balcony outside one of the rooms with iron railings round it so you couldn't fall off.' She laughed. 'She left me some money but I had to wait for it. Last week it became mine! I couldn't touch it until I turned twenty-one.'

Mrs Trott looked envious, Dora noted with satisfaction.

She went on. 'When I get my money, we're going to move to a better area. I'm going to have a baby so we shall need a garden instead of a tiny yard.'

'A baby? Oh, how exciting. Let me know if I can help when the time comes. I had two children of my own but they both died before they reached three years, poor little souls. I don't like to think about it, to tell you the truth. I wanted to have another one but then my husband was killed.'

There was a short silence before Dora said, 'Isn't it dreadful about the murders? I just don't know why the police can't catch him. He seems to cock a snook at them!'

They both laughed but Dora was now anxious to see the back of her neighbour. Suddenly guilt seized her. She felt that she had said too much. John must never know. As if sensing her anxiety, Mrs Trott rose to her feet and brushed down her skirt.

'Well, I must be going. Let me know if

the custard helps. And it's been nice talking to you.'

Dora saw her out. Then she ran into the kitchen and sat down with the custard. It was as good as it looked and she ate it all. However, her stomach still churned uneasily afterwards. She washed up the dish and hid it inside the copper.

For a few hours she was able to convince herself that the custard had done her good but then the pains returned and by the time her husband came home she was in agony.

Before she could utter a word, he said, 'Don't worry, dearest. I've brought you something from the chemist. Something different to make up into a warm drink. He says it will taste rather bitter so I shall put plenty of honey in it for you. You go upstairs and lie on the bed. I shall be up in a few minutes and I can promise you, it will do the trick.'

Dora's forehead glistened with sweat and she clutched her stomach and bit back a groan. 'I don't think I can manage the stairs,' she gasped. 'Could you carry me, John?'

'Carry you? Of course I will.' Gently he lifted her into his arms, took her upstairs and laid her on the bed.

She said, 'I'm sorry to be such a worry for you, dear. I wonder if it's something to do with the baby. Maybe I *should* see a doctor.'

He shook his head. 'You were having these

pains months ago, Dora. They're nothing new. I've told you, you need to stir yourself. I talked to the chemist about you and he agreed you should be more active. And drink boiled water. Cool it in a jug and drink regularly...'

'But John, I really don't think...'

He scowled. 'Don't interrupt me, Dora! You have this morbid obsession with your health and you convince yourself you're ill. Trust me, Dora.' He seemed to realize he had spoken sharply and forced a smile. 'The chemist knows what he's talking about and you will soon be free of your pains.'

He went downstairs and she listened to him as he clattered around in the kitchen, opening cupboard doors, running the tap, heating water in the kettle. She ran her hands over her abdomen and spoke to the child growing within her. 'I'm sorry. I'll be better soon. I'll be better before you're born and then we'll all be happy.' She closed her eyes as another cramp seized her and bit her lip to prevent a scream which she now knew Mrs Trott would hear.

He came into the room, carrying a mug of the precious brew that was going to rid her of the pains. As she sat up, sweat ran down her face and neck and she struggled for breath. John put the mug on the bedside table, fetched a flannel from the washstand and wiped the sweat away.

'That's better, Dora. My poor little wife. Now sip this slowly and if it doesn't ease the pain I shall personally strangle that chemist!' He laughed and she managed a faint smile as she dutifully drank down the clear brown liquid. It was slightly warm and did taste rather odd, but not unpleasant, and she recognized the flavour of the honey.

'You're so good to me,' she whispered. She thought of poor Mrs Trott and her lonely life ... and the custard. Count your blessings, Dora, she told herself. A loving husband, a roof over their heads, a friendly neighbour – and a baby on the way. She relaxed and lay back against the pillow.

'One more mouthful and it's gone,' John urged and she obeyed willingly. 'Now snuggle down and sleep, Dora. That's what you need most. A long, long sleep.'

She did as he requested and he kissed her lightly on the top of her head. She closed her eyes and heard him tiptoe out of the room.

When she next opened her eyes she was astonished to see that it was dark. Moonlight shone into the room and she wondered what the time was. The pains had gone and she thanked God for the relief. Her eyes felt extremely heavy and she closed them again, luxuriating in the freedom from pain. Suddenly a voice said, 'Are you still with us?' Without opening her eyes she knew it was her husband – but why wasn't he on duty at the hospital? She seemed wrapped in a strange lethargy, with no energy and was finding it hard to concentrate. Dora struggled to wake up but found it hard to open her eyes. There seemed be someone in, or on, the bed beside her but that was impossible because John should be at the hospital, working...

'I think I've done it!' She could hear John's voice again.

The bed moved. She tried to speak his name but speech seemed impossible.

With an effort she forced her eyelids apart and in the darkness she was aware of a flickering light. Had he lit the candle? Was she ill?

Second by second her energy was returning. Her thoughts were less muzzy and she sensed, rather than saw, that he was now beside her.

'My God!' he muttered. 'It's done!'

Through her lashes she glimpsed his face close to her. He was holding the candle and studying her face. He was smiling.

He said quietly, 'Well, Dora my love, I promised you a long sleep and...' He took hold of her wrist and as he did so she opened her eyes.

'John!' she whispered.

To her surprise he took a step backward and drew in his breath sharply. By the light of the candle she thought he looked shocked. She said, 'I had a lovely sleep ... That medicine you brought back...'

'You ... You're...' His voice was hoarse and the sentence went unfinished.

She opened her eyes fully and was surprised by the expression on his face.

'I'm recovered. Quite free of the pain!' She struggled to sit up. 'You did it, dearest.'

'Did what?' His voice had risen and he was staring at her wide-eyed.

'You gave me a long sleep. I feel so much better.'

He set down the candle with an unsteady hand. 'That's wonderful.' He kept his distance. His breathing was ragged.

She said, 'What's the time?'

As if to answer her question the church clock chimed once. 'One of the clock and all's well!' she said. 'D'you remember the night-watchmen that used to go round the streets when we were young? They made me feel very safe if I woke in the night ... John?' She peered at him through the gloom. 'Are you all right? Shouldn't you be at the hospital?'

'Yes. That is, no! I ... I was worried about you. You fell into such a deep sleep I was afraid to leave you. I thought ... I was afraid you might die.'

'Die? Why should I die?' She reached out a hand and, after the merest hesitation, he took it. She placed it on her face. 'Feel me. I'm alive!' She laughed. 'Come to bed.'

'*No!* That is ... I mean ... I must go. To the hospital. I must put in some extra hours.'

For the first time she realized that he was fully dressed. Abruptly he turned on his heel and left the room. Dora closed her eyes and slept again.

Five

The briefing room at the police station in Commercial Street on the evening of 14th of September was crowded with police of all ranks who listened with grim and resentful expressions to an account of their failures. Some sat in attitudes of dejection, listening to the summary of their unsuccessful efforts to find a strong lead. Others lounged at the back, arms folded defensively, as they were brought up-to-date on the investigative measures that had been undertaken with no results.

'The public demand more,' the super-intendent told them. 'But for the life of me I don't know what more we can do.' He stopped suddenly and sniffed. 'Has someone been smoking in here?' It was his pet hate.

'No, sir!' they chorused.

'I can smell smoke!'

Douglas glared at PC Riggs who had the decency to look apologetic.

The superintendent continued. 'All the usual roads of enquiries have been followed and all have ended at a dead end – if you'll ignore the unintentional pun.' He glared at a young PC who had dared to snigger. 'We know from the results of the post-mortem that Annie Chapman died in the same way as the previous victims – throat cut, body organs removed. We know rings were missing from her hand but maybe that was supposed to suggest robbery as a motive. God knows! And if He knows, He's not letting on! So we're checking out the usual fences, pawnbrokers and so on but nothing's turned up so far.'

Someone mumbled, 'Tell us something new!' and there was ragged laughter.

Douglas wasn't listening. He didn't need to because he knew exactly what was going on and that the briefing was mainly for the men under him. They needed a pep talk to keep them interested and alert. He remembered his own time as a young constable. It was so easy to get bogged down in the routine door-to-door enquiries, feeling that the really exciting events were passing you by.

'We think he lived in the vicinity of the murder scene because it was broad daylight when he walked away from his latest victim...'

Douglas thought about the small break-through in his own case. The previous night he had waited around near the Hubbard house in Goulston Street when, by all accounts, his suspect should have been on his way to a night shift at the London Hospital. In fact, several hours later he had set off in that direction, turning left at the end of Goulston Road and along Commercial Road. However Gerald Cummings, alias John Hubbard, had then turned off down Whitechapel Road and turned left again into Osborn Street. He then waked along into Brick Lane, turned left again into Fashion Street and ended up at No 4, White Street.

'We've taken witness statements galore and none very likely to be of use. Most of the suspects we've rounded up have been released...'

'What about the German, sir? Isenschmid?'

'Not German, Riggs, he was born in Switzerland. He was examined but no blood-stains were found on his clothes or person.'

'They say he's mad, sir.'

'He has his mad moments, shall we say, but we've checked him out and he's not our man. Now...'

'Is he...?'

'Riggs!'

'Sorry, sir!'

Douglas felt his head falling forward and jerked upright. Dozing off on the job! Thank heavens no one had noticed. Too little sleep was taking its toll and his concentration was faltering. Tomorrow he would call at No 4, White Street.

'Any questions?'

One hand shot up. 'Sir, I've heard they're thinking of bringing in bloodhounds to sniff round the murder scenes.'

'It's a possibility. We're prepared to try anything.' He glanced round. 'Yes, Buller.'

'My aunt's got a friend who's a medium, sir. She can find things with a bit of thread and a pendulum.'

Someone jeered and there was laughter.

'No, sir! It's the truth, sir!' Buller protested. 'She can also go into a trance and talk to the dead. She might be able to find the murderer.'

There was an outburst of ribald comments.

'I shan't dignify that with an answer, Buller. Now, show's over. All of you get back to work. Keep your eyes and ears open for any local gossip. You never know. The smallest clue could lead us to him. He's out there and we've got to find him.' He rubbed his eyes wearily. 'We've got the public on our backs, the politicians and the newspapers. We desperately need a break in this case. God! We've got to nail this blood-thirsty villain before we lose all credibility.'

Someone muttered, 'I thought we'd already lost it!'

'I heard that, Scott!'

The next morning, the 15th, Bella woke up to find the sun shining in through the bedroom window and Lloyd asleep beside her. She smiled sleepily and felt a great sense of contentment. Her husband looked tousled and handsome even in sleep and for a moment she enjoyed the sight of his long dark lashes, the fine curve of his cheek and the firmness of his mouth. She was a lucky, *lucky* girl, she reminded herself. Today, she decided, would be a happy one. No more talk of murderers – she would not allow it! No more trouble between Lottie and Lloyd. It was Sadie's birthday and she and Lottie would go round to her room and take her their presents. She dressed hurriedly, kissed Lloyd to wake him and then hurried down-stairs. On the way she knocked loudly on Lottie's door to make sure she came down to breakfast on time.

She splashed cold water over her face and dried it on a tea towel then filled a jug with hot water and carried it up to Lloyd where she found him sitting up in bed, stretching his arms above his head and yawning. He smiled at her as he slid out of bed.

She said, 'It's Sadie's birthday. We're going

round to her place after breakfast.' She poured the hot water into the bowl on the washstand.

'Give her my best wishes.'

'I will. I've some bacon rashers for your breakfast.'

Downstairs she hummed cheerfully. She had crocheted a white collar for Sadie and Lottie had made her an elaborate birthday card with feathers, ribbon and gold paper. She would fry him some bacon and add a slice of fried bread. Lloyd must have a proper meal before setting out on his working day. She and Lottie would have porridge with milk and sugar and toast.

Ten minutes later Lottie had still not come down and Bella went along to her room to hurry her along. Seconds later she was screaming for Lloyd. Washed and dressed, he joined her in Lottie's bedroom. Bella pointed to the empty bed.

'She's not here!' she cried, her face pale with shock. 'Her bed's been slept in but ... Where could she have gone? She would never go out in the dark! You know how scared she is of the dark!'

Lloyd stared round, as puzzled as she was.

He said, 'Maybe she went out early this morning before we woke?'

Bella pointed to her cousin's clothes, which were carefully folded over the chair. 'She isn't dressed!' She turned to him in a panic.

'Heavens, Lloyd! She's gone out in her nightdress. We must fetch the police. She's been out in the streets all night with that murderer on the loose!' She clapped a trembling hand to her mouth and tears sprang into her eyes. 'Help me, Lloyd! We've got to do something. We've got to...'

He placed a firm hand on her shoulder. 'Bella! Calm yourself! You'll do no good by becoming hysterical. Now I have to go to work, remember. You get along to the police station or find a constable on the beat and ask for help.'

'But Lloyd, can't you stay with me? I mean, you haven't had any breakfast. I...'

'I don't have time this morning. I have clients waiting. An early appointment. Lottie's *your* cousin. *Your* responsibility.' He pulled out a handkerchief and wiped her tears away. 'She may be perfectly all right. She may have been sleepwalking.'

'Lottie doesn't walk in her sleep! You know she doesn't!'

'Maybe she does now. We know she's getting worse. The police will sort it all out, Bella. Don't look so tragic!' He laughed lightly. She tried to cling to him but he prised her fingers loose and hurried into the hall for his jacket. He ran down the stairs and out into the street without glancing back. Seconds later the door on to the street slammed to behind him. He had gone and

Bella was left alone. Dazed, she hesitated for a moment then ran to the front door in search of help.

Mr Tuttle, who rented the shop below, was carrying a bundle of clothes and greeted her with, 'Morning, Mrs Massie.'

He was overweight with a fleshy face and small blue eyes and his podgy fingers were covered with cheap rings. He smelled as stale and dusty as his shop.

'Mr Tuttle! My cousin's missing. You haven't seen her, have you?' Bella followed him into the shop where he dumped the clothes on the counter, took off his bowler and tossed it into a corner.

'Gone missin'? Lord love us!' Showing little real interest, he scratched his untidy hair. 'Not as I know of. I'd recognize her, I reckon.'

'You couldn't miss her because she's in her nightclothes. My husband thinks she must have been sleepwalking.'

George Tuttle had rented the shop for as long as Bella could remember but she hardly knew him. He always paid his weekly rent on time, leaving the coins in an envelope on the sixth stair. Never troubling himself to climb them and hand it over personally.

He said, 'I never see'd anyone in their nightclothes, that's for sure!'

'I can't understand it. And I'm worried she won't find her way home. Or she'll meet that dreadful murderer!'

Tuttle began to separate the clothes, holding each item up for inspection and then giving it a shake. Dust flew as he shook out a woollen shawl. 'Moths have been at it!' he grumbled. He rolled it up and put it aside and detached a man's jacket from the bundle. Holding it to his nose he sniffed. 'Mothballs!' he said, pleased, then glanced back at Bella. 'Try that chap over the road. He might have seen something.'

Surprised, Bella saw that a man waited on the other side of the road, his hands thrust into the pockets of his long coat. She went outside and called to him. He hesitated, glancing along the road where Lloyd could be seen turning the corner. Crossing the road, Bella clutched his arm eagerly.

'Please! I need help!' she cried. 'My cousin! She's disappeared. In the night!' Still he hesitated and she shook his arm impatiently. 'Could you find a constable, please? She might be in trouble. She's still in her night-clothes and...'

He said politely, 'Madam, I *am* a policeman. Detective Sergeant Douglas Unwin.'

Bella frowned. He was not in uniform but perhaps he was on what they called 'plain clothes' duty. She had heard of that. She studied him carefully. He had fair hair and nice blue eyes. His voice was soft and he seemed kindly but he didn't look tough

124

enough to be a policeman. However, she didn't have time to be choosy so this one would have to do.

As if sensing her doubts, he produced a card from his pocket and showed it to her. The sight of a badge reassured her

He said, 'Should we talk about it inside?'

Bella realized with a shock that several neighbours had appeared at their windows and she hastily led Unwin inside and up the stairs.

Once they were seated, he took out his notebook and Bella began an account of what had happened. 'Lottie has never, *never* left the house in the middle of the night. She had a difficult birth and her mind is not quite right, but she's scared of the dark.'

'So are you thinking she's been taken away? Is that what you're telling me? You think she's been kidnapped, for want of a better word?'

'I think so but I can't think why such a thing would happen. We couldn't pay a ransom – we're not rich.'

'What exactly does your husband do, Mrs Massie?'

'He's a private investigator and he has an office ... somewhere. I'm not sure where exactly because I've never been there. He doesn't want me involved with his work because it's so dangerous.' She smiled briefly. 'We've only been married a few weeks but he's looking after me very well. Me and Lottie, I mean. He doesn't mind her living with us. After all, it is her house – at least it was her mother's and it was left to me for the two of us to live in because Lottie isn't capable of living alone and managing bills and things. So she left it to me instead.'

He regarded her gravely. 'But doesn't your husband own it now, since you have married?'

'Yes, I suppose he does.' She frowned. 'But, excuse me for saying so, aren't we wasting time when we should be out searching for poor Lottie? That murderer might have got hold of her somehow. She might be in dreadful danger.'

'A moment or two longer then we shall spring into action. We need to know the whole picture first, Mrs Massie ... Does your husband have any relatives living in Goulston Street?'

'No. I don't think so.'

'Is there anyone your cousin might have gone to see? A relative or friend?'

Bella blinked. Why hadn't she thought of that? 'She might have gone to my aunt. Sadie. She's also Lottie's aunt. She lives in Thrawl Street, not far from here.' Suddenly she felt hopeful. That is where they would find Lottie. 'Shall I go there?' she asked.

'We'll go together, Mrs Massie. Then if she's not there I'll report her missing and we'll put out the word for any sight of her.'

Striding out beside DS Unwin made Bella feel a great deal happier. He seemed to know what he was doing and her confidence returned. They would find Lottie at Sadie's place. Now she wished she had thought to bring the birthday card and the new collar. Never mind. It would be enough to be re-united with Lottie who hopefully would be found safe and sound.

Sadly, it was not to be. Sadie was recovering belatedly from a pre-birthday drink with friends the previous night. As usual, her room was in total disarray and smelled stale and dirty. Bella regretted bringing the detective with her. She saw the look in his eyes as he glanced round at the scattered clothes, the unwashed crockery and the general muddle. Looking sullen and bad-tempered, Sadie insisted she was too ill to get out of her bed so, since she hadn't seen Lottie, they left her to it and went back downstairs. On the way they met the land-lady and DS Unwin asked if she had seen Lottie. The answer was again in the negative and Bella's worries returned in a rush. Her stomach seemed to churn as she was once again faced with the prospect that Lottie had come to some harm.

The policeman said, 'You must go home and wait, Mrs Massie. You need to be there in case your cousin finds her own way home.

She would be most upset if you were not waiting for her and she might even go off again.'

Faced with this alarming prospect, Bella reluctantly agreed and made her way home alone. The detective had promised to keep in touch and to let her know of any developments. He was going to check the local hospitals in case she had been knocked down by passing traffic.

Finding the flat empty, Bella went upstairs to the flat of the Hungarian couple, who welcomed her in and listened to her story with expressions of alarm.

'We haf not seen her,' Mr Schwartz assured her. 'This is not good. Not good at all!'

His wife nodded timidly. 'Anything can happen to a woman on the streets at night – especially in Whitechapel!'

They offered her a cup of tea but Bella declined and hurried back down the stairs to Mr Tuttle's shop where she quickly filled him in on her conversation with the policeman.

'He says I must wait in for her in case she comes back, so I will. I wondered if you would ask all your customers if they have seen a woman in her nightclothes.'

'That I will.' He had hung the jacket on a hanger and was brushing it down. 'That looks a treat,' he said proudly. 'That's going in the winder, that is – unless you'd like it for your new hubby. It's a nice bit of cloth and the linings not too bad. I could do you a good price.'

'I don't know if it will fit him,' Bella said tactfully. She was sure her husband would be mortified by the notion of buying second-hand clothes from Mr Tuttle. 'If he's interested, I'll send him down when he gets home.'

'It'll be well gone by then. It'll fly out the winder, that will!' He picked up a pair of grey kid shoes. They were stained and down at the heels. 'Now look at these. They look your size. Slip 'em on. You can have 'em for twopence and I'm robbin' myself!'

Thankfully they were too small and Bella pretended to be disappointed. Then she hurried to the door before he could find anything else. 'You'll remember to ask your customers about Lottie,' she reminded him.

'Any news and I'll send 'em straight up!'

'Thank you, Mr Tuttle.'

As she made her way up the stairs she crossed her fingers and muttered a prayer for Lottie's safe return.

Time passed very slowly and Bella longed for Lloyd to come home. She had a dreadful image of Lottie being whisked off to Soho where everyone knew the slave trade was still flourishing. Or else her cousin was lying in a ditch with blood oozing from her head. Whatever had inspired Lottie to run away like this? If she *had* run away, of course, and not been taken against her will. Suppose they were sent a ransom note! How would they pay it? What would she do if Lottie was dead and they had to bury her? Life would never be the same again. Somehow Bella knew she would always blame herself if Lottie had come to a bad or sad end. She had promised her aunt that she would look after her. She sighed heavily. She thought angrily about Aunt Sadie and the state she was in. Would she, Bella, have ended up like that if she had not had Lottie to think about – and if she had not met Lloyd Massie? It didn't bear thinking about.

While Bella sat at home, twisting her hands in frustration, Mae Dunnley was leaving a common lodging house on Batty Street where she had spent the night. Mae had no home of her own and regularly slept in such places when she could afford it. When she couldn't raise fourpence, she slept under nearby arches with other unfortunates. This morning she was creeping past the owner of the lodging house when she was halted in her tracks.

'Oi, Dunnley! You get back here!'

Groaning, Mae turned back from the front door and went into what passed as a kitchen at the rear of the house. Mrs Levington, the landlady, stood with her hands on her hips and a frown on her face. Fifty-one years of life struggling to survive in London's East End had given her a permanently sour expression.

'What?' Mae demanded crossly.

'You know what! That one you brought in last night. You brought her in, you take her out! You're not dumping her on me.'

Mae scowled, already regretting her kind action. 'But what will I do with her? I don't *own* the poor girl. All I did was...'

'All you done was talk me into giving her a bed for the night. More fool me, I say. I should have had more bloody sense! I'm getting soft in my old age. Now you go up and wake her and get her out of here. I'm not running a charity.'

Mae tossed her head derisively but she didn't argue the point because Mrs Levington *had* taken the woman in without payment. Mind you, it was either that or set her up as the murderer's next victim and no woman in her right mind would do that. Especially not to someone like Lottie who was obviously not all there.

Mae hesitated. 'What am I supposed to do with her?'

'Don't ask me! It was your idea to bring her here and I was fool enough to go along with it. Lost me fourpence, that has. I've got a living to earn, in case you hadn't noticed. Get her out into the street and tell her to go home!'

'She might not know the way.'

'Then find out from her where she lives and take her home.'

Mae bridled at the image this created. 'But she's in her nightgown! I'm not walking through the streets with her like that.'

'Call a policeman, then. They look after stray dogs. They can look after a stray woman for a change.'

'Well, me and the police don't exactly hit it off.'

Mrs Levington shrugged. 'You sort it out, Mae. You're responsible for her now.'

Muttering obscenities, Mae made her way upstairs and over to the bed where Lottie was sleeping. She looked so young and innocent, Mae wanted to cry for her but tears didn't come easily to her after the life she'd led. Instead she shook her awake.

'What's your other name?' she asked as the young woman struggled to a sitting position and stared round her in obvious confusion.

By way of answer, Lottie screamed and hid under the threadbare blanket. She clutched it round her and refused to abandon the bed or utter a single word. Mae rolled her eyes and gave up on her. She had more important things to do, she told herself, than struggle with this crazy woman. Turning from the bed, she tiptoed downstairs and out of the house. 'That's what you get for doing a good deed,' she told herself angrily as she almost ran down the street, and she vowed never to repeat the mistake.

An hour later DS Douglas Unwin arrived at the lodging house and claimed knowledge of the woman who had been reported to the police by Mae Dunnley.

'We think she may have been walking in her sleep,' he told Mrs Levington.

'I don't care what she was doing. I just want her out of here.'

Together they approached Lottie, who was still wrapped in the blanket, her face hidden. The policeman spoke gently to her.

'Lottie, I want you to come along with me,' he began. 'I've been talking to Bella and she's very worried about you. She wants you to come home with me. You don't want to stay here, do you?'

A muffled voice came from the blankets. 'No!'

Mrs Levington, her hands on her hips, regarded her sourly. 'Last time I do anyone a favour! Nothing but a nuisance she's been. Crying all night and keeping honest folk awake. I've had complaints about her from my regulars.'

Ignoring her, the policeman patted the hidden form within the blanket. 'Poor Bella. She's waiting at home. She thinks you might be dead. She's probably crying, she's so unhappy.'

Mrs Levington snorted and flounced out of the room. Her footsteps clattered scornfully on the bare wooden stairs. Douglas waited until he was sure she had gone.

'Mrs Levington has gone downstairs,' he said. 'You can come out now, Lottie. You can come with me and I'll take you home.'

Slowly, Lottie untangled herself and allowed herself to be seen. She said, 'It was Lloyd! He said I was to go with him but I wouldn't. I don't like him. I really don't!'

Douglas stared at her, shaken by her words. 'You mean it was Lloyd Massie who took you out into the street?'

Lottie rubbed her face. She looked exhausted, he thought, and near the end of her tether. He tried to imagine how she had felt, alone and helpless in the dark, foggy streets, lit only by the flickering gaslights.

He asked, 'Would you like to go home to Bella now? I can take you home.'

'He put something over my face.' Lottie frowned. 'It made me go to sleep ... and then I was in the street and Lloyd was running away and I thought it was a nightmare but it was real.' She looked at him anxiously. 'I hate him. I do!'

Thinking furiously, Douglas glanced round the room. Nothing but four dilapidated beds, each with a dirty pillow and one flimsy blanket that had seen better days. No room for a table or chairs. This was where homeless women spent their nights. There was probably another room for men. He sighed. What a dreadful existence.

Lottie said, 'He hates me. He said so.' She pushed a lock of hair back from her face and he could see that her eyes were red, her cheeks blotched and her skin pale.

'Out you get!' he said, as briskly as he could manage. 'Time to go home.'

When she threw back the blanket, he realized that the white nightdress would make them very conspicuous so he draped the blanket over her shoulders. She had no shoes and he wondered how long she had been on the streets before Mae Dunnley took pity on her.

Downstairs, before Mrs Levington could protest, he tossed her a sixpence. 'Buy another blanket,' he told her and led Lottie from the house and out into street.

They attracted a certain amount of comment as they made their way along Commercial Street and into White Street. Lottie stumbled along, waif-like, in her strange outfit, muttering to herself, unaware of the stares she drew from passers-by. She refused to let Douglas hold her arm to steady her and he felt it unwise to insist. However, as soon as Lottie recognized where she was, her expression changed to one of relief and they were soon waiting on the doorstep of No 4.

Lottie's ravaged face broke into a broad smile. 'Home again!' she said.

Bella, watching from the first-floor window, rushed down the steps to let them in and hugged and wept as she welcomed her cousin back.

'I thought you were dead!' she cried, heady with delight. 'I thought the murderer had got you! Oh Lottie, whatever were you thinking of, to go off like that? You've worried me half to death!'

She made some warm milk and honey while Lottie was sent up to her room with instructions to have a quick wash, put on some day clothes and comb her hair. While Bella and the policeman were alone he told her what he had gleaned from the little conversation he had had with Lottie and Mrs Levington.

'From what she says, it sounds as though she's accusing him of using chloroform on her. It sounds as if...'

Bella's mouth fell open. *Chloroform?* But that's ridiculous!'

When he had finished what Lottie had said about Lloyd's part in the drama, Bella shook her head.

'It's absolute nonsense! She has taken against him,' she explained. 'Poor Lloyd. He wouldn't hurt a fly! And he's very good with her. Firm but fair. He doesn't want her to end up in an asylum. That would be awful ...

but she does seem to be getting worse these last few weeks. I think she hates sharing me with my husband. She's rather like a first child when a second child is born. I'm sure she'll come round to liking him eventually.'

'So you don't think she *might* be telling the truth?'

'Telling the truth? You mean about Lloyd?' Bella was shocked. 'Most certainly I don't! It isn't the first time she has made up stories about him.' She told him about the ruined curtains and the wet bed.

He wrote in his notebook. 'I'll have to make a report,' he told her. 'Unfortunately this incident has wasted police time on a day when the whole force should be out searching for the Whitechapel murderer.' He wrote again then closed the notebook. 'I'll see that you don't get into any trouble over it. If your cousin isn't telling the truth about your husband, it might be worth your while to find out what really did happen. If she did go sleepwalking, you could get a better lock on your front door – or lock her in her room each night.'

Bella nodded. She was longing to get Lottie alone so that she could give her a 'talking to'. There was no way she dare let her husband know of Lottie's accusations. He would be furious with her.

As the clock struck eight that evening, Lottie

137

sat at the table in the parlour trying to finish the jigsaw of the Houses of Parliament. At least, she was supposed to be doing it but instead she was straining to hear the argument going on in the kitchen between Lloyd and Bella. She knew what it was about. She knew Lloyd was angry with her, Lottie, about what happened in the night. She had tried to tell Bella and the policeman but they hadn't believed her. She slotted in a piece of the window into the puzzle and beamed with satisfaction.

'I can do it!' she crowed. 'I really can!'

She tried not to think about what had happened the previous night when she woke up to find herself slumped against a cold wall in a dark street. She tried because Bella had told her not to think about it, but she couldn't help herself. The memories kept returning. She remembered Lloyd hurrying away, his shadow made long by the flickering gaslight. She had called to him to wait but he didn't hear – or didn't want to hear. When he had gone, she had sat up and cautiously looked about her. A cat had slunk past, head down, tail stiff, looking for trouble. A cat was better than nothing. She remembered thinking that a cat would be company but when she called, it fled into a darkly shadowed doorway and disappeared.

When she at last managed to stand up, her legs felt strange and wobbly and she started to cry because Bella wasn't there to help her. The street was empty and there were no lights in any of the windows which meant that everybody had gone to bed because it was night time. It was all very mysterious and not a bit friendly.

'Don't think about it!' she reminded herself. She found a piece of sky and that fitted, so she pushed aside the worrying thoughts and thought instead about the jigsaw.

Lloyd and Bella came into the room and Lottie could see that her cousin had also been crying.

Lloyd said, 'What you did last night, Lottie, was a very bad thing. It was unkind. You made us both very unhappy and worried.'

Lottie muttered, 'You made me!'

Bella gasped. 'Oh Lottie dear, *don't*! You must stop trying to blame poor Lloyd.'

Lloyd sat down next to Lottie and took hold of her hand. She wanted to snatch her hand away but she knew it would make Bella cross.

'This is serious, Lottie,' Lloyd told her. 'It was dangerous to go out so late. There's this very nasty man around – the one who murders people. He might have murdered you! Don't you understand?'

She was surprised that he was being so nice. 'I called you but you didn't hear me,' she said.

Bella opened her mouth to protest but

Lloyd gave her a warning look. Lottie recognized it as such and was silent.

'This is your last chance, Lottie,' Lloyd said. 'The doctor says you need to go away. If you do anything else bad, that's what will happen to you. You won't live here with us any more You'll go and live in a place where bad people go. Do you understand?'

Lottie stared at him. Her heart was thumping and horrible thoughts crowded her mind. She wanted to stay with Bella. 'I'm not bad!' she stammered.

'Then why did you go out last night?'

'You said we would have a nice walk and you said...'

Bella groaned. She closed her eyes. 'Stop it, Lottie! Please! You mustn't tell lies.'

Lottie frowned. If only she could make Bella understand what really happened. 'There was another man,' she began. 'He came towards me and said I should go with him but then he was sick in the gutter.'

For a moment they both stared at her. Bella said, 'She's remembering things!'

Lloyd snorted. 'Of course she's not. She's making it all up.'

Lottie looked at Bella. 'He said, "Who you staring at, you trollop?" What is a trollop?'

Lloyd turned quickly away and stared out of the window.

Bella, shaken, said, 'She couldn't have made that up, could she?'

Lottie said, 'While he was being sick I ran away. I didn't like him.'

Lloyd faced them and now he didn't look at all kind. He looked cross and mean.

'She's making it up, I tell you. She's not the little innocent you think she is, Bella. She's a wicked little trouble-maker and the sooner you realize that, the better for all of us!' He put a protective arm around Bella. 'We mustn't let her ruin our happiness, dearest. She's obviously jealous, but you can't see it. You're blinded by love for her but I can see quite clearly what's going on. I won't let her spoil our marriage. You don't want to have to choose between me and her, do you?'

'No, Lloyd. You're right, dear.' Bella looked very pale.

'Then go into the kitchen and wait for me there. I'll deal with Lottie.'

Bella looked at Lottie, her mouth trembling, but then she obeyed her husband.

Lloyd moved towards Lottie. The look in his eyes chilled her. 'You've had your last chance, do you hear me? You be very careful, Lottie.' He pointed to the jigsaw. 'Now get on with that.'

'I don't want to!'

'I don't care what you want!' His voice rose angrily. '*I* want to see it finished so you just work at it until I tell you to stop. And from now on, keep your silly tricks to yourself!'

'You made me!' she insisted doggedly.

Lloyd swung his hand back and slapped her face then walked out of the room, slamming the door behind him so hard that a small ornament shuddered and fell from the mantelpiece. Lottie stared at the jigsaw with mixed emotions. At last a faint smile lit up her wan face. She picked up a piece of the jigsaw, carried it to the window, pushed up the lower pane and pushed the piece of puzzle out. Now Lloyd's jigsaw would never be finished.

Six

When Dora awoke on Monday, the 1st October, she thought at once of the baby she was expecting. There was something wrong, she was certain, but John was so convincing she was now thoroughly confused by her symptoms. She had begged to be allowed to visit the doctor but John was adamant that she was fussing over nothing and that all expectant women had aches and pains. She had spent another restless night, tossing and turning in an effort to find a suitable position, but all the while abdominal cramps had caused her considerable discomfort and her heart had raced unnaturally. She also felt feverish so that she woke several times drenched in perspiration.

A knock at the front door surprised her. The church clock had only just struck eight. Who could be calling at this hour? She tried to get up but immediately doubled up as she felt a sharp spasm in the place where she believed the child was growing. There was no way, she decided, that she would be able to get down the stairs, but John had thoughtfully considered this. He had left the front-door key beside her on the bedside table and now she clutched it as she staggered towards the window.

'It's me, Mrs Trott.'

With an effort Dora pushed up the window and leaned out. 'I'm sick,' she cried. 'I'll drop the key and you can let yourself in.'

While she waited, she made her way back to bed and lay there, panting.

'Come in!' she called as the footsteps paused outside the bedroom door.

Emily Trott looked fresh as a daisy, Dora thought enviously, and wished she had felt able yesterday to wash her nightdress. She felt crumpled and stale, and pushed her hair back from her face. 'You'll have to excuse me,' she said. 'I'm not at all well and John doesn't want me to bother the doctor. It's the pains.'

Mrs Trott kept a reasonable distance but was obviously excited by something unconnected to Dora's condition.

'I haven't seen you for nearly a week,' she began breathlessly, 'and wondered if you'd heard the news. Yesterday there were *two* new murders. *Two!* Can you believe it! The man's a monster. What's more he's sent a letter to the newspapers. His name's Jack and he calls himself "the Ripper"! Isn't that awful? Can you imagine?'

In spite of her pains, Dora was intrigued. 'Jack the Ripper? Oh, how ghastly! That's horrible, that is.' For a moment she forgot her own troubles. 'He had the cheek to write to the papers? The man's some kind of madman.'

'And that's not all. He killed the last two in just one hour! Soon after midnight, they think, the night before last. Can you believe the cheek of the wretch? I hope he burns in hell!'

Dora screwed up her eyes as the pain deepened. When it subsided she said, 'When they catch him he'll hang. If they ever do catch him.'

'Jack the Ripper!' Mrs Trott rolled the words across her tongue. 'He sounds like some kind of fiend. Maybe he's the devil! You know ... Why can't they catch him otherwise? Because if he is the devil then he can use magic to vanish after he's done his grisly deeds.'

They regarded each other soberly. Dora

said, 'You mean black magic. Magic spells and satanic whatnot?'

Mrs Trott shrugged. 'Well, he can't be an ordinary man, can he, the things he does?'

Dora sank back against the pillow. 'He brings me this stuff from the chemist. John, I mean. At times I think it makes me worse.'

Mrs Trott walked to the window and looked down into the street. 'I saw that man again. In the long coat. Some while ago now. Mr Undershot.'

'The debt collector?'

'Yes. He followed your husband one day. It was very odd. I was cleaning my bedroom window and I saw him but he didn't see me. He was leaning against the wall just this side of the gaslight and then Mr Hubbard came out and Mr Undershot followed a few yards behind him.'

'I expect he wanted to ask him questions. He's still trying to find that man that owes all the money.' She clutched her abdomen and let out a stifled scream.

Mrs Trott looked startled. 'You really should see your doctor,' she said.

Dora recovered her speech. 'Could you go downstairs and find my medicine? I'll take an extra dose and maybe I'll sleep for a while. It's in a brown bottle on the shelf next to the kitchen window.' Too late she realized she hadn't washed up yesterday's supper things.

She struggled into a sitting position and when Mrs Trott returned with the medicine, Dora reached for it eagerly. 'I'll give myself a bit extra,' she said. 'The chemist said I could. The pain's really bad this morning.' Reaching for the glass on the bedside table she poured a generous helping and gulped it down. Mrs Trott watched with interest. The mixture immediately brought relief and Dora visibly relaxed. 'That's better. It's wonderful stuff.'

Mrs Trott folded her arms and prepared to go on with her news. 'Anyway, the first one was called Lizzie Stride but she wasn't cut up at all so that's a blessing – although she's still dead, of course!'

Dora shuddered.

'The other one's called Catherine Something ... Eddowes, I think, and she was ripped to pieces if you can believe the papers. Found in Mitre Square – off Mitre Street, by the Aldgate. Not that far from Berner Street where the first one was done. They're saying it could be two different murderers. Is that supposed to make us feel better? I mean, one's bad enough!' She shook her head. 'And the letter! Written in red ink, they reckon, to look like blood – and full of jokes. *Jokes!* Sick, that is. Joking about murdered women.' With narrowed eyes, she leaned a little closer to the invalid. 'You all right?'

Dora smiled faintly. 'Much better, thanks.'

She closed her eyes and her head lolled to the left.

Mrs Trott said, 'Well, I'll leave you to it. Hope you feel better soon. If you want someone to come with you to the doctor, let me know.'

'You're very kind ... Just close the door. Leave the key with me.'

When the front door closed behind Mrs Trott, Dora poured herself another large measure of the medicine and settled down in the bed, already feeling much happier.

As soon as Douglas Unwin set foot in the police station later that evening, the desk sergeant beckoned him over.

'You're to get round to Goulston Street pronto, sir – that man you were investigating – what's his name? – he's reported...'

'John Hubbard?' Douglas forgot that he was weary from lack of sleep and spoke sharply. 'What about him?' He thought that if the wretch had fled the country he would shoot himself.

'Wife's dead. Seems he found her when he got home.'

Douglas almost reeled. 'Dead? Are you sure?' Guilt filled him. This was all his fault. He had known something bad would happen to that poor woman. He should have done something! But what? He had nothing to go on except intuition, and the Ripper

147

killings had taken precedence over every-thing else.

A shapeless but well-dressed woman was standing at the desk beside him and now she gave him a stern look. 'I was here first, if you don't mind!' she snapped. She turned back to the desk sergeant. 'She's white and very curly and her collar's brown leather. She answers to the name of Binkie...'

Douglas asked the desk sergeant, 'How did she die? Do they know?' I know, he thought, his agitation increasing. She was poisoned, like Edmund Cummings.

The woman gave him a fierce look. 'She's not dead! She's run away – and stop inter-rupting. I'm talking to him, not you!' She jerked a fat forefinger in the direction of the desk sergeant. 'Binkie's a very friendly dog. She wouldn't bite anyone.' Her face crump-led. 'But she is valuable. She may have been stolen.'

The desk sergeant ignored her. 'Cause of death unknown. Best get round there.'

Douglas set off at a run. He remembered his conversation with Dora Hubbard and with the neighbour. He imagined Dora Hub-bard lying still and silent on a slab at the morgue. There would be a post-mortem, surely. They would discover the crime. His obsession with the case would be justified officially ... but wasn't it his job to *protect* the public?

As he pounded through the sombre streets his heart was heavy with remorse. He slowed eventually to a walk, still wrestling with his conscience. He should have done *something*! He should have warned Dora Hubbard in some way. But how could he have done it without arousing suspicion? That had been his problem ... and now she was dead.

He arrived at the door of No 16 to find it standing open. A small group had gathered outside and Mrs Trott was among them. To her he said, 'What's the story?'

Mrs Trott had been crying and now two more tears trickled down her face. 'Poor woman! I blame myself. I was round here this morning, talking to her. She was alive then. She took her medicine and settled down again. When I left her she seemed fine. Smiling, even. Oh, to think that she just up and died. It's terrible.'

Douglas shouldered his way into the narrow passage and found a young police constable in the bedroom, talking to the man who called himself John Hubbard. He was immediately tempted to call his bluff there and then. Perhaps to call him Massie or Cummings and see his reaction. He wanted the wretch to know that his present wickedness had been discovered but he dared not take the risk. He had to know the results of the post-mortem before he could arrest him. The last thing he wanted was for him to take fright and disappear. Instead he addressed himself to PC Riggs. 'I'll take over now,' he told him.

Riggs tried unsuccessfully to hide his disappointment. Probably the first time he'd been first on the scene of a murder, thought Douglas, but it won't be his last.

PC Riggs nodded but was not giving up all his trump cards. He said, 'Right, sir. This is Mr Hubbard...'

'We met some years ago.'

PC Riggs went on. 'Mr Hubbard is the dead woman's ... I mean, the victim's husband ... that is...' He hurriedly studied his notebook, giving Douglas a chance to address the man he had been hunting for so long.

'Very sorry to hear of your wife's death, Mr Hubbard.' Somehow he kept his tone neutral.

'Thank you. It's such a shock! So unexpected! She seemed so happy. She was expecting our first child.' Hubbard's gaze was fixed on the empty bed. 'Poor Dora. She's always been a bit of a hypochondriac but I never expected her to do anything like this!' He passed a hand over his eyes.

PC Riggs looked up eagerly. 'Sir, Mr Hubbard assumes she died by her own hand.'

'Oh? On what grounds, Mr Hubbard?'

Hubbard glanced up. 'She had convinced herself she was going to die in childbirth. A

150

friend of her family did just that. Died giving birth, I mean, and poor Dora...' He appeared to be overcome by emotion and Douglas saw genuine sympathy in the young constable's face and wished he could manage something similar. He was uncomfortably aware that by comparison he himself sounded brusque and uncaring, and struggled to at least make a convincing pretence of understanding.

He said, 'You must have had a terrible shock, Mr Hubbard.'

'Thank you. Yes. I was explaining to your constable that I came home and found her in bed. I thought she was asleep and then ... later I noticed she wasn't breathing.'

'So how do you think she killed herself?'

Hubbard indicated the empty medicine bottle. 'That was almost full when I left home. She's supposed to take a measured amount. She was having stomach cramps and the chemist gave me this. She found it very soothing.'

'The chemist?' he snapped. 'Didn't she see a doctor?'

He shrugged. 'She wouldn't go to him. We argued but I gave in to her. I put a lot of it down to her nerves ... and this conviction that she was doomed to an early death. A particularly sad way to go, I'm sure you'd agree.'

Riggs, his face pale, said, 'Dreadful!'

Douglas wondered if he had a young, possibly pregnant wife. He said, 'Take Mr Hubbard down to the station, PC Riggs, to give a statement. I'll finish up here. Make a few notes and contain the crime scene. Get rid of the neighbours.'

'Crime scene?' Hubbard's head jerked up. 'There's been no crime, officer. If my poor misguided wife took her own life ... That is, no one else was involved. No one *killed* her.'

Riggs said, 'Suicide is a crime, Mr Hubbard.' He put away his notebook.

Douglas nodded. 'There'll be a post-mortem, I'm afraid, Mr Hubbard.'

'A post-mortem? Oh no! That's so savage. My poor dear Dora.' Hubbard covered his face with his hands and the two policemen exchanged glances.

Douglas said grimly, 'Take him down to the station, Riggs. I'll be along later.'

Hubbard said, 'We mustn't assume ... That is, she may *not* have intended to kill herself. It may have been an accident.'

Douglas fixed him with a cold stare. 'But you told PC Riggs that you suspected that she had deliberately taken an overdose. Because of the childbirth worry. The family friend who died. Remember?' Damn! He had forgotten he was supposed to be neutral.

Riggs looked at him, then fished out his notebook again and began riffling back through the pages for confirmation.

Hubbard looked flustered. 'I–I think I may have said something like that but it doesn't mean I was right ... I'm not thinking straight, officer. The shock. I mean, Dora was obsessed about her health but...' He threw up his hands. 'Can't we forget all that? For her sake. A suicide means an unmarked grave. No proper burial. I couldn't bear that for her. God knows how much I loved her!' His voice shook, but whether with fear or grief wasn't clear.

Douglas said, 'Take him to the station, PC Riggs – and keep him there until I get back. There are other procedures, Mr Hubbard. You will need to formally identify your wife's body.'

Now Hubbard looked frightened, Douglas thought with satisfaction.

'But I won't be kept in overnight or anything, will I?' Hubbard asked. 'I'm not in any trouble, am I? I haven't done anything wrong.'

Douglas narrowed his eyes. 'Not as far as we know, sir. The incident has to be properly investigated, you understand.'

PC Riggs said, 'It's only a formality. Don't...' He stopped abruptly as he caught sight of Douglas's expression. 'Sorry, sir!'

Hubbard was recovering. He looked from the constable to the detective. 'Of course. You have to do your duty.'

Riggs touched his arm and the two men left the house. Watching them go, Douglas took comfort from the fact that Hubbard was obviously rattled.

Now's my chance, he thought. He had the house to himself and he would search every inch of it. He would even lever up the floor-boards if it seemed likely that there was anything of interest to be hidden under them. He took out his own notebook and a pencil and laid them on the kitchen table then drew in a long satisfied breath. He may have been too late to save Dora Hubbard, but if there were any clues in this house that would lead to Hubbard's arrest, he, Douglas Unwin, was determined to find them.

In the kitchen he began with the space beneath the sink, which was hidden from view by a grimy curtain strung on a wire, and there he found a variety of buckets and cloths, a large bar of carbolic soap, soda and a scrubbing brush. He also found mouse dirt, a mouse trap, a few dried potato peelings, dirt and mould – but nothing suspicious. The kitchen cupboard contained an assortment of crockery, basins and a large brown teapot with a broken spout. On the bottom shelf he discovered a few medicines, most of which he was familiar with: Anderson's Pills ('to cure all maladies'), a bag full of dried herbs, a jar containing Epsom salts and assorted proprietary packets containing powders to soothe the digestion or regulate the bowels. Not forgetting Daffy's Elixir which claimed to cure almost everything. Douglas smiled at the sight of it. His mother swore by it.

'But no laudanum, no strychnine!' he muttered with a sigh and moved on.

The parlour was equally unproductive. The furniture was limited to a small round table, two armchairs, a few fire-irons and a coal scuttle. A small glass-fronted cupboard had been screwed to the wall and this held a small china doll, a glass paperweight, a musical box and a small dish of artificial rosebuds. The mirror over the fireplace was showing signs of age. There was no sideboard and nowhere to hide anything.

Upstairs, the bedroom contained very little. A double bed – with nothing hidden under the mattress – did however, produce a sad rabbit's foot. Douglas found it between the pillow and the pillowslip.

'Poor Dora,' he whispered. 'It didn't bring you much luck, did it?'

But at least she presumably died peacefully, if the overdose of soothing medicine was to be relied upon. He would have to find the chemist who had prescribed it and see if the recipe tallied with any potentially noxious substances found in Dora's stomach. He would also ask about the quantities involved to find out if Dora had been deliberately given a massive overdose.

A chest at the bottom of the bed contained a frayed blanket and a pair of mildewed button-boots. A bedside table and a chair completed the room, but behind the door Douglas found a man's overcoat on a hanger and a cotton wrap which Dora would have worn over her nightdress.

On the small landing there was a chest of drawers containing nothing but the expected clothes. The small spare room had obviously been treated as a box room. It contained empty teachests, old newspapers, and a broken rocking-horse with peeling paint, no tail and the remains of a moth-eaten mane. Douglas ran his hands over the wooden back and wondered if this had been Dora's favourite toy. He tried to see her as a young girl, her tiny feet tucked into the stirrups, curls tumbling over her shoulders, rocking to and fro in delight and patting the horse's glossy neck. A tattered but treasured remnant of what might have been a happy childhood. His eyes darkened. All her hopes of happiness for the future had come to nothing because she had married the wrong man. Somehow she had stumbled into the path of a handsome villain who had brought her young life to an abrupt end.

'I'm sorry, Dora,' he whispered – then cursed himself for being a sentimental fool. 'Get on with the search,' he told himself, angry at his lapse of concentration.

Now it was time to check the two trunks and three small suitcases. Surely there must be something incriminating in the house; some small item the wretch had overlooked. Closing his eyes he uttered a short prayer for divine help but when he opened the trunks they were both empty. The suitcases contained only crumpled tissue paper, a few old letters of no significance and one suede glove.

'Nothing of interest. Damnation!' For a moment frustration filled him with a feeling of helplessness. He straightened up slowly. He made no effort to tidy up or hide the signs of his search. Let the man know his place had been turned over, Douglas decided. If they had to release him, he would know that he was being scrutinized and hopefully the pressure on him would make him careless.

Douglas put away his notebook and pencil, closed and locked the house and went back to the police station, his spirits somewhat depressed.

Two hours later, Lloyd was sitting at a table opposite Unwin. In front of him was a mug of tea which was getting cold. He had told the DS that he didn't want tea – he wanted to be released, but so far that hadn't happened. The detective sat back in his chair and stretched his legs. Damn him, thought Lloyd. He was trying to rattle him but he, Lloyd, was too smart for that. Those tricks might unsettle a lesser man, but not him. He folded his arms and stared at the policeman with what he hoped was a scornful expression.

'Let's go over that again Mr Hubbard alias Massie alias Cummings. You're now telling me that the deceased woman was *not* your wife. So why is her name Hubbard, the same as yours?'

'It's not the same as mine. My name's Lloyd Massie and I'm married to Bella. We live at No 4, White Street.'

'So since we last met you have married two wives. Is that what you're saying?'

Lloyd longed to throttle the man. Anything to wipe the smile off his face. 'Dora believed that we were man and wife but we weren't. We went through a – a *sham* ceremony.'

DS Unwin leaned forward. 'A sham ceremony! Well, that's original.'

Lloyd shrugged. 'You don't have to believe me.'

'I *don't* believe you! I think you're lying through your teeth!' He leaned closer and instinctively Lloyd shrank back a little, startled by the animosity he saw in the blue eyes.

'I suggest you are a bigamist, Mr Hubbard – or is it Mr Massie?'

'And I've explained that I'm not! I've told

you once and it's really not difficult to understand.' He hoped the man would recognize the jibe but policemen were not very bright, in his opinion. 'I lived with my father, Edmund Cummings. He was beginning to lose his mind but as you know I cared for him until his death. We went through all this at the time, you recall. Later I felt free to marry. I married Bella, a woman I had admired for some time. It's in the church records. A legitimate marriage.'

'But the marriage included a problematic cousin. You must be finding that rather irksome.'

'Lottie, yes. Bella and I deal with it. We do whatever we think best for her.'

He reached for the cold tea and sipped it. Had he convinced this sharp-eyed policeman?

He had gone over the rest of the story in his head a dozen times and knew it was open to misinterpretation. Would this man believe it? Probably not. They had crossed swords when his father died but DS Unwin had been forced to let the investigation die. Now, here they were again, face to face.

DS Unwin stood up abruptly and began to pace about the small room. Lloyd ignored him. There was a door with a grill in it so that officers outside the room could see and hear what was said and done. No one was going to ill-treat him, he told himself. It was

159

just a matter of time. He must not get rattled. If he stuck to his story they would have to let him go.

'So,' the policeman continued, 'when did you *pretend* to marry Dora? And why?'

'I've already told you.'

'I want you to tell me again.'

'You have a short memory!' Lloyd stared at him with loathing. *Detective Sergeant* indeed. The jumped-up detective was hoping he'd slip up. He wanted him to forget the details of his story and be caught out in a lie, but he'd be disappointed. Lloyd felt in control. He had no fear of this man.

'I discovered that my father had – had molested the girl. She was a servant from the house next to us.'

'So she would have known your name was Cummings and not Hubbard?'

Lloyd, rattled, tried to keep his expression steady. He breathed deeply, keeping his gaze on the detective without flinching.

'Yes, she knew me as Cummings. She was going to make a fuss. She was threatening to go to the police and I had to stop her. So I offered her marriage in exchange for her silence. But I didn't want to go through the ceremony in my real name in case later I wanted to make a genuine marriage.'

'So had you met Bella at this time?'

'No. I told Dora that I was Edmund Cummings's stepson and my real name was Hubbard.'

The detective's laugh was scornful. 'And you expect me to believe all that nonsense? D'you take me for a fool, Mr Massie?'

Lloyd shrugged. 'It's the truth. I can't prove it but I'll swear on the Holy Bible...'

'We don't have one to hand!'

'That's not my problem.'

'You don't have any problems, do you, Mr Massie, because *conveniently* your father died suddenly while in your care? So he can't deny any of this cock-and-bull story.' He sat down again and leaned close. 'People die on you, don't they, at the most convenient times! Now it seems, poor Dora, this innocent servant girl, who is *not* married to you, was expecting a child by you.'

'So you say,' Lloyd challenged, 'but where's your proof? You say a neighbour told you. Really! Do you believe everything you hear?' He gave a short laugh. 'Dora may have thought she was in the family way but I can assure you that is impossible. I ought to know.'

'Her doctor might confirm it. I haven't spoken to him yet.'

'She didn't visit the doctor. She wasn't ill. She liked to see herself as an invalid and was always imagining that she was ill. She was in good health but a malingerer.'

'So she didn't see a doctor. That, too, is very convenient! But she will see a pathologist at the post-mortem. He might confirm that she was with child.'

'If she was it was another man's child.'

'Which means she was unfaithful, Mr Massie. Didn't she love you?'

'She never did. She was grateful to me for marrying her – as she thought. We were never in love.' He was beginning to sweat under the unrelenting barrage of questions and hoped it didn't show. His hands were moist and he could feel perspiration on his scalp. He longed to take out his handkerchief and wipe his face but that would please the detective. No, he must brazen it out. He was more than a match for the police. The thought came to him that if he ever met DS Unwin in a dark, deserted alley he would give him a good beating.

The detective smiled thinly. 'And now your so-called legal wife will find out about Dora! Very awkward.' He shook his head with mock regret but the next words snapped out. 'So when's Bella going to die? She's next, isn't she? Or will it be Lottie? And what little stories are you thinking up for them?'

With an effort Lloyd held himself back. Striking a police officer in his own police station would not be wise.

Instead he said, 'I love my wife. And she loves me. I imagine you hate to hear that. You spend so much of your time with the dregs of society it must warp your feelings.

You hate the idea of a perfectly normal, happy couple. I'm sorry for you, Detective Sergeant Unwin. You and all your nasty-minded colleagues.' He pushed the mug across the table. 'Now, I want to go home. If you want me to stay here any longer you'll have to arrest me and you can't. You have nothing. No evidence whatsoever. I've told you the truth. For the last time – I've done nothing wrong! I suggest you get back to something that really matters. Stop hounding me and find Jack the Ripper, why don't you? Unless he's too clever for you...'

The detective stepped outside and spoke to someone else. Lloyd strained to hear what was being said but failed. To his surprise, however, the detective seemed to have reached the same conclusion. Opening the door he said, 'You're free to go, Mr Massie. Thank you for your co-operation in this matter. We may, of course, talk again some time – after the post-mortem on Dora's body. I shall look forward to that little chat.'

As Lloyd walked past him the policeman said softly, 'I've got my eye on you, Massie. Think on that.'

Lloyd, refusing the bait, walked out of the room without another word, his head high, his eyes gleaming in triumph. They could hound him for a year and a day but they could never win. Innocent until proved guilty. That was the law. And they had no evidence.

Outside the police station, he clenched his fists and grinned then strolled casually away in case Unwin was watching. He knew things that the detective had not yet discovered and he felt good. He felt *safe*. His future was looking bright. He was now the legal owner of the not-so-small legacy left to Dora by her grandmother, though he would allow a little time to pass before he claimed it in case the police got wind of it. He didn't want to hand them another weapon.

Crossing the road, he sighed. He would have to tell Bella about Dora, which would not be easy. He had kept the secret well until now but the police might tell her. He certainly didn't trust DS Unwin to keep quiet about it. So he would confess to Bella and the sooner the better, He wasn't too worried at the prospect. He would bend the truth a little and she would accept it because she loved and trusted him – and because she *wanted* to believe in him.

When he had survived this little crisis, he would turn his attention to Lottie.

At five past nine, Bella sat alone in the parlour, both hands round an empty mug which had recently held cocoa. She was still waiting for her husband to come home. Lottie had gone to bed as ordered at nine o'clock sharp and Bella was trying to think clearly about Lottie's behaviour and what, if anything, should be done about it. Normally a cheerful girl, she followed her mother's advice and tried to look on the bright side. She had been a bright, bubbly child and she had grown up expecting life to be fun. Only Aunt Sadie had offered a rare warning that life was not all beer and skittles and that she must take the rough with the smooth. Now, she told herself, she was encountering some of 'the rough' and must deal with it sensibly.

She kept hoping that there would be an improvement in her cousin's behaviour but it seemed slow in coming and she knew Lloyd was becoming less tolerant as the days became weeks. In her heart she didn't blame him because he didn't love Lottie the way she did. The latest escapade, running off in the middle of the night, was serious because Lottie might have met Jack the Ripper. He could have killed her. Bella could imagine the headlines in all the newspapers. Another killing! The thought of poor Lottie lying dead on the pavement in a back alley was too awful to think about.

The front door opened and shut and she jumped up from her chair in the parlour and ran to greet her husband. To her dismay he looked dishevelled and there was a strange expression on his face.

'Dearest!' she cried, throwing her arms round him with her usual exuberance.

'What's kept you? You look terrible! Has there been an accident? Or another murder?' She steered him into the parlour. 'I'll fetch your slippers for you. Sit down and...'

He held her at a distance. 'I'm all right, Bella. Don't fuss so! Just sit down with me and listen. I have something to tell you that will come as a shock, but you need to hear it from me.'

Bella stepped back, looked questioningly at him and then sat down heavily. 'What?' she cried. 'What's happened?'

He sat down opposite her and she saw the way he searched for words.

'Oh no,' she whispered. 'It's Lottie, isn't it? The doctor's said something. You're going to take her away. Oh Lloyd! I can't bear it!' Her worst nightmare was coming true.

Lloyd shook his head. 'A policeman might call here tomorrow. A Detective Sergeant Unwin. He'll be asking you questions about me.'

As she began to protest, he held up his hand. 'Please, Bella. Let me tell you the whole story and then you can ask me anything you wish.' He took a deep breath. 'I've never told you, but I have had to share a home with a young woman named Dora...'

Bella cried, 'Share a home? How do you mean?'

Ignoring the interruption he went on. 'My father, who was losing his sanity, assaulted

166

her and she was threatening to tell the police.'

'You have been living with another woman?' She began to tremble, partly with shock but more with anger. "So it's all been a lie – our marriage!'

He closed his eyes to avoid her anguished expression. 'My father would have been arrested,' he went on doggedly. 'He would have been sent to prison. I had to save him so I – I came up with a plan. I offered to marry Dora and she accepted.'

Bella sank back in her chair, her eyes wide, her breathing rapid and shallow. She tried to speak but was unable to utter a sound. Her mind was spinning and her heart thudded within her chest. Had she heard him correctly? Had she misunderstood?

Lloyd continued. 'I simply found a house, paid the rent and visited her from time to time. She thought I was working a night shift at the London Hospital. She thought I was a doctor. That way I could come home to you most nights.'

At last she found her voice. 'You *married* her? God Almighty, Lloyd! Tell me it's not true!'

'It's not true that I married her. She...'

'But the police!' Bella stammered, her throat dry with fear. 'You said the police would be calling. Have you done something to her?'

'I've done nothing, dearest. You must believe that. I did what I did to save my poor father – who, sadly, has since died. The police are involved because Dora has died. Yesterday, in fact, and we think she died by her own hand by an overdose of her medicine. She was always very worried about her health. A hypochondriac, in fact. Also, she was expecting a child but we don't know who the father was.'

A *child*! Bella put a trembling hand to her throat. 'But it's not yours?'

'Mine?' He regarded her with astonishment. 'How could it be mine? She wasn't my wife – although she thought she was. We had a ceremony but it was not a real marriage service. The truth is I bribed a clergyman to pretend we were married.'

Bribed a clergyman? Wasn't that fraud? Bella thought she would faint if she heard any more. In fact, she wished she *could* faint. Anything to get away from these terrible revelations. Faced with Lloyd's confession, the problems with Lottie suddenly paled by comparison. Poor Lloyd! What a dreadful time he had had, she thought. An insane father who did terrible things to young women and now the same woman had committed suicide. How he must have dreaded revealing the truth.

'My poor Lloyd!' she whispered. 'How I wish I could have helped you through this nightmare. I feel I have let you down. I might at least have been able to comfort you.' She left her chair and crossed the room to kneel beside him. 'Tell me how I can help you, dearest. You need not face this alone.'

He put his arms round her and held her close. 'Oh my darling. What a relief to hear you speak so bravely – and with not a word of reproach. My wonderful Bella. I have been so anxious. So terrified of losing your affection.'

'Losing my affection? That you will never do!' Bella reached up to kiss him. 'We'll see this through,' she murmured. 'You will tell me what I must say to the policeman and I will say it. I'll be your alibi!'

'Alibi?' He held her at arm's length. 'I have no need of an alibi, Bella. I've done nothing wrong and you must say nothing to DS Unwin that might make him suspicious. I am not charged with anything, you under-stand. Nothing!' He stood up and moved to the window. 'We may never find out who has put the girl in the family way. The wretch has probably taken to his heels by now.'

Bella stood in front of the fireplace, strug-gling to keep up with the revelations. A new thought entered her mind and she gasped. 'Oh Lloyd! You don't think ... I mean, sup-pose that same man has murdered her? He might well have done.' Her voice was rising. 'He may have forced his way into the house and ... and *forced* her to drink an overdose. Or ... Good Lord! He might have forced poison down her throat!'

Lloyd turned from the window and his expression silenced her immediately. 'Poison? Now you are being ridiculous!' he snapped. 'If you are going to make comments like that to the policeman, you might as well hang me.'

'But why, dearest? I wasn't talking about *you*. I said "that same man". Meaning ... well, I thought you'd know what I meant.'

He strode across the room and took both her hands in his. 'I'm not angry, Bella, but you do have to be careful what you say to the police. If you go putting wild ideas into their heads, goodness knows where it will lead. You must promise me to think twice before you say anything to them. Be sure in your own mind before you speak. They might try to frighten you into saying something foolish about me. You must see that they want to arrest *somebody* for the crime. *Anybody*.' His expression was anguished. 'Do you want it to be me?'

Bella, shocked and verging on hysteria, burst into tears and Lloyd was quick to comfort her. He finally persuaded her that he was in no real danger and then she, in turn, convinced him that she would say nothing untoward when questioned.

'I'll pretend to be very innocent,' she

promised through her sobs. 'I'll keep saying that I don't know ... or I don't remember. They won't learn anything from me, Lloyd.'

Ten minutes later, when she had recovered, they moved into the kitchen for a cup of tea and some cold sausages with chutney, and, after they had eaten, Lloyd rehearsed her in preparation for the inevitable questions.

'I shall pretend to be the policeman,' he explained. 'I'll ask you some searching questions and try to trick you into saying the wrong thing.'

She nodded dutifully, crossing her fingers. She must not be caught out, she told herself. She must never say anything that would be misunderstood.

Lloyd adopted a stern posture and said, 'So did you ever suspect that your husband was a bigamist?'

She thought carefully. 'No, sir. I never suspected a thing.'

Lloyd rolled his eyes.

'What's the matter?' she asked indignantly.

'You made it sound as though there was something wrong but you didn't suspect it!'

He closed his eyes. Bella felt crushed. She had fallen at the first hurdle.

He said, 'You must say, "Certainly not! The idea never entered my head".'

Bella repeated Lloyd's answer.

'Next question ... Mrs Massie, do you

think your husband capable of committing a crime of any sort?'

'Well, he's a very capable man but ... but a crime? No. Certainly not.'

Lloyd looked pleased. 'Much better! You're a good girl, Bella...' He frowned, searching for another question. 'Has your husband been behaving strangely at all lately, Mrs Massie?'

Bella pursed her lips. This time she would come up with a very good answer.

'He has been rather irritable but that's because poor Lottie has...'

'No! You've just suggested that I *have* been behaving strangely! You've said that I've been irritable. Think before you speak, Bella.'

'I did think and you have been irritable. I think that if I stick to the truth I can't possibly...'

'Bella! Whatever you do, don't *think*! Just do as I tell you. You will say, I haven't been behaving differently. You can say that Lottie exasperates me but I never lose my temper. Don't you see? It's Lottie who's behaving differently, not me.'

Bella looked sullen. She didn't see the need for this stupid rehearsal and she didn't see why he should shout at her when she was doing her best. She said, 'I'm going to bed.'

She made to move away but he caught her by the wrist.

'You'll go when I say you'll go!' he told her.

'Why shouldn't I go to bed? I'm tired!'

'Because we haven't finished!'

Bella's temper flared suddenly. She had had a miserable evening, hearing about the hateful Dora and Lloyd's horrible father. The thought of him visiting another woman and pretending to be her husband had left her shaken and confused. How had they behaved together, she wondered. Had he kissed her? Had he done other things that married couples do? Had he enjoyed being with her, knowing that his real wife was at home waiting for him? Lloyd had explained how it had come about and it sounded logical, but she resented him keeping the secret for so long. He should have confided in her before they were wed.

She said again, 'I want to go to bed!'

He released her. 'Go then!'

She hesitated. This was beginning to sound like another quarrel and they had been married only a short while. Tears pricked at her eyelids as she stumbled from the room and went upstairs. Only one thought gave her comfort. Tomorrow she would go and consult Sadie. 'And, please God, don't let her be drunk,' she whispered to herself.

Seven

Detective Inspector Warne regarded Douglas through narrowed eyes. 'You look as if you've been dragged through a hedge backwards!'

'I'm all right, sir.' Douglas looked up from the incident board he had been studying. 'This message, sir? Chalked on the wall last week. Do we know it was from him?' The DI shrugged. 'Could have been. Who knows?' He quoted, *'The Juwes are The men that Will not be Blamed for nothing.'*

'What's it supposed to mean, sir?'

'God only knows! Could mean nothing. Could refer to something other than the Ripper.'

'But it was found just after the double killings on the thirtieth of September. Eddowes and Stride.'

'Right – but did our Jack do both of them? Only Catherine Eddowes was mutilated.'

It was five to eight in the morning on the 9th October and the room was filling up with police officers of various ranks. The

174

conversations were muted and the air was fraught with failure. The police and everyone else knew that they were no nearer the discovery of the murderer, and morale within the force was at an all-time low.

Douglas said, 'How did the trials go today – with the bloodhounds?'

The DI rolled his eyes. 'Bloodhounds! I ask you! What next?'

'But they did work, sir, with that case in Blackburn some years ago. They tracked *him* down. Made quite a stir at the time, so I heard. It was more than ten years ago but everyone remembers it.'

DI Warne nodded. 'Actually they did quite well but, of course, they weren't tracking a real murderer. It was only a trial and holding it in Regents Park early in the morning made the tracking easy. The park was empty so there was no one to walk across the trail and confuse the dogs. Bit different on the streets of Whitechapel. Still, the dogs performed well enough, I grant you that.' He shrugged. 'Did what was expected of them. But we'd have to have the dogs on hand when there's a murder and that's difficult. The dogs' owner lives in Scarborough.'

Douglas nodded then risked a question about the death of Dora Hubbard. 'Have they done the post-mortem yet, sir, on Hubbard?'

The DI gave him a frosty look. 'Never

mind Hubbard, DS Unwin. You keep your attention on Jack. If we don't catch the blighter the police force will never live it down.'

Sadie was sober and Bella muttered a prayer of thanks as she followed her up the neglected stairs and into her small attic room. It looked as bad as ever, smelly and untidy, and Bella wondered how her aunt could bear to live like that. An hour's work with a dustpan and brush and a soapy cloth would transform it. Well, maybe two hours! thought Bella. There were two large baskets containing clean but unironed clothes and, in spite of the warm weather, the fire had been lit and two irons stood facing it in preparation for Sadie's work.

As the door closed behind them Bella demanded, 'Where have you been this last week? I kept coming round and you weren't here. The landlady says you didn't come home at all for five days.'

'Trust her. Nosy old cow!' Sadie sighed. 'If you must know, I met this chap. Nice fellow. At least I thought so. He asked me to go home with him and promised me a shilling.' She held up a hand. 'And no! I didn't ask for money. Nothing like that. He offered.' Avoiding Bella's startled gaze, she spread an elderly blanket over the table to create an ironing area then took a skirt from one of the baskets and shook it to free some of the creases. She arranged it over the blanket and reached for one of the irons.

Bella blinked. 'You went home with him? What ... you mean ... He was going to *pay* you?'

Sadie spat on the iron to check that it was hot enough. It sizzled and she went to work on the skirt. 'Yes, Miss Prim! That's what I do mean. He seemed nice enough. I'd had a few and I thought, Why not? Who cares?'

'Are you mad?' cried Bella. 'Going home with a stranger! He might have been Jack the Ripper! He might have murdered *you*!'

'Well, he didn't, did he? And a shilling's not to be sneezed at. It would have come in very handy. Not that he gave me a shilling. Rotten sod!'

'So how long did you stay with him? Five days?' It was a different side of her aunt, thought Bella, shocked. Had her aunt often gone with strange men, she wondered, or was this something new? If she *had* done it before, she'd never admitted as much, but maybe, now that Bella was a married woman, Sadie saw her as more worldly and thought it safe to talk about such things. Bella was intrigued and also a little dismayed. Was this how the unfortunates started? she wondered. A first step on the slippery slope to ruin?

Sadie was smiling to herself as she recalled

the time she had spent with him. 'He bought me a mutton pie and we went to a dog fight near Battersea. He's a bit of gambler. Won half a sovereign that first night so he asked me to stay for another night and promised me another shilling. I s'pose I should have guessed it was too good to be true!'

She ran the iron round the hem. A hot smell of soap filled the air and Bella wrinkled her nose.

Sadie noticed Bella's expression. ''Orrible, isn't it? They don't rinse them properly.'

Bella said,' So what happened with this man?'

Sadie scowled. 'Bet on a horse race and lost all his money and wouldn't pay me so I hopped it. Miserable devil!'

She exchanged the rapidly cooling iron for the hotter one and Bella thought what a dreary way it was to earn a living.

'So he didn't pay you anything? After you'd...'

'After I'd warmed his bed for him? No he didn't. When I got back here I found a note from one of the ladies I iron for. It said that as I wasn't here to do her ironing she'd found someone else. Blooming sauce! Silly old cow!'

Bella had lost interest in the story. Quickly she began her own account of her conversation a week earlier with Lloyd. She told Sadie everything. Sadie became so wrapped up in her account that she became careless and scorched a flannel nightshirt. 'Oh Gawd! Now look what you've made me do!' she cried. She took it to the sink and rubbed it with soap and excessive energy. The scorch mark was less noticeable but the fabric had been frayed by Sadie's energetic rubbing. She tossed it back on to the ironing blanket. 'If they say anything I shall swear it was like that before.'

Bella went on, 'And I do trust Lloyd. Of course I do, but...'

'I don't. I trust Lottie.'

'What's that supposed to mean?'

'Well, his story about her going out at night didn't match Lottie's story, did it? If I had to choose, I'd believe Lottie.'

Bella stared at her. 'What, you believe that Lloyd made her go outside?'

'And then left her alone? Yes.' She folded the nightshirt and placed it on the growing pile and reached for a petticoat. She held it up, scowling. 'Look at this! All these blooming frills!'

Bella drew in a shaky breath, feeling as though Sadie had punched her in the stomach. How could she ... How *dare* she suggest that Lloyd would do such a terrible thing?

Sadie went on, blithely unrepentant. 'I mean. I can't see Lottie making up that bit about having something over her mouth and watching Lloyd walk away and calling after him. It's not like her to invent that – and why should she? I know you don't want me to say this, but you should be careful, Bella. How much do you really know about Lloyd?'

'I love him! I don't care what you say! He's a good man!'

Sadie put the iron back in front of the fire and ignored the second iron. She sat down opposite Bella. 'Right then. Have it your way. Now tell me what happened when this policeman came and talked to you?'

'He asked me about what happened to Lottie and about what I knew about Lloyd. Whatever he asked me, I said I didn't know or I didn't remember. That way I couldn't betray him.'

Sadie closed her eyes then opened them. 'How could you betray him if he hasn't done anything wrong?'

'I don't know ... Lloyd got me so confused. He said it was better that I didn't actually answer anything properly. I was just to say I didn't know or...'

'You've said that already!' Thoughtfully Sadie picked at her already broken finger-nails. 'If you're worried, Bella, you could go round to where this Dora lived and talk to her neighbours. Ask them what they know.'

'About what? What will they know about Lottie?'

'I don't mean about Lottie. I mean about this Dora woman. Maybe she really *was* his wife. Maybe...'

Bella jumped to her feet, breathless with fear and anger. Anger that Sadie had dared to voice her own doubts, and fear that she might be right. 'If you're right – which you're not! – then you're saying that I married a bigamist and I'm not legally married to Lloyd! That's the most hateful thing you could say, Sadie! I never thought you'd say such things to me about the man I love. About my husband.' She was clasping and unclasping her hands. 'Oh, I know you're jealous because you've never had a man of your own but I didn't expect you to be so spiteful! And I didn't...'

Sadie prised herself from the chair, her face reddening. 'Can't you see that I'm trying to help you? Maybe to save you and Lottie?'

'Save us from what? We're not in danger!'

'How can you be so sure?' Sadie threw up her hands in despair. 'Don't you see, love? If the police are suspicious of him there just might be something about him that you don't know? Why did none of his friends or relations come to your wedding? We thought it odd.'

Bella hesitated. She had thought the same thing but had pushed the doubts to the back of her mind. 'What's the wedding got to do with it? That was months ago. They couldn't come. It couldn't be helped and it didn't matter.' She thought rapidly. 'Maybe he's fallen out with his family and didn't want to say so. Families fall out sometimes. Maybe they did all live abroad, like he said. I'm sure it was perfectly innocent.'

'You might be, but you would! You think the sun shines out of his ar—'

Bella screamed, 'Don't you dare talk about him like that! You know nothing about him!'

'And neither do you! You say he works as a private investigator. So, where's his office? You have no idea.'

'His office?' Bella floundered momentarily. 'I don't need to know where it is. I'm not one of his clients, am I?'

'If he has any clients! You want to ask a few more questions, Bella. Ask him to take you to his office. Talk to his secretary.'

'He doesn't have one. He does his own paperwork. He told me.' Bella's throat was dry. The more Sadie probed, the less sure she became. 'He says it's dangerous work and he doesn't want to involve me.'

'And what's all that about his father? You told me ages ago that his parents died in an accident.'

'Did I?' She recognized the truth of this immediately. 'I suppose he wanted to spare me the truth.' Her stomach churned. Lloyd had lied to her once. Perhaps he had told her other lies. Her mouth felt dry, but she quickly rallied. Damn Sadie. She was trying to turn her against her husband.

Sadie grabbed a shirt from the basket and snatched up an iron. As soon as she laid it on the garment there was a strong smell of scorching and smoke rose. 'Oh! Sod it! That's your fault, Bella. Distracting me!' She held up the shirt which now had an iron-shaped hole in it. In frustration she hurled it across the room, her mouth quivering.

Bella knew that her aunt would have to pay for the ruined shirt. Serve her right, she thought. I'm sick of her! I came to her for help and all she's done is upset me and say bad things about Lloyd.

Sadie towered over her. 'Just go away, Bella. I'm done with talking to you. You take your chances with your precious Lloyd. Why should I care? Calling me jealous and spiteful. Your own aunt. My God, girl, you've gone too far this time. I'd rather have no man than the one you've got.' Her eyes almost bulged and flecks of spittle flew from her lips. 'Get out of here, Bella, and don't come back. But if anything happens to Lottie, I'll blame you. Got that? I'll blame you!'

Frightened by her aunt's vehemence and thoroughly upset by the words themselves, Bella rushed from the room and almost fell down the stairs, trying to hold back her tears. Her aunt had overstepped the mark, she told herself, and had said unforgivable things about poor Lloyd.

'I'll never, never set foot in No 9, Thrawl Street again!' she promised herself. Sadie could be dying and she wouldn't lift a finger to help her. She reached the bottom of the stairs and slammed the front door behind her. What sort of woman was Sadie, anyway, she asked herself, to go off like that with a strange man? Who was she to lecture Bella on taking risks and being in danger? As she fled along the street in the direction of home, she was sobbing and had never felt so frightened and alone.

As she turned into White Street, Bella felt a slight lessening of anxiety. She was nearly home. She would tell Lottie that they were no longer friends with Aunt Sadie and that she was to stay well away from Thrawl Street. But how could she explain to Lloyd about her quarrel? He would be furious if he knew what Sadie had suggested about him and there would be more trouble. Bella longed for her life to return to that tranquil time before her wedding when she and Lottie had lived together in peace, and Sadie was a welcome visitor. That time, however, would never come again and she must learn to accept that.

A carriage passed her and she caught a glimpse of two men in white coats and a third person who sat between them but, wrapped up in her own troubles, Bella gave it no further thought. The moment that she reached the front door it opened and Lloyd stood in the hallway. His face was pale and his left hand was swathed in a large bandage.

'It's Lottie!' he told her. 'Come in, Bella, and talk with the doctor. He was on the point of leaving but...'

'Lottie? What's happened to her?' Panic stricken she rushed past him as Doctor Hague appeared at the kitchen door. 'Is she hurt? Where is she?'

Lloyd said, 'All this concern for Lottie. No concern for your husband?' He held up his bandaged hand, his eyes full of reproach.

Bella stared from him to the doctor, unable to believe that her troubles, far from being at an end, were multiplying. 'What's happened? Oh Lloyd, your hand! Has there been an accident? Where's Lottie?'

The doctor said, 'Come and sit down, Mrs Massie. I'll explain. Your cousin has come to no harm but has volunteered to enter the asylum. Temporarily, you understand.'

Taking her arm, he steered her to a seat and handed her a glass of water. The two men also sat down and Bella sipped the water fearfully.

The doctor smiled gently. 'Your cousin had an attack of irrational rage and attacked your husband with a knife.'

'Oh no!' For a moment Bella thought she would faint as a wave of dizziness swept through her. She looked at Lloyd, who nodded gravely.

'She tried to kill me, Bella. I put up my hands to defend myself and she slashed it with the knife. I've cleared up most of the blood. I didn't want you to be frightened.' He pointed to a large kitchen knife on the draining board.

She was at once full of concern for him. 'Poor Lloyd! Is it very painful? I wish I could have been here.'

The doctor said, 'It's a good thing you weren't. She might have gone for you instead of your husband. She might have killed you. It was some sort of mental seizure.'

'Quite unprovoked,' Lloyd told her. 'She suddenly sprang to her feet and...'

'But what were you doing here? You left for work as usual.'

'I was working nearby in Bishopsgate Street, following a suspect, and lost him so I thought I would look in on you as I was so near. Lottie was behaving rather strangely when I came in. Sitting at the table, mumbling to herself and refusing to speak to me. I didn't know where you were and...'

'I went to see Sadie.' Bella couldn't bring herself to say any more about the visit. The less said the better, she told herself. She would think of an acceptable way to tell the story before she told her husband anything about it.

Lloyd continued. 'Suddenly she jumped up, snatched up the knife and tried to stab me. I was taken by surprise, stepped back and...'

'Wait! Did I see her leaving here – in a carriage? Was that her with those two men in white?' Her eyes widened in horror. 'You mean they've taken her away! Oh poor Lottie! I can't bear this. I must go to her. She'll be terrified.'

The doctor exchanged a meaningful glance with Lloyd. 'Mrs Massie, you must understand that your cousin is in a very disturbed state. Disturbed mentally. She needs to rest and she needs to be examined by the doctors. Your long-suffering husband was very good. He insisted that she went in as a voluntary patient.'

Lloyd smiled at her. 'I did my best, Bella dearest. You must believe me. If I hadn't agreed, the doctor would have had to call the police and she might have been arrested.'

'More than likely!' the doctor confirmed. 'She attacked your husband with a knife. It might have been attempted murder.'

Bella gasped. 'But that's nonsense. Lottie wouldn't murder anyone.'

'It was an irrational attack of rage, Mrs Massie. That means that she didn't know what she was doing.' He turned to Lloyd. 'You must get some stitches in that nasty wound,' he said. 'I have my carriage outside.

If you come with me to my surgery I'll deal with it.'

Lloyd thanked him and turned to Bella. 'You've had a bad shock,' he said. 'I'll be back before too long and we can talk about it. Don't fret about Lottie. She is in good hands and will receive the best treatment. Hopefully before too long she'll be back with us – her old cheerful self.' He kissed her briefly. 'Now make yourself a pot of tea – or better still, have a small brandy to restore you.'

Bella watched the carriage drive away and closed the front door with a strong sense of foreboding. She was shocked by the speed with which her life had been shattered. She would never speak to Sadie again and now she had lost Lottie. Thank heavens she still had Lloyd.

Lottie woke up the following morning and wondered where she was. She remembered being taken away by the two men in white coats and she remembered coming to a very big house with lots of people in it. A doctor gave her a drink of something pink that tasted of coconut and then she must have fallen asleep because she didn't remember anything else. Cautiously she opened her eyes and looked around. She found herself in a large room with a great many beds in it. She sat up in amazement and was surprised to find a wooden rail around her bed. Stranger still, she was tied to the rail by thick cords around her wrists. She sat up with difficulty and counted the beds. Thirty! 'What a big bedroom,' she muttered.

An elderly woman in the next bed hissed, 'Lie down! Don't make then notice you!'

Lottie smiled nervously but said nothing because she didn't know what to say to this strange woman who had almost no hair and who was also tied to her bed. Another careful scrutiny of her fellow inmates showed her that they were all tied to their beds.

Outside the large windows it was barely light.

'Lie down, you idiot!'

'I'm not an idiot!' How many times had Bella told her to say that? No one must call her an idiot, Bella had insisted. She was a little slow, that was all. 'I'm a little slow, that's all.'

The woman cackled with laughter. 'Course you're an idiot. We're all idiots here. This is an asylum. Did you think it was a hotel or something!' Amused by her own joke she cackled again and Lottie saw that she had no teeth.

'Where have all your teeth gone?' she asked, intrigued.

'They took 'em all out because I bite people.'

Lottie regarded her with alarm. 'I don't

bite people. I really don't!'

'No. You stab people with knives! We've heard all about you. You tried to kill someone. You're dangerous, you are!' She cackled again and further down the room another woman joined in the laughter.

At that moment a large nurse appeared and clapped her hands. 'Time to get up! Wake up!' Groans and murmurs of disquiet followed this but the nurse ignored them and made straight for Lottie. 'You're being assessed at nine o'clock,' she told Lottie. 'You have to wash and dress and eat your breakfast first and I want no monkey business. One step out of line and you'll end up in a padded cell.'

Lottie had no idea what a padded cell was but she understood that she might not like it. As the nurse untied the first cord Lottie said, 'When am I going home? When is Bella coming for me?'

'Bella? Who's she?' The second cord was untied. 'Now get up and follow me – and if you try anything you'll get the back of my hand!'

Lottie scrambled from the bed then stared down at herself. 'This isn't my nightgown!' Her voice rose anxiously. 'Mine's blue. I don't like this one. I want my own nightgown! I really ... Ow!' She clutched the right side of her face as the nurse carried out her threat and slapped her hard with a meaty hand.

The next hour was relentless. Lottie stumbled from one crisis to another in floods of tears. The nurse hated her, she decided. She stood naked under a cold-water shower and was then told to dress in an ugly and ill-fitting garment made of a coarse grey material.

In a vast dining room with no cutlery on the tables, Lottie choked down a large brown rusk and drank a glass of watery milk then followed the nurse along endless corridors, past a variety of inmates in differing stages of insanity.

One elderly man leaned against the wall of the corridor crying, 'I'm a lunatic. I belong here!' over and over again. A young woman with a wild expression crouched in a corner, sobbing. A man in a doctor's coat steered an elderly man who was manacled to him and two men in short white jackets held a frenzied woman against the wall and called for extra assistance. Lottie found it strange and distinctly unpleasant and wished fervently that Bella would hurry up and rescue her.

'I want to go home,' she told the nurse's broad back, scurrying to keep up with the woman's firm strides. 'I really do. I want to go home with Bella. We have toast for breakfast. I don't like it here.'

The nurse stopped abruptly outside a door marked 'Mr Bannerman'. She knocked then turned to Lottie. 'I don't like it here either but I'm not making a fuss. My advice to you is speak respectfully to Mr Bannerman and don't try anything or, believe you me, you'll like it even less!' With a mirthless smile she opened the door and ushered Lottie inside.

Bannerman was a dejected man of fifty-five, depressed by the six years he had spent as a consultant in the asylum where hardly any of the patients were helped by the various treatments available. He regarded Lottie despairingly, ran his fingers through his thick grey hair, and nodded to the chair in front of the desk. 'Sit down Lottie.' He returned to her notes.

A voluntary admission ... backward from birth and has little education ... attacked her brother-in-law ... wandered the streets in the middle of the night ... backwards mentally but physically sound ... has an irrational distrust of her brother-in-law and tells lies about his behaviour.

'Hmm!' He glanced at her. Not unattractive, he thought, but the childlike expression was a giveaway. Her movements were sharp, almost birdlike and her manner towards him was suspicious. Hardly worth trying any drastic treatment, he decided, unless she was properly committed and would be there at least a year. Maybe he would give her a few written tests and a personal assessment followed by interviews with Doctor Craythorne. Then send her home – if she wanted to go.

Mr Bannerman hated these half-hearted attempts to correct what he saw as 'a minor incapacity'. For him, someone suffering from a severe paranoia or a complete mental breakdown was more of challenge, of more value and more to his taste. Perhaps he would simply add her to Craythorne's list and hope for a more stimulating case to present itself.

'So, Lottie, you don't like your brother-in-law?' He leaned closer. 'You don't like Lloyd? Is that it?'

She frowned. 'He tells lies. He gets me into trouble. He really does.' Folding her arms, she stared down at the well-polished linoleum covering the floor.

He said, 'Do you realize that you cannot go home? You have to stay here until your behaviour is more acceptable. You have to stop telling lies about him and you have to stop hurting people. You have a very nasty temper.'

'He doesn't like me!'

'I'm not surprised!' He raised bushy eyebrows. 'Are there any other men you don't like?'

She appeared baffled by the question.

He asked, 'Do you like me?'

'Yes ... No. I don't know. I really don't.'

'You don't like men at all, Lottie, do you?'

She frowned, searching the room for inspiration. 'I don't know. '

Dr Bannerman wrote 'immature and uncooperative'. He wondered if she was a virgin. If there had been an unpleasant sexual encounter, that might account for her attitude towards men. Towards Lloyd Massie in particular. Had he perhaps taken advantage of her? If so, the incident might have tipped her over the brink and exacerbated her problems. He glanced at the clock on the wall and decided he would take a break and go to the staffroom for a cup of tea. This was going nowhere and he was losing interest.

'Do you know any men?' he asked, returning the pen to the inkstand and leaning back in his chair. 'Do you have any men who are your friends?'

'Lloyd tells lies.' Her eyes narrowed. 'He walked away and left me in the street. It was dark. He said if there was any justice in the world I would meet Jack the Ripper and he might work the miracle!'

Surprised by her coherent answer, Dr Bannerman sat up and gave her a long appraisal. This was more interesting. The words she had quoted had a genuine ring to them. And it seemed she *could* string more than a few words together and she *could* recall details!

He nodded with satisfaction. He would keep this one on his list for a while longer and see what developed.

Several days passed during which Bella made repeated trips to the asylum in an attempt to visit Lottie and talk with her and with her doctor. All these attempts failed but Bella did not give up. On the fourth day she walked straight into the reception area and demanded to see her cousin.

The woman behind the desk consulted her list and shook her head yet again. 'I keep telling you that they don't like visitors during the first week of the patient's stay. It unsettles them something chronic and...'

'You told me that yesterday and the day before!' snapped Bella. 'If I can't talk to her then I want to see her. I have to satisfy myself that she really is in here.'

'If she's on this list then she's in here.' The woman regarded her balefully. 'I don't make the rules, so don't get snippy with me!'

This time Bella had come prepared for rejection. She said, 'Do the rules allow you to tell me which ward she's in? That would be all right, wouldn't it?'

'She might be in solitary! If they get too upset, or they threaten the other patients, they have to be shut away on their own. It's awful then because they keep on screaming to be let out and they use terrible language.

Cursing and blinding and...'

'I see.' Bella gave her a straight look. 'If I give you a sixpence, could you find out for me?'

The woman glanced round to see if they were being overheard. Then she whispered, 'No ... but I'll do it for a shilling!'

Bella handed over the money and the woman flicked through a large leather-bound ledger. 'She's in the main ward for women on the first floor. If I was to drop something on the floor and bend down to pick it up and you was to run off and go upstairs and I didn't notice and raise the alarm ... Well, it wouldn't be my fault, would it?'

Bella saw the crafty glint in her eyes and guessed that more money would be needed. After some haggling another sixpence was passed over and the deal was struck. The woman dropped the ledger on to the floor and then dived down behind the desk to pick it up again.

Bella took her chance and ran along the corridor and up the stairs. She tried to ignore the various patients whom she passed as they wailed and mumbled their way from A to B with blank expressions or exaggerated smiles. She dodged the clutching, out-stretched hands and was deaf to the pleas for help. The fact was not that that she was cold-hearted or oblivious to their plight, but that she was frightened by them. The crazed look and the incoherent muttering unnerved her and it took all her courage not to turn and run back down the stairs. She passed a doctor in a white coat, but although he gave her a surprised glance he had his hands full with a screaming woman who was scratching frantically at her own face.

Bella was in luck. The first double doors each contained a glass viewing panel and the ward was full of women. Some were in bed, others ambled slowly about and one stood by the window, her hands clutching the bars, her face pressed against the glass. Even in her dreary uniform, Lottie was recognizable. Bella caught her breath, shocked by the sight. How, she wondered, could poor Lottie bear it? Seeing Lottie pressed against the window tore at her heartstrings and she longed to rush in and rescue her. Common sense came to her aid, however. Even letting Lottie see her would unsettle her and there was nothing Bella could do but retrace her steps. But at least she had seen that Lottie was indeed in the asylum and had not been locked away in solitary confinement. Half blinded by tears, she stumbled down the stairs and cannoned straight into a man with grey hair who wore a white coat.

'Can I help you, madam?' he asked suspiciously.

'Thank you but I've been attended to,' she

stammered. 'I'm just leaving.' She almost ran along the corridor in her haste to be out of the place and fearful that her deceit had somehow been noted. She had just reached the door when a man came up the steps towards her.

'Mrs Massie?' he said with a smile.

She stared at him. 'Detective Sergeant Unwin. Fancy meeting you here!'

'Let me guess, you've been to visit your cousin Lottie.'

Bella wanted to hug him. After her experience in the asylum it was a great relief to see a familiar face. In a low voice she described her abortive visit in vivid detail.

He frowned. 'Demanding money for information is a felony! She had no right.'

'Oh no! It was my fault. My idea. I bribed her. I don't want her to get into trouble because of me.'

Taking her gently but firmly by the arm, he led her down the steps and a few yards from the entrance. 'I'm here to ask your cousin a few questions of my own about the night she wandered the streets, and also about her attack on your husband.' He hesitated as he saw her expression grow wary.

Bella was remembering her quarrel with her aunt and wondered uncomfortably what the policeman had to say to Lottie. Was it true, what Sadie had said – that the police believed Lottie?

'I'm sorry she made all that up about poor Lloyd,' she said quickly. 'She didn't realize how much trouble she would cause. She's trying to get him into serious trouble and I know she can't help it but I don't want you to think she's telling the truth.' Lottie had told lies, but so had Lloyd. She pushed the uncomfortable thought away. 'Lottie can't be telling the truth because that would mean ... because if she is telling the truth then...' Her voice faltered and she swallowed hard. If Lottie was telling the truth, that made Lloyd truly wicked. She looked at the policeman appealingly. Don't believe it, she willed him silently. Don't even think such a thing!

His smile had vanished and he was looking at her strangely. Was it pity she saw in his blue eyes? Her stomach seemed to lurch and suddenly her throat was full of bile which she forced back down. Coughing, she pulled a handkerchief from her pocket and wiped her mouth.

He said, 'Mrs Massie, I'd be failing in my duty as a policeman if I...'

'Don't!' she cried. 'I won't listen to a word against him. You're wrong! *Wrong!*'

'I've just come from the mortuary. I spoke to the pathologist who—'

'No!' She felt cold inside and thought she might faint. She turned to run but he caught hold of her sleeve.

'Dora Hubbard's post-mortem revealed

the cause of her death. She was poisoned!'

'No,' she whispered. She swayed and would have fallen but DS Unwin caught her and sat her on the asylum steps. Then he sat beside her.

He went on slowly. 'Her stomach contained large traces of laudanum which as you know is opium mixed with wine. There were also several other noxious substances in small quantities. None in sufficient quantities to kill her but together they proved lethal. The small doses of strychnine would have given her a lot of stomach pains.'

Bella found it difficult to breathe. 'So are you saying it was murder?'

'The investigating officer – the man who was first on the scene – thinks it was suicide.'

Hope flared. 'There you are then. She killed herself.'

'I think it was murder. Lloyd Massie's father died in exactly the same way. Don't you think that's too great a coincidence?' He regarded her gravely.

She struggled to her feet. 'No I don't! I think it's just terrible luck. Poor man.' She glanced back up the steps to the asylum. 'You won't get any sense from Lottie. It will be all gobbledygook! She doesn't know what she's saying.'

The detective also rose to his feet. 'Oh, but I think she does. I want to speak with the doctor who's handling her case. I don't want to make any mistakes, you see. I don't want to spoil our chances of a conviction—' He stopped suddenly.

'You want to see my husband hanged!' she exclaimed. Anger and fear came to her rescue and her courage returned. Glaring at him, she wondered how anyone could think him handsome. The blue eyes appeared cold and hard. The smooth fair hair seemed weak and unattractive on a man. Even his kindly manner seemed to be a way to hide his cruel nature. 'My husband is innocent, DS Unwin, and you will never make me say otherwise. I love him and I shall believe in him until the day I die!'

He frowned at the unfortunate choice of words. 'I'm doing my best, Mrs Massie, to ensure that you stay alive for as long as possible.' His expression was sad. 'Don't you see that I am on your side? If I can prove that Lottie hasn't lied, she can come home to you. Isn't that what you want? Is it fair that she should be locked away? Don't you care that this may be a major injustice?' When she didn't answer he sighed heavily. 'Have you had any pains lately?'

'No!' She saw at once where his questions were leading. 'And I haven't been given any so-called medicine ... nor any laudanum! I'm in perfect health!' She was longing to be gone but a terrible fascination gripped her.

He said gently, 'Mrs Massie, did it enter

your head to wonder who the father of Dora's child was?'

She swallowed painfully. 'I didn't have to wonder. My husband told me that Dora has ... has been with another man but he doesn't know who he is.'

'And you believed him?'

'Yes! *Yes!*'

'I've spoken with their neighbours and they are adamant that...'

'DS Unwin!' Bella cried. 'Don't you understand anything about love? I love Lloyd Massie with all my heart and soul. I shall never, *never* help you in any way.'

'Not even if I could *prove* him to be a murderer?'

Bella stepped forward and struck him across the face. He was taken by surprise and stumbled backwards. Only then did she realize that she had struck a police officer. Was that a crime? She began to tremble. 'I'm sorry! Oh please! *Please!* I didn't mean it!'

He sighed, shaking his head. 'It doesn't matter.'

'But you're a policeman.' She shrank back. 'I'm sorry I hit you.' Terrified, she realized that she was getting deeper into trouble with each day that passed. This hateful man would be the undoing of her. 'If you hadn't said such terrible things about Lloyd...' she began. 'If you would only leave us alone. I don't need your advice. I want to be left alone. Is that too much to ask?'

'It's for your own good, Mrs Massie.'

'My own good?' Her voice rose. 'How can it be for my own good for you to tell me my husband is a ... a suspect in a murder case? You're hounding me, DS Unwin. Hounding us both.'

He regarded her helplessly. 'I'm trying to help your cousin. Don't you understand how hard I am trying to save you ... both of you! Don't you see that I care about you?'

'We don't need saving and you *don't* care! We were perfectly all right before you came along. Now look at us.' She threw up her hands in despair. 'Please leave us alone.'

He stepped closer and took hold of her hand but she snatched it away, alarmed. He began to say something but she was too upset to listen and before he could utter another word she gave a small cry, turned and fled. If she never saw him again it would be too soon.

Eight

Annie Unwin sat in her chair by the window later that evening, sewing by what remained of the daylight. She was repairing her son's best jacket where the seam around the sleeve had come undone. He was home later than usual but she was resigned to his dedication to his work and rarely grumbled. Tonight she kept his supper hot on a plate over a simmering saucepan of water. A nice beef and oyster stew with onions and potatoes and carrots. It had been her husband's favourite meal, she thought, smiling to herself. She remembered how excited he'd been when their son was born ... and now she was cooking the same dinner for the same son who was now twenty-seven. He'd been such a friendly, biddable child but now he was a senior policeman with responsibilities. Where had the time gone? She glanced up at the photograph on the mantelpiece – the only one she had of her husband and son together. Douglas sat on his father's knee, staring at the camera as ordered. His father had an arm round Douglas's waist and looked very proud of his young son.

Snipping the thread, she eyed her handi-work with satisfaction and began to put her needles and cottons back into the old tin tea caddy where they were kept. She stood up and shook the jacket to get rid of any stray threads then draped it over the wooden hanger and took it back upstairs to his room where she hung it in his wardrobe. As she went downstairs he let himself in at the front door and, as usual, her heart lifted at the sight of him.

'You're back!' she said. 'You must be tired. Your supper's waiting for you. I made your favourite today. Remember how your father loved beef and oyster...' Her expression changed. 'What is it? Is something's wrong?'

He shut the door. 'It's nothing, Ma. Just a wretched day. Everything going wrong.' He allowed her a kiss as he took off his jacket and hung it up. 'How are you?'

He followed her into the kitchen and snif-fed appreciatively. 'Smells good.' He washed his hands in the sink and she handed him a cloth with which to dry them. With a tired smile he said, 'Stop looking at me like that. I'm all right. Tired and hungry but otherwise all right.'

She knew he was hiding something from her but said no more. She bustled about, getting his meal on the table and, when he had started, said, 'I mended your jacket. The sleeve.'

'Thank you.'

'You are so like your father, Douglas. You both have broad shoulders. I was always having to mend his jackets round the sleeve. The sleeve seam always gave way...' She studied him carefully. 'So it was a bad day?'

He nodded, his mouth full.

A sudden thought struck her. 'Have you been in any danger?' Her eyes widened. 'Oh, Douglas! Is that...'

'No, Ma. Just a set of disappointments. Nothing turning out the way I hoped.' He gave up the pretence. 'I'll tell you as soon as I've finished. Don't want it to get cold.'

Annie smiled. I can always tell, she thought. He can't hide anything from me for long. Even when he was a baby. I suppose being an only child and me a widow brought us closer. I had more time for him although I was working after his father died.

Minutes later Douglas put his knife and fork together the way she had taught him and leaned back in his chair. She waited. No point trying to hurry him.

He sighed. 'This woman, Bella Massie...'

Annie caught her breath. Something in the way he had said the woman's name alerted her to the fact that she was important in some way.

'I'm ninety-nine per cent certain that her husband is a murderer but she won't believe me! I can't get through to her. They've only been married a couple of months or so and she thinks he can do no wrong.'

'Well dear, she would, wouldn't she? If she loves him she *won't* believe ill of him. If you were married, your wife would never entertain such an idea. It's called love, Douglas.'

'But her life's in danger. I'm sure of it. I can feel it deep inside me. She will be his next victim. How do I convince her?'

'You probably never will.' She looked at him with a deceptively casual expression. 'What is she like, this woman?'

His silence seemed to echo in her mind and her heart sank. This wretched woman *meant* something to him. Oh Lord!

After deliberation he said, 'Young, pretty and very vulnerable. Very trusting but so ... so naïve. She's cheerful by nature and I doubt if she's ever been without friends and family to support her. Now she's alone with this ... this killer! It's my job to protect people like her, but how can I? She sees *me* as the villain of the piece. She's never going to trust me enough to confide in me.'

'Why can't you simply arrest this man?'

'Because we couldn't hang on to him indefinitely with the evidence we have so we'd have to let him go. And if he felt we were getting too close he might kill her and disappear.'

'He's not ... Oh Douglas! He's not Jack the

Ripper, is he?' Her heart was racing. Douglas might be the one in danger, she thought tremulously. The killer might kill *him*!

'No, Ma. We're certain of that. He's a killer – a poisoner – but he's not Jack.'

He leaned back and rubbed his eyes. 'There's a rumour doing the rounds that they know who he is but think he's skipped the country. I can't say more than that because it's all very secret but...' He shrugged. 'A woman reported that her lodger had blood on his sleeves and the cuffs of his shirt. But he went away for a few days and hasn't returned. Conveniently for him, he has disappeared into thin air!' Under his breath he muttered, 'Bloody typical!'

Her sharp ears caught the words and she stiffened. 'Douglas Unwin! What's come over you, using such language? Your father would turn in his grave if he could hear you.'

'I'm sorry. But it's so bl— So *very* disheartening. Not to mention humiliating. The papers are full of cartoons and verses ridiculing the police. Somehow they got wind of the test with the bloodhounds and have written a mocking poem about it! When I was in the asylum earlier today I heard one of the patients reciting it! Not so daft as he appeared, I thought to myself, for it's quite long. I wouldn't find it easy to learn off by heart.'

'Maybe not, dear, but you have work to do

and he, poor fellow, is locked up with nothing much to think about. He's got time to learn poems. It might be good for his brain – learning something by heart.' After a moment she leaned forward. 'What were you doing in the asylum, dear? Looking for the poisoner?'

'No. Bella Massie's cousin is in there but only as a voluntary patient. I went to question her about our suspect and ... Do you know, Ma, I thought that, for all her problems, she was telling me the truth. About him, I mean. He had her put away by saying that she went for him with a knife and he does have a nasty wound on his hand. She says he came in from the kitchen and his hand was already bleeding. She insisted that she did nothing to hurt him. So why, I ask myself, does he want her locked away? Because he's going to poison Bella and he doesn't want any witnesses. He wants—' He stopped abruptly.

His mother felt her pulse quicken again. He had used the woman's Christian name. She said nothing.

He rolled his eyes then glanced at her to see if she had registered the slip.

She smiled. 'This poor woman sounds very nice, dear. I'm sure you'll help her if you can.' So this was it, she thought, fighting down a sense of dread. Her son was falling in love with the wife of a murderer. Whatever would her husband say if he knew? 'You say she has lots of friends. Won't they keep an eye on her?'

He seemed not to hear her question. 'She's quite sweet, Ma, and has this amazing red hair, all curly with a slight frizz. Her eyes are the most wonderful blue and she's so ... so honest and trusting. I can quite see how she would be impressed by this wretch. He's quite handsome in a dark way. The thing is, he might be slowly poisoning her! I've tried to warn her but ... Well, she hates me for it. Everything I say has to be against the man and she loves him.'

'That's unfortunate, dear. I see your problem.' Annie could see more than one! 'But if you manage to arrest him – she'll hate you even more!'

He shrugged. 'And if I don't arrest him he'll probably poison her for her money. She's the owner of the place they live in. There's a shop downstairs – a second-hand clothes shop. And above them there's a foreign couple living. Hungarians. Jewish, I expect. But if Bella dies and he lives and is not incarcerated – he'll own it all!'

'Oh dear! That sounds dreadful, Douglas. Where is this place they live in?'

'White Street. It's a poor area but they're better off than some of their neighbours.'

Annie was torn between wanting her son to have the woman he wanted, and hoping circumstances would separate them. She tried to imagine the woman – frizzy ginger curls! Goodness! This Bella sounded rather colourful. Not the sort of woman she would have expected her son to choose. She would have preferred someone more sober but it was Douglas's choice and he had said she was 'quite sweet'. And she had blue eyes. Annie had no objection to blue eyes – her son's eyes were blue – but it all sounded very doubtful and she wasn't happy about it. Poor Douglas. She wished she knew how to advise him. He had finally found a woman who excited him only to face the fact that they might never be together because she was already married to this wretched poisoner who might kill her. She decided to go to church twice on Sunday and pray hard for a happy outcome.

The following morning, Bella woke up and immediately panicked as the memories of the past few days swept back into her consciousness. She felt dreadfully alone and helpless. She was no longer on speaking terms with Sadie, Lottie had been locked away, and the hateful policeman insisted on saying that her beloved husband was a murderer. She sat up, slid from the bed and crossed to the windows to see what sort of day it was. Outside, a steady drizzle had dampened down the dust in the road but

White Street still looked mean and unloved. A baker's van turned into the street and the horse clip-clopped past the window, shaking its head fretfully as if it had problems of its own to worry about.

She said, 'I know how you feel!' and smiled wanly. What did horses worry about? she wondered. Where the next bag of oats was coming from, perhaps. Life would get better, she reflected as she stared gloomily out of the window, when they had bought a new house and moved away from this depressing area.

There were footsteps on the stairs. Mr Schwartz on his way to work. From the bedroom window she watched him walk briskly along the street, his head down, turning up the collar of his shabby coat as a protection against the rain.

'I have to *do* something,' she said to herself. But what could she do? The long day stretched ahead. With Lloyd already on his way to his office, and no Lottie to talk to, Bella felt she must get out of the house. Before *he* turns up again to hound me, she thought.

Galvanized into action at the thought of a return visit from DS Unwin, Bella made a snap decision. The policeman had started to say something about Dora Hubbard's neighbours. She would go and talk to them. She would find out what it was that they were so adamant about. Buoyed up by the prospect of a challenge, Bella scampered through her morning routine and gobbled down a slice of bread and jam.

I'll go and talk to them, she decided. Minutes later she was out of the house and, huddled beneath her umbrella, on her way to Goulston Street.

On the way, she thought about how she would approach the task. Should she pretend to be somebody else or admit that she was Lloyd's rightful wife? Did they know that poor Dora Hubbard had been tricked into believing that she and Lloyd were married? As she walked along Goulston Street she convinced herself that honesty was the best policy. She had done nothing wrong and had nothing to be ashamed of so she would be totally honest about herself and her curiosity but she would try not to mention the police. No one needed to know that Lloyd had been questioned about the suspicious death.

The door of No 18 was opened by a nervous-looking woman who was wiping her hands on a damp cloth.

'Yes?'

'I'm Bella Massie. I would like to ta' you about...' She lowered her voice. '   *t* the people next door at number sixt'

Emily Trott's eyes widened. 'Wh'   *u?* What do you know about them'   *oo,* kept her voice down. 'Is it about the suicide?' Her eyes filled with sudden tears. 'Poor Mrs Hubbard. I was talking to her just hours before she died. She was in...'

'Yes, it is about her. May I ask your name?'

'I'm Emily Trott. I'm actually very busy at the moment. I overslept and didn't wake until gone eight. But...' Curiosity won over her caution. 'Well, all right. Come in – but I'll have to carry on with my work. I'm a homeworker now for Bryant and May. At least I am until September comes and then I go...'

'Hop-picking?'

'You guessed.' She looked wistful. 'I love Kent. Be nice to live there when I'm old but...'

'But the countryside's quiet and you might get bored.' Bella smiled. 'Everyone says that. I worked for a time at the B and M factory. I missed the other girls, though, when I left. We had some fun one way or another. It was dull work but I was never bored.'

She followed Emily into a small kitchen and saw at once the sort of work that she did to keep the wolf from the door. There were sheets of thin wood veneer with the shape of boxes stamped into them. In a separate box there were sheets of thin paper on which were printed words and pictures – the matchbox labels. On the table there was a of what looked like glue and a damp

214

cloth on a chipped plate. While Emily helped Bella off with her coat she kept up a stream of nervous chatter, explaining how the veneer shapes were pressed out and folded into shape.

'Then they're covered with the paste, and the paper wrapper is stuck round it and, hey presto ... a matchbox!' She gave a short laugh.

Bella sat down on a chair and watched for a few moments, pleased that they had found something in common.

Mrs Trott was well-practised and her fingers were nimble. She said, 'I'm very quick. I can make twopence an hour.'

Bella smiled. 'I was a packer but I can try and help you. You need to catch up if you overslept.' She thought the woman might refuse but Mrs Trott found another brush for the glue and they began to work on the boxes together.

Fleetingly the thought crossed Bella's mind that she might be reduced to work of this kind if Lloyd was ever taken from her. No, she decided. She couldn't face the loneliness. It would drive her mad. She would rather find a job as a barmaid. She was young and pretty and would earn good tips and at least the atmosphere would be jolly.

As calmly as she could she told her new-found friend the truth about the Hubbards, as she understood it, while Mrs Trott listened open-mouthed. 'I understand how my husband was driven to do what he did but ... Well, I wanted to find out for myself.'

'I suppose you would!' Mrs Trott was trying to hide her surprise. She was both fascinated and horrified as she listened to the unhappy story. 'So they weren't really man and wife?' She tossed a matchbox on to the pile and reached for another. 'Well! All I can say is that the walls are very thin and he certainly behaved as if he had rights ... Oh! I'm so sorry!' She clapped a hand over her mouth. 'I shouldn't have mentioned it! He was your husband, too. Or rather, *is* your husband.'

'It doesn't matter,' Bella said firmly, but she was suddenly breathless, her confidence badly shaken. She had hoped to hear that Lloyd and Dora had not been a very devoted couple; that they quarrelled. She needed to believe that the baby Dora had been carrying was not Lloyd's. Now she was unsure. At least the baby was dead, she thought, but felt immediately guilty. The baby had not been to blame.

Mrs Trott dipped her brush into the paste pot and continued. 'I reckon she might have been with child but he wouldn't take her to the doctor even though she was in pain. He's not going to be a very good father, I thought, but some men aren't, are they? Mind you,' she added hastily. 'It seems she was a bit of a malingerer and must have tried his patience. Do you have any children, Mrs ... What did you say your name was?'

'Massie. Bella Massie. I do believe, Mrs Trott, that it was not his child. He assured me they were not ... doing that ... and hinted that she had been seeing another man.' Bella added another matchbox to the pile. She was making one to Mrs Trott's three but at least it was some help.

Momentarily distracted from her real purpose, Bella asked, 'Did the homeworkers go on strike in July with the rest of the match girls?'

'The way they all walked out! It was amazing what they did.' Mrs Trott laughed for the first time. 'But no we didn't. Leastways *I* didn't. It was only the factory girls. I would have starved without this – or ended up in the workhouse like my aunt, poor old thing. Mind you, it was very brave of them. They might all have lost their jobs.'

'Might have but didn't.' Now Bella was speeding up. Soon she would be making two boxes to Mrs Trott's three.

'Still, it worked out well in the end. The strike was in all the papers. It must have been exciting but I'd rather work at home. I like to keep myself to myself, as they say.' For a few moments she worked in silence, her fingers moving in the familiar pattern: press, fold, glue, wrap.

At last Mrs Trott said, 'But about your hubby. I suppose he had to change his name. I've always known them as Mr and Mrs Hubbard.'

Bella leaned forward. 'Did you see anyone who might have been the father of Dora's child here?' Bella was willing her to remember something that she could tell the policeman when he next called – something to show Lloyd in a better light. 'Or could she have slipped out to meet anyone without you noticing?'

Mrs Trott thought about it. 'She might have done but if she did, I never saw it. I don't reckon she was well enough to have another man. She was always very sickly and pale. I used to think she should pull herself together. I mean, she wasn't a very cheerful sort. Always moaning about her aches and pains.'

'So you never saw any other men come to the house?' Bella prayed she would say 'Yes' but Mrs Trott shook her head.

'Never. But why should she want another man? Mr Hubbard's a fine-looking man.' She laughed. 'Well, you should know! He'd easily turn a girl's head. I do like a man with a moustache. My dear departed had a moustache. He was very proud of it ... But poor Mrs Hubbard. She must have been lonely. Bit of a ... what do they call those people who live in caves?'

'Hermits?'

'Yes. Those. I mean, poor soul was alone most of the day and he was out most nights doing his work at the hospital. At least...'

Bella looked up sharply. 'He was with me every night,' she said. 'Sharing my bed! He certainly was not at the London Hospital because he wasn't a doctor ... although he told her that he was. He's a private investigator. He has an office and he goes to it every day.'

Even as she uttered the words, a small doubt surfaced. What had Sadie asked her about the office? Did it exist? Her throat tightened. Of course it existed. She would ask Lloyd to take her there – or she would follow him one day to discover the address. The latter idea might be safer. If she asked him outright he might think she was challenging him and be angry with her. She might hurt his feelings and that would never do. She drew a deep unhappy breath. How she hated these suspicions and the mistrust that was forming. He was her lawful wedded husband and she should be dutiful. Being here would hardly meet with his approval.

Mrs Trott looked puzzled. 'But he was at home for some of the day. He has to get some sleep ... Not that I've seen him since she killed herself but then I daresay he would not feel like being in the place. Ghosts and suchlike. Unhappy memories ... Well, not so

219

unhappy.' Confused, she added quickly, 'It wouldn't mean so much to him, them not being really married.'

Avoiding Bella's eyes, she wiped her sticky fingers on the damp cloth and carried on with her work. Bella wondered how many thousand matchboxes she would make before she died.

Mrs Trott glanced at her, frowning. 'So if he's *not* a doctor, how come he was making up medicine for her? I saw her take some. Funny old business, isn't it? I can't make head or tail of it and that's the truth!' She stood up. 'All this chatting. I do go on a bit. It's living alone, I suppose. I think we could do with a cup of tea.'

The pile of matchboxes grew over the next half hour and Bella was pleased to find that her fingers speeded up with practice. Surreptitiously, she surveyed the kitchen. Presumably the house next door would look similar and she tried to imagine Lloyd sharing it with the sickly Dora. It hurt unbearably and she was forced to blink back tears, but if Mrs Trott noticed, she tactfully said nothing.

When at last Bella decided it was time to go home, she braced herself to ask the important question. As she slipped her arms into the sleeves of her coat and picked up her umbrella she asked, 'How were they together – the two of them? Would you say they were a … a devoted couple?' Unable to watch Mrs Trott's face, she stood on the doorstep and fumbled with the catch of the umbrella.

'I wouldn't say "devoted". Not really. He often sounded very impatient with her, especially when she wasn't well. Not that I spoke to him much. Sometimes we exchanged a "good morning" if he happened to be coming home when I was whiting the step. Now that I know the truth – that it was all a sham – I suppose I can understand it.'

Bella breathed a sigh of relief. 'So he didn't love her?'

Mrs Trott hesitated. 'Not in the way you mean. He wasn't affectionate towards her. Not when I was over-hearing them, anyway.'

Over-hearing them? Bella had a vision of Mrs Trott with her ear pressed to the shared wall between the two bedrooms. The thought of her listening to their love-making appalled her but there was nothing unusual about the situation. She uneasily wondered who had started the love-making. If Dora had been sickly most of the time she would hardly have been interested in encouraging Lloyd. Which meant that Lloyd had encouraged *her*! She swallowed hard, trying to banish the thought that she, Bella, had not been enough for him. Struggling to find an excuse for his actions, she decided that probably Lloyd had felt it his duty to pretend. They were supposed to be married after all –

and hopefully he hadn't really enjoyed it. Taking a little comfort from this reasoning, Bella gave him the benefit of the doubt.

Mrs Trott smiled wistfully at her. 'It's been really nice to have someone to talk to. Do call in again if you think of any more questions. And thanks for making all those matchboxes.'

Bella grinned. 'Let's hope all the matches don't fall out!'

They shared the laughter and Bella realized belatedly that she felt marginally better for having shared the awful secrets with a sympathetic listener. As she turned to go she said, 'Please don't tell my husband that I came round to see you. I don't think he'd be very pleased. Things are a bit difficult...' She let the sentence trail into silence.

'I can imagine!' Mrs Trott patted her arm. 'Your secret is safe with me, Mrs Massie, but suppose that man comes snooping and asking questions – the policeman who pretended to be a debt collector. What shall I say if he asks me about you?'

Bella hesitated for a moment then tossed her head. 'Tell him the truth. I'm not afraid of him!' It was still raining so she raised her umbrella. 'I've done nothing wrong and neither has my husband so he can put that in his pipe and smoke it!'

And on this cheerful and positive note they parted company.

* ★ *

For two days Bella mulled things over in her mind, unwilling to believe anything bad about Lloyd, but her faith in him had been dented by her visit to Emily Trott. After much deliberation she made up her mind to check certain things out. One of these was her husband's office. Another was the whereabouts of the church where Lloyd had pretended to marry Dora. Lodged at the back of her mind was a suspicion that Lloyd might have married Dora legally and that her *own* marriage was the sham. Left alone all day without Lottie's company, she felt the hours drag by full of dreadful uncertainties and she decided to do a little investigating of her own.

When Monday morning arrived she rose early, much to Lloyd's surprise, and announced that she would go to the office with him.

'Come to the office? What on earth has got into you, Bella? You would be hopelessly bored...'

'I'm bored at home, Lloyd, without Lottie. I used to have someone to talk to, but now the days are so long.' She pouted. 'I thought you'd be pleased to see me taking an interest in your work.'

'I would, dear, but today is not a good day. First I have a client coming in at nine o'clock for a confidential meeting and then I have an observation to conduct which *would* bore you, followed by compiling a detailed report on the observation which will take me at least an hour. Some other time, Bella dear.'

Bella smiled sweetly. 'If you promise, Lloyd.'

'Of course I promise. Have I ever broken my word to you?'

You've lied to me, Bella thought, but merely shrugged.

As soon as he left the house she put on her own coat, snatched up the umbrella and rushed out into the rain to follow him. She kept about fifty yards behind him and kept her head well down behind the umbrella in case he should turn round and see her. After about five minutes it dawned on her that he was not heading for the station. So where was this office of his? It must be nearer than she thought. Ten minutes later he had turned into Goulston Street and finally he let himself in to No 16. As Bella hesitated, shocked and angry, she saw Emily Trott open her door. She had a pail of water and a scrubbing brush and Bella realized she was going to clean her front step. Before she could decide whether to turn and run, Mrs Trott caught sight of her. Bella put a finger to her lips and Mrs Trott left the pail and hurried towards her.

Bella whispered, 'He doesn't know I'm here.'

'I expect he's come for the funeral. It's in half an hour. Mrs Betts over the road told me. It's got to be a very quiet affair. Suicide and all that. Not that they're certain, of course.'

'The funeral? Do you know where it's being held?'

Mrs Trott mentioned a nearby church and Bella thanked her.

'I take it, Mrs Trott, that you won't be going.'

'Not me. I hate funerals. You know what they say. Bad luck comes in threes! My mother went to my uncle's funeral many years ago and within three weeks she was dead herself. Fell down the stairs for no good reason. The doctor said she must have fainted or something. Her cousin died on the way back from her funeral. She was very old and the doctor said the journey had brought on a heart attack, so that made three. I steer clear of funerals. Well, I must get on,' she said. 'Mondays are always a rush because of the washing. The step, the wash and the matchboxes!' She laughed. 'Not very exciting, but it has to be done.'

Bella agreed but felt that her own life was a little *too* exciting at times. Undecided, she withdrew to the end of the road. Would there be a hearse? she wondered, for people to follow. Suicide was a wicked sin in the eyes of the church and people who took their own

225

lives were relegated to an obscure corner of the churchyard and buried during the night. But what about people who might have been murdered? Not that Dora *had* been murdered, she corrected herself hastily. She knew that was quite ridiculous.

For about ten minutes she loitered on the corner of the road, half hidden by the trunk of a large and sooty plane tree. Then the rattle of hooves alerted her to a closed van that was approaching from behind her. It was painted black and it passed her and came to a halt outside No 16. Ornate writing on the side of the van announced that it was the property of Billings Funeral Parlour. The peeling paint and rusting wheels announced that it was cheap. So had Lloyd ordered it to bring Dora's body to her last resting place? Was Dora's body in a coffin inside the van? Bella moved closer, using the umbrella to shield her face from any passers-by.

Lloyd appeared at the front door. He locked it behind him and took his place behind the hearse where he was joined by a woman from the house opposite who Bella presumed was Mrs Betts. At the last minute a few others joined them and the horses set off at a walking pace. Grey skies and steady rain made it a dreary sight, but Bella decided to follow at a distance. She was sure that her husband would not want to see her because that would mean she had found him out.

There was no client waiting urgently for his appointment at nine o'clock.

As Bella followed the pathetic procession she was trying to make excuses for Lloyd's lie. He might not want her to know that he was attending Dora's funeral. But why not? He had pretended to be Dora's husband. It would have looked very suspicious if he failed to turn up. Yes, that was it! She drew in a relieved breath. On any other day Lloyd would have taken her to the office. It was bad timing on her part. Dearest Lloyd was trying to spare her the pain of knowing that he was still involved in the charade.

Five minutes later as they reached the church, she slipped behind a cypress tree to watch the coffin being carried into the church. Bella smiled as she huddled beneath the umbrella. Dora was no longer any kind of threat. She was dead and soon she would be buried! Even as the unkind thought flashed into her mind, she felt ashamed. Dora was a poor servant girl who had been abused by an old man. Lloyd had taken her under his wing, so to speak, and had done what he thought was best for her in the hope of protecting his father. Lloyd hadn't even *met* Bella at that time so he hadn't realized how awkward the situation would become. Then he had met and fallen in love with her. And she with him! Her smile broadened. Now Dora had killed herself, but that wasn't

Lloyd's fault. He had helped her in her hour of need.

The sound of ragged unaccompanied singing came from the church. This would be a short service with no frills. Of course Lloyd might feel some regret, but he must also be highly relieved to be done with Dora. And Bella was also glad to know that from now on her husband would be hers and hers alone. When they moved to another house, DS Unwin would never find them. They would be free of him, too.

'A penny for them!'

Bella jumped. Turning, she discovered that DS Unwin was standing right next to her, his footsteps obviously muffled by the grass. He was leaning against a tall tombstone and she wondered how long he had been next to her.

'Speak of the devil!' she snapped. She was embarrassed to be caught spying on her own husband. Damn DS Unwin!

'I wondered what you were thinking,' he said. 'It's a wretched business.'

Taken aback by his tone, Bella said, 'My thoughts are worth more than a penny. Anyway, what are you doing here?'

He sighed. 'I'm here because I failed. I wanted to save her but circumstances were against me. Jack the Ripper is partly to blame for Dora's death. If he hadn't taken up all the police resources over the past few weeks...' He shrugged. 'But that's water under the bridge. At least I feel that I did what I could.' He looked at her with an expression she could not fathom. 'I don't want to attend your funeral, Mrs Massie.'

Bella tossed her head. 'That's good, because I'm not planning to die.' She knew she must appear confident but his words had sent a shiver down her spine.

'Poor Dora Hubbard didn't exactly *plan* to die!'

'So you say. The trouble with you policemen is you can never see the good in people.'

'And your problem, dear Mrs Massie, is that you cannot see the bad.' He straightened up. 'Now I'm going to show my face inside the church. Do you want to come with me? It might be interesting to see the look on Lloyd Massie's face.'

'No I don't! He's showing his last respects. He was kind to the poor girl. Surely you understand kindness, DS Unwin.'

'I also understand the criminal mind and it's not pretty. Why *did* you come here? I'm curious.'

'It's none of your business!' Bella glared at him. 'And I don't have to stand here listening to your nasty remarks. Goodbye.'

She turned to go but he caught her by the hand and pulled her back. 'If you want a nice walk, Mrs Massie, I recommend a stroll in that direction...' He pointed along the road.

'Take a left turn and then another and then go right. You'll come to a church. Ask for the Reverend Amos Stanning. He'll show you the church records if you ask him.' His eyes darkened. 'I think you should, Mrs Massie. To please me and to satisfy your own curiosity.'

Quelling the panic that flared within her, Bella stammered, 'I most certainly *won't*! I ... I don't have any curiosity. I have my husband's word.'

Turning too quickly in her efforts to be gone, she tripped and fell. Lying in the tangled grass and weeds she felt totally humiliated and burst into tears. For a few moments she lay there, hating the thought that he was watching her downfall and dreading the moment when he would pull her to her feet again. Seconds became minutes and eventually she scrambled to her knees to find she was alone. So, he had gone into the church to upset poor Lloyd. She stood up and brushed herself down. Unobserved, she blew her nose, wiped her eyes and tried to put the past few minutes out of her mind.

But she was no coward and she thought about what he had said. Left, left and then right. Well, she decided grimly, she would go and find this Reverend Stanning and she would look at his church records. If she *did* find an entry concerning the marriage of

Lloyd and Dora, she would only know that he had bribed the vicar. With her mouth set in a grim line, she set off with her head held high.

Nine

The Reverend Amos Stanning was an elderly man with a halo of white hair and a sweet expression. Bella was at once reassured by his benign appearance, and quickly explained her request. She did not, however, explain the reason behind it.

'A relation of yours?' he asked. 'Oh dear! You do know, I suppose, that she has recently gone to meet her maker? Poor soul. Such a short life. But when our Father calls us to be by his side...'

'Not exactly a relative,' Bella admitted, 'but I did know of her and was sad to hear that she had died.' A lie but never mind.

He led the way to the vestry and took a heavy book from one of the many shelves and laid it on the large oak desk which filled much of the small room. With practised fingers he riffled through the pages and then turned the book towards Bella. With a plump forefinger he underlined a section of writing. 'There we are. I can't pretend to remember her – we have so many brides through our doors, but I can assure you it was a legal ceremony. That is what you want to know, isn't it?'

Bella read the words with a terrible ache in her heart. It sounded most convincing. She said, 'And the words of the ceremony – they were accurate?'

He nodded.

'So there couldn't have been any mistake? I mean, you wouldn't have agreed ... that is, no vicar would agree to...'

He shook his head gently. 'I can't speak for all of us,' he said. 'But I have never falsified a marriage. The detective told me you would need to know the truth. Dora and Lloyd were joined in Holy Matrimony.'

For a moment Bella simply stared at him as the full truth dawned on her. It was she, and not Dora, who had gone through a sham marriage. She shivered. 'How would a vicar know if the husband was already married? My husband ... that is, the man I thought I had married, is called Lloyd Massie.'

'The banns are always called, my dear. That is the time for anyone who knows of just impediment to come forward. There is also a chance during the ceremony. *If any man knows just cause or impediment why this man and this woman may not be joined together in Holy Matrimony...*'

232

She looked at him with growing desperation. 'But surely the vicar would make some checks.'

'Why should we? We don't expect every man or woman to be a bigamist.'

Bella stared at the carefully written lines that seemed to show that she was not Lloyd's wife. 'Does this mean that I'm living in sin?'

He looked unhappy. 'Perhaps that is a question you should ask the vicar who married you.' Gently he removed the book and closed the pages. 'If you wished to have your marriage annulled I could copy the relevant page for...'

'No! I want to stay married! But...' She looked up suddenly. 'Suppose we were to marry again – that would be legal, wouldn't it? Dora is dead, which means that Lloyd is free again.' The words that echoed in her ears had a hollow ring to them. Did she *want* to be married to Lloyd under these circumstances? She drew in her breath at the very idea that, given such a choice, she might not want to be Mrs Lloyd Massie. Was it possible to even *think* such a thing? Anger flooded through her. This was DS Unwin's fault. He had twisted her mind and filled her head with awful doubts ... but he had been right! She was not Lloyd's wife. She swayed as the pressure mounted and would have fallen but the vicar saw what was coming and pushed a chair into place. She sat down heavily, her vision growing cloudy and her hearing weakening. She knew the vicar was saying something but the words were unclear. When she recovered he was handing her a glass of water and she drank greedily.

He said, 'Shall we go to the altar and pray together? God will give you the strength to face whatever is ahead.' He held out his hand and she took it, and moments later they were kneeling together and despite the vicar's hopeful prayers on her behalf, Bella felt she had reached the lowest point in her whole life.

More days passed and Lottie was still incarcerated in the asylum. She had been given a bed in the women's ward where she was most unhappy. Solitary confinement hadn't suited her either and now she was sinking fast into a dark despair. She found it easier not to try and converse with any of the other patients, some of whom had tried to befriend her. Her stock answer to anyone except the doctor was, 'Bella is coming for me. Really she is.'

Somehow, during her sessions with Dr Bannerman, she managed to retain the threads of her story about Lloyd, insisting that he took her out into the streets and then abandoned her. She also continued to accuse Lloyd of cutting his own hand and blaming it on her.

Dr Bannerman was a nice man, she decided, and she liked talking to him. But she hated everyone else and woke every morning with the fixed idea that *that* was the day Bella was coming to take her home.

On Thursday, the 18th October, she washed and dressed without speaking a word and went down to breakfast. She sat in the vast dining room and averted her eyes from the vacant stares and lopsided grins of the unfortunate patients who were all around her. Lottie hated to see the ugly ways in which they ate their food and the amount of food and drink that ended up in their laps or on the floor. They ate everything with their fingers, being denied the use of knives and forks for safety reasons. Only spoons were allowed but this morning the meal was bread and jam with a glass of milk. Lottie had been brought up to eat properly and today, for the third day running, she refused to eat or drink anything. She was hungry and felt rather faint.

'Bella will give me some porridge when we go home,' she told the nurse. 'She will. I'll wait until Bella comes.'

'She's not coming,' the woman told her. 'Eat.'

'I'm not hungry.'

An elderly woman opposite Lottie smiled at the nurse. 'I'm eating mine! I'm a good girl, aren't I?'

The nurse glared at her then addressed Lottie again. 'Drink your milk then. You can't go on like this. D'you want to be force fed? It's not pleasant.'

'Bella will...'

The nurse slapped her arm hard. 'That's enough about your precious Bella. Just *eat*! If you don't, I'll tell Dr Bannerman and you'll be for it!'

Lottie gave her a dreamy smile. 'I like Dr Bannerman. I really do.'

'Yes, well, he wants you to eat your breakfast and stop this nonsense about Bella.'

Lottie's smile broadened. 'I can do jigsaw puzzles.'

The nurse towered over her. She was a large mean-looking woman in a dirty apron. 'Eat your breakfast,' she ordered her, 'or I'll give it to someone else.'

'I'll have some porridge when Bella takes me...'

The nurse snatched away the bread and jam and handed it to the elderly woman sitting opposite Lottie. The woman snatched it from the plate and tried to stuff it all into her mouth at once. The nurse rolled her eyes. 'Pigs! The lot of you. No better than pigs!'

She turned angrily on her heel and walked away.

When the bell rang there was a loud scraping of chair legs as all the patients rose, filed out of the dining room and made their various ways back to the wards or the duties that had been assigned to them. Some patients cleaned windows, some helped out in the kitchens by washing up, others swabbed down the long corridors. Lottie was given a mop and a pail of water which smelled of disinfectant. She accepted her task without protest because she found it made her almost invisible. She moved slowly along the corridor, working earnestly and trying above all to avoid anyone's displeasure. At any moment she expected Bella to arrive to take her home.

While Lottie worked in the asylum, Bella was answering the door to a small grey-haired woman. She wore a neat but faded jacket and skirt and a matching straw hat in dark blue.

For a moment neither woman spoke. Bella was trying to recognize the woman and, if she failed, to guess who she was and what she wanted.

Bella asked, 'Do I know you?'

'No, dear, but I would like to speak to you for a few minutes if you would allow me.' She smiled faintly. 'I'm quite harmless.'

Bella hesitated. In her present state of mind she was suspicious. 'What's it about?'

'It's about your cousin Lottie ... and other things.'

'Lottie?' Fearfully Bella laid a hand over

her heart. 'Oh no! Don't tell me...'

'No, no! It's nothing bad.' She glanced nervously up and down the street. 'If we could talk for a few minutes...'

Bella opened the door wider. If it concerned Lottie she must hear it. She led the way into the parlour and they both sat down.

'Who are you exactly?' Bella asked.

'I'm a friend,' the woman replied. 'If you will let me be your friend, I can help you. I know you're troubled and in need of advice and...'

Bella was intrigued.

'My name's Annie Unwin and I'm Douglas's mother.' She swallowed hard. 'You can throw me out if you wish but I beg you to give me a few moments first.'

Bella's eyes widened. 'Unwin? Not ... You don't mean you're *his* mother – or do you? DS Unwin?' She jumped up from the chair as a spot of angry colour burned in each cheek. 'How dare you trick your way in here! That man is trying to ruin our lives!'

The woman shook her head. 'I know exactly what you are feeling, Mrs Massie. The point is...'

'The point is I want you out of this house! Now!' Dramatically, Bella pointed to the door.

'Please sit down, my dear.' Mrs Unwin sighed. 'I won't go until I have done what I can to help you. Douglas says you are very isolated. That your cousin has been taken away against her will and you have no one to turn to. I hoped I might be able to advise you. I certainly would like to change your opinion of my son.'

'There's no chance of that!' cried Bella, remaining on her feet. 'If he has sent you round here...'

'He doesn't know I'm here. He'd be very angry if he knew I'd taken it into my head to come round here. I knew you lived in White Street so I asked at several of the houses because I didn't know the number. I want you to know that my son is deeply concerned for your safety. I know you don't believe him. I understand also that you are very much in love.' Her smile was sympathetic and, despite her reservations, Bella felt herself drawn to the older woman. She missed Sadie more than she would admit.

Mrs Unwin went on. 'Men don't understand women when it comes to love, Mrs Massie. My father forbade me to marry my husband Donald because he was born with a club foot. I had to run away from home to be with him and we were very happy until he was killed in an accident at work. Love is blind to the faults of the beloved and that's how it should be.'

Bella had listened without interruption but now she said, 'I adore Lloyd! I couldn't live without him.' At that moment, the doubt re-entered her head. Was there anything else Lloyd had not told her? If the worst happened, could she live without him? Suppose she was *forced* to live without him?

'It's terrible for you.'

Bella sat down, as the temptation to talk about Lloyd overtook her reluctance to share any confidences with this woman.

Mrs Unwin said, 'My son admires you so much. He wants to help you to get Lottie away from the asylum.'

Bella's expression changed. 'Could he?'

'I know I'm speaking out of turn but I do want to help you.' She frowned. 'He says that she didn't sign herself in as a voluntary patient. He's seen the documentation. It's signed by your husband. Since he is not legally responsible for her, you could bring her out of the asylum on a technicality.'

Bella was staring at her in delight. 'Then I can go right now and collect her?'

'You would need Douglas to go with you and I'm sure he would never do that as things stand. He thinks that your cousin is safer in there for the time being. Out of harm's way, if you take my meaning. Douglas thinks that your husband will kill her.'

'Oh no, that's nonsense! I won't listen to this!'

'He thinks the same about you. He's desperately worried, Mrs Massie. It's eating into him. You see, he was trying so hard to save

Dora Hubbard and he failed.'

Bella's excitement had faded. 'It was suicide. She drank all the medicine at once. Lloyd had warned her never to do that.'

'Do you know what Dr Bannerman thinks? He's the doctor treating Lottie. He thinks Lottie is telling the truth about your husband. He thinks he led her into the streets that night in the hope that something would happen to her. He, too, believes that she should never have been admitted to the asylum...' She leaned forward and rested a hand gently on Bella's knee. 'But if Lottie stays there long enough she'll get worse and then they'll never let her out.'

Bella groaned and covered her face with her hands. 'This is so terrible,' she whispered. 'You can't imagine what I'm going through. Who should I believe? What should I do? I'm desperately confused.'

'You need your mother at a time like this, dear.'

'Ma's dead.'

'You poor soul! I do wish you'd let me help you. Even if all we do is talk ... Or I could come with you to the asylum. We could ask to see your cousin and talk with her. Just to reassure her that she hasn't been forgotten.'

'Forgotten?' Startled, Bella uncovered her face. 'How could I forget her? I miss her so much. We grew up together. But if she is settling down in there, would it be fair to remind her of home? I swear I don't know what to do for the best.'

'I don't think she is settling down. Douglas is keeping an eye on her for you and he says she's not eating.'

'What? Oh Lord!'

Mrs Unwin pushed herself up from the chair. 'I daren't stay too long in case your husband finds me here. Or my son! They'd most likely both be furious but for different reasons.'

In a daze, Bella led her to the door, but before she opened it Mrs Unwin said, 'I want you to be very careful, Mrs Massie. My son will be ... very upset if anything dreadful happens to you. I can see why he thinks so highly of you. You're a very pretty young woman, Mrs Massie, and I'm sure your heart is in the right place. Here, take this.' She opened her purse and took out a folded paper. 'It's our address. If you ever need any help, come to us.'

'But your son? What would he say? He doesn't know you've been here.'

'I shall have to confess sooner or later. We don't hide things from each other for long. I shall choose the right moment.' She turned to go.

'So did *he* say I was pretty?' The words were out before Bella could stop them.

Annie Unwin smiled. 'Not in so many words but he described your hair, which is indeed beautiful, and he spoke of your blue eyes.'

Bella hesitated, flattered and vaguely comforted that in the midst of all her worries someone still appreciated her – even if it was the last person in the world she wanted to impress. She wanted to say something nice to this kindly woman who had taken the trouble to track her down and offer a warning, but a niggling doubt persisted. Suppose this was all the detective's idea – to make use of his mother to weaken her resistance and to fill her mind with doubts and fears. She longed to trust Mrs Unwin but something held her back. Partly she feared that to put any faith in DS Unwin's mother would be a betrayal of her husband.

Mrs Unwin paused on the doorstep. 'I'm glad we met,' she told Bella. 'Maybe at some later date we will meet in different circumstances. Take care of yourself, Mrs Massie. My son fears for your safety.' She took a few steps and then turned back. 'Will you tell your husband I called on you?'

Bella's chin jutted out. 'Probably. Sooner or later. We don't hide things from each other for long.'

Mrs Unwin chuckled at the neat way Bella had turned the words against her. 'You deserve to live!' she said. 'I do hope you do!' And then she left Bella in a turmoil of indecision.

★ ★ ★

That afternoon Bella decided to abandon her cold treatment of Sadie because she desperately needed to confide in her. The visit from Mrs Unwin had left her wavering faith in Lloyd badly dented and she had to share her fears with someone she could trust. Her aunt was *family* and that counted for something.

The rain had stopped and Bella set off for Thrawl Street through the muddy streets; a strong breeze blew dead leaves around. With her head down and her thoughts elsewhere, Bella failed to watch where she was going and collided with a man who was pushing a hand-cart. The collision, although not violent, made her stumble and she lost her balance and fell. Her shrill cry of alarm mingled with the costermonger's oaths.

'Look where you're going, you stupid cow!' he shouted.

Bella gave him a baleful look. 'Don't help me up, whatever you do!' she snapped, as she struggled to her feet. 'Because the shock would be too much! You don't look like any kind of gent to me!' She examined her knees and hands and brushed down her skirt. 'Anyway, you shouldn't be pushing that load of tat along the pavement. You should be on the road.'

'And you should be getting your eyes looked at. Blind as a bat, that's what you are.' He

244

made a pretence of examining his load of shabby furniture. 'Luckily for you nothing's broke,' he muttered.

'And lucky for you I'm still in one piece! I might have been bleeding on the pavement and waiting for an ambulance.'

A woman pushing a pram full of very young children yelled, 'You tell 'im, Missus! Ruddy costers and their ruddy carts!'

The man held up two fingers in a rude gesture to both of them. Bella tossed her head and marched on. The small fracas had momentarily distracted her from her various cares and woes but she now returned to her main worry with renewed concentration. Annie Unwin seemed nice enough but she came from the enemy camp. Sadie could be a downright pain but at least, when push came to shove, she was on Bella's side. The truth was that Bella had forgotten what their quarrel had been about and hoped that over the past days Sadie had done the same.

She wanted to talk with her aunt about Lottie, but that meant she would have to mention Mrs Unwin's visit and her advice that they should leave Lottie in the asylum for the time being. She wanted to ask Sadie what she thought about Mrs Unwin's offer to try and help Bella get in to the asylum to see Lottie and reassure her that it was a temporary stay. It worried her enormously that Lottie was refusing to eat. Suppose they neglected her to such an extent that she wasted away and died! Bella would feel responsible and the guilt would never leave her. She might even admit that the detective thought Lloyd might kill Lottie if she came out of the asylum although she knew how Sadie would gloat. It would be humiliating, but Bella was determined to do what was best for Lottie.

Were her own feelings toward her husband changing? she wondered nervously. She seemed to be the only person who believed in him and she was finding it increasingly difficult to go on trusting him. Mrs Unwin had said that her son believed Bella might also be in danger. Was it possible? She pushed the thought away.

'For better, for worse!' she whispered but the words did nothing to resolve her confusion.

Perhaps Sadie would go with her to the asylum instead of Mrs Unwin. Bella pursed her lips doubtfully. Sadie could be very forceful – but she could also be very rude and over-bearing and sometimes downright outrageous. She might even turn the staff at the asylum against them.

'We must talk directly with Dr Bannerman,' Bella muttered as she hurried around the last corner. Perhaps as a gesture of goodwill she would do a bit of a 'tidy-up'. Sadie always appreciated a bit of housework since she so rarely did any herself. Half an hour would make the place half decent. She would tidy away all the clothes that were lying about, sweep up and wash the pots and pans. She might even persuade Sadie to open the window if they could, and let in a blast of fresh air.

The landlady opened the front door to her and her face held an expression Bella recognized.

'Your aunt's been on one of her benders!' she announced, the disgust in her voice obvious. 'Three days now since she's set foot outside her room. And don't look at me like that. It's not up to me. I'm not her mother. Just the landlady. But I can tell you this, Bella, if it happens again she'll be out on her ear, so I hope you've got a spare bed. Giving the place a bad name, she is.'

Bella's spirits sank to a new low. She could not think of anything to say except, 'Sorry.' After all her aunt was not her responsibility.

'Don't apologize. It's not your fault.'

So Bella merely shrugged and started up the stairs. Ginger Ted, another long-time lodger, opened his door to see who was coming upstairs and grinned when he saw her.

'Rather you than me, my old duck! Police brought her back. Collapsed blind drunk in the middle of the road, see, and caused a jam.' Laughing at Bella's discomfort, he closed his door.

She stuck out her tongue. 'Stupid fat toad!'

When she reached the top landing she knocked loudly on Sadie's door. 'Sadie! It's me, Bella! Let me in!'

There was no answer and she knocked again. She could imagine her aunt, snoring loudly, spread out on the bed like a beached whale. She decided to let her sleep on while she tidied up. There was still no reply so she rattled the handle and to her surprise the door opened. Sadie hadn't locked it. Of course. How could she lock the door if she was blotto?

She became aware, as she stood in the doorway, that the room smelled worse than usual and she wrinkled her nose. 'God! Sadie, you're your own worst enemy.'

The curtains were half pulled, making the room dim. At the far end Sadie lay exactly as Bella had imagined, stretched out on her back on the bed, still fully dressed. But not snoring. Bella tiptoed over to the bed. 'Sadie! It's me, Bella!' She uttered a brief prayer, asking God not to let the landlady turn Sadie out of the room. Sadie, homeless, would be one burden too many, she thought with growing despair. Seconds later, however, she noticed a few flies that scurried purposefully across her aunt's face —one up into her nose and another across her open eyes.

'Not that! Please not that!' Bella whispered.

Terrified, she watched Sadie's chest, pray-
ing for a rise and fall, no matter how slight.
There was nothing. No movement at all. She
leaned close to Sadie's face and listened for
the slightest sigh. Silence.

'Only my heart thumping,' muttered Bella
brokenly. 'Sadie!' she muttered. 'Oh Sadie!
Don't be dead!'

Overcoming her fear, she reached out and
touched her aunt's out-flung hand. With a
gasp she drew back. Her hand was stone
cold. Ginger Ted's words came back to her.
'Collapsed in the middle of the road...' So
was Sadie already ill or dying when they
brought her back to her room? Why didn't
they call an ambulance and take her to hospital? The sad truth was, she guessed, that
Sadie had outworn everybody's patience.
They had given her up as a lost cause. With
a trembling hand she drew Sadie's eyelids
down over her eyes and, fishing in her
pocket, produced two pennies and placed
one over each eye.

Shocked, Bella sat down on the nearest
chair. She tried to tell herself that Sadie had
gone to a better place. Her body had finally
given up the struggle and had betrayed her.
Was Sadie better off dead? It would help to
believe that she was. Even if she wasn't
better off, there was nothing to be done

about it. At least she hadn't known she was dying and she hadn't killed herself, so she could have a proper funeral with flowers and a few hymns ... and the bell could toll. With an effort she knelt down and kissed Sadie's plump hand.

'Goodbye old thing!' she said as tears rushed into her eyes. She glanced round the room and decided to do the housework anyway before she alerted the landlady.

Having something positive to do helped her through the next half hour but she sobbed as she tidied and cleaned and dusted. The window still resisted all her attempts to open it. Finally she turned her attention to Sadie herself. She arranged her clothes more decorously and found a comb and ran it through her hair. When the room and its owner were presentable Bella made her way slowly down the stairs but, on the way down, the uncomfortable thought came to her that with Sadie's death her last ally had been snatched away.

The landlady tutted with annoyance when Bella passed on the bad news. 'Dead, is she? Well, it doesn't surprise me, the way she was with gin. Couldn't get it down fast enough! She'd throw up, have a drink of water and then straight back to the gin! She may be your aunt, Bella, but she was a gin-sodden wreck for years! Had to happen! Let's hope the Good Lord has a few bottles stashed away somewhere up there else she'll wish she'd gone to Hell!'

Bella felt too unhappy to argue with her. If only they hadn't quarrelled, she thought uneasily. If only she, Bella, had popped round a few days earlier, poor Sadie might well be alive today. I neglected her, she thought miserably. I was just so mad I neglected her. I could have saved her from herself.

An hour later most of the formalities of a death had been completed. The doctor had attended to announce Sadie dead and a form was completed to the effect that she had died of an excess of alcohol. A woman had been brought in to wash the body and lay her out ready for her coffin. Bella had contacted Charles Franks, the undertaker, who had measured Sadie's body and discussed the coffin with her.

'Call in tomorrow,' he suggested, 'and we'll discuss the funeral. You will want a decent interment for your loved one and I can arrange everything to your exact specifications.'

The next day Bella turned up promptly at the Billings Funeral Parlour and was shown to a seat in the office, in front of a large desk. Mr Franks, a small, round man, regarded her mournfully.

'How many carriages would you like?' he asked, opening a ledger and dipping a pen into the ink. 'We have three but can easily call on more. We have reciprocal arrangements with other funeral directors. And mutes? We have two excellent mutes...'

His words fell on deaf ears for Bella had suddenly realized that this was the funeral service that had buried Dora. No wonder Lloyd had suggested them. She swallowed nervously, recalling Mrs Unwin's comments. Two funerals. Who would be the third? She crossed her fingers and became aware that Mr Franks was waiting for an answer.

She said, 'There won't be too many people. It will be a small funeral. My Aunt Sadie was ... She was not wealthy and left no provision for her funeral. At least none that we could find.'

Bella did wonder whether the landlady had searched the room after they all left. Had she found any money? It was most unusual for people *not* to save a little. The landlady *had* said that Sadie owed three weeks' rent...

'Mrs Massie! I don't feel I have your full attention.' He smiled thinly. 'It is quite normal for you to feel shock and grief at such a time but for the sake of the dear departed I must ask you to concentrate. I am asking you about a decorated cart. We do have one, drawn by a small brown pony, which we can decorate with ivy and similar strands. That would be the cheapest we can offer.' He turned over his ledger. 'If you wish the body to lie in waiting in the attic room there will be difficulties in carrying it down the stairs, which are very narrow. Perhaps you have a room in your own house?'

Bella nodded. 'I suppose so.' She was beginning to wish she had allowed Lloyd to arrange the funeral.

'Or you can use our premises. We have a charming room we call the Chapel of Rest.'

'Oh yes! That would be nice.'

He wrote carefully. 'In that case there is the matter of black silk drapes and the black candles. Four is usual. Then you will want flowers...'

Bella looked at him nervously. 'How much is all this going to cost, Mr Franks? I did say there is hardly any money.'

Lloyd had agreed to foot the bill for a very modest funeral on the understanding that among Sadie's few possessions there might be a few objects of some value that they could sell. That way they might recoup some of the costs of the funeral.

Mr Franks smiled again – the same smile that touched only the corners of his mouth. 'Don't worry on that score, Mrs Massie. You can pay over a number of months. Our terms are very reasonable...'

Bella hesitated. The decorated cart sounded quite pretty but that would mean that Sadie's funeral was less elaborate than Dora's and that would never do.

He said, 'Then there's the church choir if you wish it and there will be a headstone, naturally. We can keep that very simple. A few words will suffice. We have a stonemason who works for us on a regular basis...'

With effort, Bella stood up. She passed a hand across her brow. 'I'm afraid this is all too much, Mr Franks. I am feeling quite unwell. I shall have to go home, but I or my husband will call by tomorrow to discuss the final details with you. Good morning, sir.'

Once outside she turned in the direction of home. On the way it came to her that she must not neglect Lottie. She wanted to get her out of that dreadful place before she starved to death, but suppose she really was safer in there...? Bella groaned. She didn't feel she could survive another disaster.

For the first time, when Lloyd came home that evening Bella's welcome was less than enthusiastic. Doubts about him would not go away and doubts about the legality of her marriage persisted. The problem was that to ask Lloyd outright meant telling him that she had talked to DS Unwin's mother and also to the Reverend Stanning and she could imagine how angry he would be. In fact she *was* beginning to feel threatened although she could hardly bear to admit it. How had all this come about – that she might fear her own husband? Mrs Unwin's earnest hopes for her safety had seemed totally genuine, which meant that DS Unwin had made a very convincing argument.

When Lloyd commented on her subdued mood Bella blamed it on Sadie's death.

'I feel so alone,' she said. 'Sadie's gone and Lottie's locked away in the asylum.'

'How can you be alone, you silly girl? You've got me, haven't you? I seem to remember you telling me, not so many months ago, that you would happily live on a desert island if you could be with me.'

Was he looking at her closely or was she just imagining it? Bella forced a smile but said nothing.

He said, 'I can't smell anything cooking.'

'I didn't feel up to it today, dearest. I thought I'd get some faggots and peas from the girl when she comes round. You like faggots, I know.'

He *was* watching her closely. Surely he couldn't suspect anything.

'You do look rather peaky,' he said. 'You haven't been sick at all, have you?'

'No. Just unhappy. Everything is going terribly wrong and I thought we would be so happy.'

'Because if you are sick in the mornings you must tell me immediately. And if you have any other symptoms.' He leaned forward and whispered in her ear.

'A baby? Good heavens, no! At least, I don't think so. The truth is I've lost track of the days and weeks with so many other things to worry about. Would you be pleased, Lloyd?' Would *she* be pleased, she wondered, with something like panic.

He hesitated. 'I'd rather it wasn't so soon ... because I rather hoped we'd be in our new house. Would you like to come house-hunting tomorrow? I've been making a few enquiries today. I was going to choose one and surprise you but it might cheer you up to have a look round. Naturally I have put this house on the market so that we...'

For a moment, almost against her will, Bella felt a distinct flicker of interest at the prospect but it was followed immediately by a resentment that he had put the house on the market without consulting her. 'You didn't ask me...' she began.

He put an arm round her. 'Admit it, Bella! You'll enjoy house-hunting! It will be fun.'

'But ... It was really Lottie's house. We should ask her. Couldn't we wait until she comes home?'

'This house is mine now. You know it is. You're my wife.'

But am I? Bella wondered suddenly. If we're not man and wife because of Dora then he has no business to be selling the house. And with a moment of horrible clarity, Bella saw what might happen. He would buy the next house in *his* name and she and Lottie would live in it under sufferance. If they ever displeased him he would be entitled to throw them out. The idea made her feel faint with anxiety and she was finding it hard to breathe – and even harder to appear calm and collected. Was Lloyd now the owner of Dora's home? What exactly was the situation there? She dare not start asking questions in case Lloyd was not the man she thought he was. Maybe Sadie *had* understood him better than she herself did.

Oh Sadie! Why didn't I listen to you? she thought unhappily. You were trying to help me. So is DS Unwin doing the same thing? Is he really worried about my safety? His mother says he is.

If Lloyd bought the new property in his name only, he would indeed be master in his own house and where would that leave her and Lottie? A faint perspiration broke out on her skin as fear took hold of her. Could she have been wrong about Lloyd after all? She felt sure she should not be rushed into selling No 4, White Street but how could she stop him? The responsibility seemed to press down upon her slim shoulders and she knew she must get some advice. She would go to see Mrs Unwin as soon as possible.

Ten

'You wanted to see me, sir?' Douglas stood to attention in front of the detective inspector.

'Yes. I've been thinking about your case, Unwin.' The DI leaned back in his chair. 'The poisoner. It may be the time to do something about him. It's the twenty-second today and we've heard nothing from our murdering friend Jack since the double killing at the end of last month, and in some ways the case is stalled.'

'Not for want of trying, sir.' Douglas was trying to contain his excitement. What did the man mean exactly? Was he going to allow him official time to pursue Massie?

The inspector continued. 'I dread to think that our man may have fled the country. That he's somehow slipped through the net. Not that we know for sure who he is. He's a ruddy slippery customer.'

'I've heard that rumour, sir, about him leaving the country. Let's hope not.' He bit back a question about Massie. Better to let the guvnor tell him in his own time.

'If it's true, Unwin, that we've lost him, the public will never forget – or forgive. They've seized on the idea that if Jack were killing wealthy respectable women we'd have caught him by now and strung him up. That's what the public wants to see. They want to *see* justice being done. They imagine that we don't care about a few whores.' He sat forward and stared at Douglas. 'We're already the butt of countless jokes. In the eyes of the man in the street the police are only one better than the French in the popularity stakes.' He reached for a pencil and rolled it to and fro.

'Until they need us, sir, and then we're the bee's knees.'

DI Warne smiled wanly. 'They need us? *No*, DS Unwin! They need us to catch the Ripper! But we're not doing it. Too many suspects and never enough evidence.'

'We're pulling out all the stops, sir.'

The older man nodded. He stabbed the pencil into the desk, breaking the point, and with a muttered oath, hurled it across the room. Douglas resisted the urge to pick it up. It would doubtless be the wrong thing to do.

Warne frowned. 'There's a chance the American's our man but he's gone to ground – or gone back to America. There's a lot of interference from above, too. I get the distinct impression that we're not getting the whole picture.'

For a moment Douglas forgot about the poisoner. 'D'you mean someone's being protected? Someone high up? Is that possible?'

DI Warne got up from the desk, picked up the pencil and snapped it in half. Then he tossed it into the waste-paper basket and crossed to the window. He stared out in silence for some minutes.

'Anything's possible, Unwin. Except, it seems, a conviction. It would be nice to get something right sometime soon! The ruddy press is hounding us as usual and people are up in arms. Riggs had an earful yesterday from an old man who claimed to know who Jack the Ripper is – his next-door neighbour, no less! – and the letters keep pouring in.' He rubbed a hand over his eyes. 'Roll on retirement, that's what I say. Still, I'm stuck behind this desk so we have to be seen to do something. Would it be a good time to exhume your chap's father?'

Douglas could hardly believe his ears. 'A very good time, sir. We've lost his first wife and I suspect he's going to go for the second wife any day. There's nothing holding him back except the knowledge that I have a strong suspicion about him. He knows that if his present wife also dies he'll be the prime suspect.'

'Well, we'll see if we can rattle him. Bring him in again for further questioning and let him know about the exhumation. A good fright might loosen his tongue! I'll go ahead with the request for the dig and as soon as it's sanctioned you go and fetch Massie.'

Douglas said, 'Gladly, sir!'

'And wipe that broad grin from your face. It's not part of the image.'

'Sorry, sir!'

Once outside the door Douglas had to restrain his excitement. Thank God, the Ripper had lain low for a few weeks. He could see the DI's argument. If they couldn't catch the Ripper they could catch someone else. A man who poisoned his wife would meet the bill nicely and would make great headlines. And he, DS Unwin, would feature in every article. It might even earn him a promotion. His face fell. The only one who wouldn't be pleased was Bella.

Breakfast next morning was a strained affair. Lloyd seemed preoccupied and Bella was steeling herself to ask some pertinent questions.

She smiled innocently. 'How did the meeting go with that important client? Last week some time, wasn't it?'

He regarded her blankly. 'What important client?'

'You remember, surely? I wanted to come with you to your office because I was so bored and you said you had an important

261

client and you were meeting him at nine o'clock.'

'I don't remember. I have so many clients.'

'I thought him being so important you'd remember.'

'Well you thought wrong.'

He looks shifty, thought Bella. He does remember. She spooned up the last of her porridge. 'When are they going to bury poor Dora?'

'Goodness only knows. It takes ages to arrange because it's a suicide, so it's a crime, and that makes a difference.'

Two lies in as many minutes.

He said, 'I shall take the morning off and we'll go house-hunting. And don't mention Lottie again, Bella. I want to sort out the new house before she comes out again. You know what a scatterbrain she is. She'll waste time and I'm not prepared to put up with her nonsense.'

Bella was mentally forming a plan. 'I'll wash up then while you get ready and we'll be off. You won't buy anything I don't like, will you dearest?'

Looking pleasantly surprised by the meek way his wife had agreed without argument, Lloyd reached out and covered her hand with his own. 'I promise, Bella. We will choose one that we both like.'

Bella stood up and began to gather the bowls and spoons. 'How much money have we got to spend?'

His face broke into a broad grin. 'That's my secret, my love, but it's much more than you might expect. Business has been good lately. All my hard work has paid off.'

More lies, she wondered with growing bitterness. 'Oh Lloyd!' she murmured. 'I'm so proud of you.'

As she turned away to start the washing-up, he gave her bottom a friendly slap and it was all she could do not to flinch. A cold fear was settling within her as the realization grew that Lloyd, who could surely never be a murderer, was at least deceitful and at worst determined to rob her and Lottie of the house which had been left to them.

It was also possible that she and Lloyd were not married and she wondered whether this was good or bad. If they were married, she assumed she could not legally oppose him in any way but if they were not, then they were living a lie ... And if she discovered that she was expecting a child, he would be the father!

Worse, almost, than these possibilities was the fact that she had given her heart to a man who was less than honest – and she still loved him. If he still loved her, she would, she vowed silently, stand by him through thick and thin. But she now wondered if his love for her had also been a pretence on his part.

When it was time to set out on their house-hunting trip, Lloyd produced three sets of keys which he had collected the previous day.

'Three properties,' he told her as they walked swiftly through the streets, arm in arm.

Like any other married couple, Bella thought bitterly.

'Where are we going first?' she asked.

'Mitre Street.' He glanced at her. 'I know what you're going to say!'

'I don't want to live near a murder site! That would be horrible, Lloyd. You don't mean it, do you?'

'I certainly do. The fact is, there are three empty houses in Mitre Street and nobody will buy them. So we get them very cheap and live in one and rent out the other two. That will give us a nice income, Bella. You'll be a landlady.'

'I'm already a landlady. We get rent from the shop below and the couple upstairs. Oh Lloyd, don't make me live where someone was murdered. Please don't!'

Trying to hide his irritation, Lloyd did not answer but tugged Bella along with him.

'There they are,' he said as three gaunt and sooty houses came into view. 'They don't look much now but you can clean them up a bit and we'll furnish them with second-hand stuff.'

Bella stared with disbelief at the houses. Only a corner shop separated them from Mitre Square where Catherine Eddowes had been found dead only weeks before. Before she could protest Lloyd had unlocked the front door of one of them and now held it open for her. 'You might as well look at it while you're here,' he urged. 'We still have others to look at.'

Reluctantly, Bella stepped inside and the door closed behind her. Paint peeled from grimy walls, floorboards creaked beneath her feet and the air smelled of dirt and damp.

She shuddered. 'It's very cold,' she grumbled, eyeing the stairs nervously. They looked rotten in places and Bella hoped she wasn't expected to inspect the upstairs.

Lloyd was explaining the layout. 'A small back yard, parlour and kitchen on the ground floor. Two rooms above and two more in the attic. All three houses are the same so we could choose which one we wanted and let the others out as flats or as single rooms. We'd have to provide...'

She wasn't listening. She had entered the dingy kitchen, which smelled of mice, and was peering through the broken window on to a large yard full of weeds and litter. Thank goodness, she thought. She had something to complain about. She had made up her mind not to like any of them and to ask that they should see some more properties later in the week. Delaying tactics. That was her plan. Bella turned to him. 'I can't live here, Lloyd. Please don't make me. I would be so miserable.'

He bit his lip. 'It has such potential, Bella. Think of the money that landladies, like Sadie's, must be making. When we've got some money together, we can make a fresh start altogether. Just say you'll think about it – for my sake!'

Bella made her lips quiver. 'But I thought we were going to move to a nicer house. A nicer area. That's what you said. I didn't agree to live in a place like this just to make money. You have a good job. Why do we need to earn more? I don't understand.'

His mouth tightened, but then he forced a smile. 'One down, then, and two to go.'

The second house was in Church Street off the Commercial Road – a larger, empty house and in better repair and Bella actually liked it. They explored it separately and Bella discovered a reasonable garden. It seemed that Lloyd had no plans to make money from it and was prepared to consider it.

He said, 'If ever Lottie comes out from the asylum there would be a bedroom for her...'

Startled, Bella looked at him. 'If she comes out? But of course she's going to come out. There's nothing seriously wrong with Lottie. You did say that she was a voluntary patient so why should you think she might not come out?'

'Sorry!' He held up his hands in mock surrender. '*When* Lottie comes out there will be a bedroom for her. Does that suit your ladyship?'

'Much better, thank you, Lloyd. I do quite like this house but ... Come with me a moment.' Taking his hand she led him into a back bedroom on the first floor and drew him over to the window. 'Look at the view! It's creepy, isn't it?' The creepy view was a graveyard that adjoined a church. Bella did find it rather disconcerting but now she pretended to be frightened by it. 'All those tombstones and dead people. It's most likely haunted. I could never sleep at night if I thought about it. And there might be more burials and funerals all the time. I can see why this house is for sale. The owner's probably suffering from an attack of melancholy.' She gave a realistic shudder. 'I do hope I like the third house, Lloyd. Shall we go and look at it?'

For a moment she thought he was going to refuse but, tight-lipped, he led the way out of the house and locked it up without saying a word. Then he tucked her arm through his.

'You're a very difficult person to please,' he told her. 'But I shan't give up. If you don't like the next one I'll find three more.'

She laughed up at him. 'And if I don't like those?'

His smile faded. 'Then I'll make the choice alone. I'm beginning to think you'll never be satisfied.'

Bella's heart skipped a beat. His tone had changed and his mood had shifted. Had he guessed that she was being deliberately critical? Withdrawing her arm from his, she fussed with her hair and re-pinned her hat. Ignoring his cool manner, she chattered on. 'So is the next one empty?'

'No. There's an elderly woman living in it but she's going to move into her daughter's house. She has rheumatics and can't manage the stairs any more.'

His voice was level now. The awkward moment seemed to have passed and Bella drew a sigh of relief. Feeling increasingly unsure of her husband, she was afraid of antagonizing him but she felt disloyal to be treating him this way. No wonder he was getting irritable. Probably most men would, given her prevaricating manner.

The house was in Winthrop Street; the fact that it was currently occupied meant they would see it as a home and not an empty shell. It stood out from the neighbouring houses because the windows and the step were clean. A small brass knocker shone in the middle of the door.

Lloyd said, 'I'm impressed.'

For a moment Bella said nothing. She too, found the house attractive but was determined to appear lukewarm. 'It's not a very nice road, is it? No trees.'

'Trees?' Lloyd scoffed. 'This isn't Hyde Park, Bella. This is a street in Whitechapel!'

Mrs McKinnis, an elderly stooped woman, welcomed them in a broad Scots accent and closed the front door behind them. 'You're the third couple this week,' she informed them. 'So if you like it, you must make up your mind quickly to make me an offer.' She led the way along a dull but clean passage and threw open the door into the parlour. 'This room gets the morning sun,' she told them.

Bella loved the house on sight. It was not particularly large but the furniture had once been good and was well cared for. The smell of some kind of liniment was everywhere.

'You'll be starting a family no doubt,' said Mrs McKinnis. 'There's a wee garden at the back where you could park the bairn in the pram. I brought up four sons and a daughter in this house.'

Bella stroked a tortoiseshell cat that was curled on a chair and smiled when it began to purr. She would have a cat, she decided, and maybe a canary in a cage. 'It seems very comfortable, Mrs McKinnis. You'll be sorry to leave it after all this time.'

She could picture herself and Lloyd sitting either side of the fire, chatting pleasantly together while the youngest children played on the floor with a wooden top or a push-along horse on wheels. She saw Lloyd reaching for the newspaper while she knitted a pair of socks for him. This picture of domestic bliss brought a warm glow to her heart and a smile to her lips.

Lloyd noticed. 'You like it?'

'So far!' With all her heart she wished that her marriage to Lloyd could continue in the way she had expected. The first few carefree days of her marriage seemed an age away, overtaken by the recent problems. She glanced at Lloyd who, as handsome as ever, was obviously charming Mrs McKinnis. She wanted to be able to say yes to this house, but did she dare? Instinct warned her to stay cautious. If the detective turned out to be wrong about Lloyd they could come back to Winthrop Street and see if the house was still available. The kitchen looked out on a small garden with a tiny patch of grass and an outside privy.

They followed the old woman's slow progress up the stairs and investigated the three bedrooms and a large box room that was full of years of accumulated objects that were no longer wanted. The children's toys, long since abandoned, brought a rush of tears to Bella's eyes. Was she ever going to enjoy family life or had she fallen in love with a man who had never intended to make her happy?

'I'll be sorry to leave,' the old woman admitted belatedly. 'Aye, I will, but the stairs are too much for my poor old legs and my daughter Kathleen has a room for me on the ground floor. It'll suit me fine, I've no doubt.'

They had just returned to the ground floor when a loud rumbling noise was heard. Lloyd frowned. 'Is that the railway? It sounds very near.'

'Oh, aye. It's a few hundred yards, no more. But you get used to it.'

Bella had been wondering how she could fault the house which in her eyes was so perfect. Now, guiltily, she seized the opportunity. 'It's terribly loud. Isn't it, dearest? Would it bother you, do you think?'

The sound of the train paused at it stopped at the station.

Mrs McKinnis said, 'It's a stopping train – mainly passengers but some freight.' Bella loved the way she rolled her r's. 'Whitechapel Station is quite busy – but as I told you, the noise soon becomes familiar. You won't notice it after the first month.'

Lloyd said, 'What are the neighbours like? Where we live presently they're a nosy lot.'

Annoyed by this indirect slight on her home, Bella retaliated. 'I'd love Lottie to see this house – but she might not like the trains.'

Lloyd gave her a sharp look.

Mrs McKinnis asked, 'Who's Lottie?'

Bella said, 'My cousin. She lives with us.'

At the same time Lloyd said, 'Sadly my wife's cousin is in an asylum and may never see this house.'

The woman's eyes widened. 'An asylum? Och, the poor wee lass!'

Bella forced a smile. 'Well, thank you for showing us around. We'll go home and talk it over.'

Lloyd gave her a warning look. 'There are a few more questions I'd like to ask you, Mrs McKinnis. Perhaps, Bella, you would wait outside. You are obviously eager to be gone.'

'I'll start walking home,' she said.

'You don't know the way!'

'I'll ask someone.'

Minutes later as she stalked furiously along the pavement she heard Lloyd's footsteps hurrying after her and braced herself. She had annoyed him, but it was his fault. He shouldn't have said what he did about the nosy neighbours. They were no worse than the people in Goulston Street where he had chosen to live with his stupid Dora.

'Bella!'

She quickened her steps.

'That was very childish of you, Bella,' he snapped when he finally caught up with her.

'That's a matter of opinion!'

'I can't imagine what Mrs McKinnis thought of your behaviour.' His voice was cold.

'I don't care what she thought and I hated the house. I hated them all!'

'That's a lie! You liked it. I could tell.'

'All those trains rumbling past. I shouldn't like it and neither would Lottie – and...' She stopped abruptly and glared at him. 'What exactly did you mean about Lottie? About her never seeing the house? '

She saw him waver so turned on her heel and walked on without him. He caught up with her again but she refused to speak to him and they reached White Street in an angry silence. To Bella's surprise they found a small reception committee outside the door of No 4. It consisted of DS Unwin and two constables.

'What on earth...?' Bella questioned them. Shocked, her right hand fluttered to her heart and rested there.

Lloyd gasped as the detective stepped forward and the two constables took up positions on either side of him. All Bella's anger faded. 'No!' she stammered.

DS Unwin said, 'Mr Massie, I would like you to accompany me to the police station to answer some questions about the death of your father, whose body is being exhumed as we speak. If you are not willing, you will be formally charged with being implicated in his death and will be arrested.'

Lloyd's face paled and for once he was speechless.

'You can't take him away!' Bella cried. 'When will I see him again?'

Lloyd said, 'This is all a mistake, Bella.' He was recovering. 'I'll be home in no time. Don't worry, dear.' He turned to the detective. 'I shall come with you as you wish. I'm sure the matter can be dealt with very quickly. My father took his own life. I have never understood why you persist in this ridiculous accusation.'

Escorted by the two constables, Lloyd was led away and Bella watched him go. Everything seemed unreal to her. DS Unwin hung back for a moment and Bella turned to him.

'When will you know?' she asked him, referring to the exhumation.

'Twenty-four hours if we're lucky. Try not to worry.'

Bella rolled her eyes. 'How can I *not* worry?'

'Believe me, I'm sorry to have to do this but it's for your own good. I wish I could make you believe that.'

'I wish you could. This is all a nightmare for me.'

He hesitated. 'I thought we might go to the asylum tomorrow morning to try and get your cousin released. Would you like to do that?'

'Oh yes! That would be wonderful.' Her gloom lifted a little at the prospect of seeing Lottie again. 'You are so kind ... but ... Is it safe for Lottie? You said she was safer in there than here with ... with Lloyd.'

'But your husband is with *us* now. What could he do? We shall certainly keep him overnight and possibly the day after. And maybe longer.'

'For exactly how long?'

Lloyd and his escorts were now a hundred yards away and DS Unwin shouted out to the constables to wait for him. To Bella he said, 'It will certainly be a day or two and remember, even if the examination shows nothing conclusive, Lloyd Massie now knows we're watching him. Even if we have to release him temporarily, I don't think he'd dare do anything to either of you. I think you're safe for the time being.' He regarded her anxiously. 'You must prepare yourself for the fact that he might go down for a long time. Years!' As she opened her mouth to protest he added, 'If he has killed two people you wouldn't want to live with him. No sane person would. He wouldn't be the man you thought he was. But I must go. You know where we live if you want to talk to me or to my mother.'

He hurried after his prisoner. Bella stood on the pavement watching Lloyd until he had disappeared round the corner. Would they really discover traces of poison in his father's remains and charge him with murder? She raised a trembling hand to her mouth in shock as something dawned on her – she hadn't even kissed him goodbye.

From the corner of her eye she saw the curtains twitch in the window of the house opposite and at once hurried inside and slammed the door. She remembered Lloyd referring to their neighbours as nosy. Well, perhaps they were. The minutes passed as she stood in the hallway, replaying the day's events. That last house we saw, she thought, unbuttoning her jacket. I did like it. Why couldn't everything be nice the way I imagined it would be?

Whatever doubts she had had previously were now doubled in intensity. Tomorrow was Sadie's funeral – at two o'clock – and she realized she was glad Lloyd would not be there. Maybe Lottie *would* be released and they could go together.

That same afternoon, a corner of Spitalfield's church was roped off, and uniformed constables kept curious onlookers at a discreet distance from the exhumation site. As quick as possible, the soil was removed from the grave and dumped in a heap nearby by a worried gravedigger. Albert Higgins was used to digging graves for dead people but emptying a grave to remove a coffin was new to him and he was not happy about it. A superstitious man, he wondered if the dead man would resent being disturbed in this way and might haunt him by way of punishment. He mumbled prayers as he dug, asking the Almighty to protect him from the wrath of the man inside the coffin.

The detective beside him said nothing, but watched grimly. Albert paused to wipe his brow with his shirtsleeve, and glanced at the policeman.

'This ain't right!' he growled. 'Disturbing the dead. I don't like it and that's a fact! It ain't Christian, if you want my opinion.'

'I don't, thank you. Just get on with it.'

Albert leaned on his spade. 'He'll be rotted away by now.'

'That's our business, not yours.'

'How much am I being paid for this ungodly work? That's what I want to know.' He glared at the detective, hawked and spat.

'I've no idea and I don't care, but if you don't get a move on I'll have you sacked and then you won't get a penny piece.'

Albert sighed heavily and resumed his work, muttering under his breath about the way people grind down the honest poor, but the detective had lost interest in him and moved away to speak to one of his colleagues.

Albert worked on resentfully. 'Like to see you do an honest day's work,' he grumbled at the retreating policeman. 'You can't even catch Jack the bloody Ripper and him doing the women in, left, right and centre, right under your blooming noses.'

When, twenty minutes later, the coffin came into sight, the gravedigger was sent away and the police team began their work. The cheap wooden coffin was carefully lifted out and wrapped in a blanket for its journey to the mortuary. There, various tests would be made on the remains of the body which had been interred less than eighteen months ago and hopefully would surrender the desired information and prove Lloyd's complicity in his father's death.

Douglas followed the coffin all the way to the London Hospital where it was going to be examined. He, too, was a superstitious man and his fingers were crossed. He would ensure that the body was safely delivered and then go round to call on Bella Massie and arrange to take her to the asylum.

Eleven

The following day they were walking up the steps together. At the desk, Douglas asked to see Dr Bannerman and explained that, although he was not a relative of the patient, he was there at Bella's request.

'Dr Bannerman will be with patients until

his break in fifteen minutes,' they were told. 'I'll let him know you are waiting and perhaps he'll agree to see you.'

Bella and Douglas sat side by side but neither spoke. Bella was fiercely hopeful, but equally fiercely fearful that Lottie would not be released. When at last they were directed to Dr Bannerman's office, Bella felt faint with emotion and sank gratefully on to the chair where he indicated she should sit.

'So you feel there was something illegal about the way your cousin was committed to this asylum?' The doctor eyed Bella with interest. 'We were told that Mr Massie was a relative and that it was in his power to supervise her voluntary commitment. She refused to sign so he signed instead.'

Bella leaned forward in her chair. 'At that time my husband – the man I thought was my husband – was doing what he thought best for her. At least, I think he was.'

'You *think*?' He raised his eyebrows.

Bella was trying hard not to betray her husband while trying to secure her cousin's release. She was weighing each word before she spoke. 'I mean, I didn't know he was bringing her to you until it was too late and then ... I had thought I was her legal guardian. I believed that I was responsible for her before I was married, but I *had* been married ... at least I thought so but...' She glanced desperately at Douglas.

He said, 'Mrs Massie now thinks that her marriage to Lloyd Massie was not legal because it appears that Mr Massie was *already* married. Therefore he was in no way responsible for Lottie and we are therefore hoping to take her home.'

The doctor frowned. 'May I ask why you are involved, DS Unwin? Are you a relative or friend of Mrs Massie?'

'Neither, Dr Bannerman, but I'm working on a criminal case which involves the man she believed was her husband. Mrs Massie and I are both of the opinion that Lottie has done nothing wrong and should never have been admitted.'

'Aha!' He raised his eyebrows again. 'Are we now talking about the patient's accusation that she was taken from her bed into the streets in the early hours of the morning? On that matter, I must admit, I am convinced that she is telling the truth.' He watched their expressions before continuing. 'Also about the attack on Mr Massie.' He turned to Bella. 'Your cousin has never wavered from her declarations of innocence and, from what she tells me, I'm inclined to believe her. I was planning to ask you here to discuss the matter. I agree that there would seem to have been a serious miscarriage of justice but, naturally, I was waiting to make a final judgement. It would be improper to release her back into society if she *were* found to be dangerous.'

Bella cried, 'Lottie has never been dangerous! She was fine until my husband arrived and then she seemed to go to pieces...' As soon as the words were out she realized what she was saying and felt enormous guilt. Now she *was* betraying the man she loved; the man she had *once* loved, she corrected herself.

Seeing that both men were staring at her she said, 'She once cut up the curtains!' Poor Lottie. More guilt flooded through her. She should have trusted her cousin instead of Lloyd. Because of her infatuation for Lloyd, she had let Lottie down. She blinked, shocked by her thoughts. *Infatuation?* Her face crumpled despairingly. Had she really thought of her feelings for Lloyd as *infatuation*? What was happening? The familiar confusion flooded back.

Dr Bannerman nodded. 'Lottie insists that Mr Massie suggested she should do it. She claims that he said it would be fun. Which suggests that he behaved maliciously, perhaps in an attempt to get rid of her from the household. Probably he found her intrusive.'

Douglas looked grim. 'Or was trying to enrich himself at her expense. Remove Lottie from the equation and it would be easier for him to take the house from his so-called wife and sell it and put it in his own name.' Bella groaned and covered her face with her hands. 'I'm afraid he is very clever. Very devious.'

Dr Bannerman sighed. 'Don't blame yourself, Mrs Massie. How could you have guessed? He has been very clever.'

Bella looked up slowly. 'How could I have been so stupid?'

The doctor said, 'You are being too hard on yourself, Mrs Massie. It's obvious he was very convincing. What matters is that we have, between us, discovered the truth.'

Douglas nodded. 'So when can Lottie go home?'

The doctor steepled his hands thoughtfully. 'We really have no grounds on which to keep her here. She has certainly shown no signs of hostility. Her only real sign of what we might call defiance has been her refusal to eat and that is worrying us.' He sat back in his chair. 'Being in here is doing her no good at all but she has coped reasonably well. Every day she has repeated her conviction that she is only here until you, Mrs Massie, arrived to collect her.' He paused. 'What I am going to suggest is that she comes home with you today for what we will call "an opportunity to be rehabilitated". In fact, if she shows no worrying symptoms she could then be considered out of the wood, so to speak.'

At last Bella's stricken expression gave way

to a smile. 'That would be wonderful, but this afternoon our aunt is being buried. Would that upset her?'

'Not really. She has to know that her aunt has died. I'm sure if she is with you, she will cope. You will no doubt be able to comfort each other.' He reached for a pad of printed forms and uncapped the inkwell. 'You, Mrs Massie, will have to sign this as Lottie's guardian. She will also have to sign it to say she wishes to leave and return home. It's only a formality, you understand.' He scribbled on the form, filling in various sections, and then Bella signed. They all rose to their feet.

Dr Bannerman smiled. 'Let's go and give her the good news.'

They found Lottie in the day room, standing at the window. When she turned and saw Bella, her eyes lit up. 'I was waiting for you to come, Bella,' she cried and the two young women rushed to hug each other.

Dr Bannerman said, 'You can go home now, Lottie, but first you have to sign this form.'

DS Unwin watched as the signature was added to the form and then he grinned at Lottie, who returned the smile shyly.

The doctor held out his hand and after a moment's hesitation, Lottie shook it.

'I shall miss you, Lottie. You've been a very good girl.'

She beamed at him. 'I am good, aren't I? I really am.'

Outside the asylum, DS Unwin made his excuses and left them to walk home on their own. Lottie slipped her arm through Bella's. 'I like that man, but I don't know who he is.'

'His name is DS Unwin and he's a policeman. A detective sergeant. Don't you remember him?'

Lottie shook her head. As they came into White Street she slowed down and looked nervously at Bella. 'Will Lloyd be there?' she whispered.

'No. He's away at the moment – on business.' Bella could not bring herself to say that he had been arrested. The less said about Lloyd the better.

'His hand was bleeding.'

'Yes, I know, but we have to forget all about that, Lottie.'

'He left me alone in the dark and when I called...'

'It's best if we don't talk about him,' Bella said sharply. They reached No 4 and Bella unlocked the door. 'Let's have a nice cup of tea and some buttered toast,' she suggested.

'We had porridge and it was burnt.'

Bella wondered what other details would come out about Lottie's time in the asylum. She supposed it was natural for her to want to reminisce and resigned herself to hearing about it. At least Lottie seemed untouched by the experience and hadn't been hurt by any of the other patients. Bella vowed to find ways to make up to her cousin for what had happened. 'We'll make some cakes later, shall we, Lottie? You can stir the mixture for me and add the currants.'

Lottie's face glowed. 'Oh yes! The little currant buns. I like those best. I really do!'

Bella, with tears in her eyes, threw her arms around Lottie and held her close. 'And out of all the people in the world, I like you best, Lottie! I really, *really* do!'

At two o'clock the funeral began. In the event, Bella had been forced to choose a plain coffin with cheap handles and the horse that pulled the funeral cart was elderly, but Bella told herself Sadie would have understood. A few friends waited at the church, mainly Sadie's old drinking friends. Stan Welby was there and Jon the barman. The vicar mumbled the mercifully short service. At least there was an organist – a very young man whose legs barely reached the pedals – but he could play, which was something to be welcomed since the standard of singing was lamentably poor. Both Lottie and Bella shed copious tears and Bella asked God to forgive her for neglecting her aunt.

Earlier, Bella had gently explained to her cousin that Sadie had died. To her surprise and relief, Lottie appeared undismayed by the news.

'Mary died in the asylum,' she told Bella in a matter-of-fact way. 'She was a lunatic so John said it didn't matter and nobody cried.'

'Oh dear! What did she die of?'

'Someone pushed her down the stairs and she hit her head and blood came out, but it didn't matter. The nurse said it was quite definitely an accident and we mustn't bother the police because they were so busy looking for Jack the Ripper.'

Startled, Bella blinked. Had she heard her right? 'Are you sure somebody pushed her?'

'Quite sure. I saw John push her but he said it didn't matter. Lunatics don't matter. They really don't.'

Afraid to learn more, Bella had quickly changed the subject.

The service came to an end and they followed Sadie's coffin outside and watched it lowered into the grave. Poor Sadie. What a wretched life she had had. No husband. No children. Probably very little real love. And now, long before her time, she was gone, her passing celebrated by a cheap funeral and few mourners. Bella was determined to find enough money to pay for a nice headstone.

As the vicar recited a final prayer over the grave, Bella's thoughts wandered to the police station where Lloyd was being questioned by DS Unwin about his part in his father's death. And Dora's death. She shuddered. Suppose he *did* come home again. Would she and Lottie be in danger? She must ask DS Unwin. And was she, Bella, now simply unmarried or did she have to go to court or somewhere to prove that their marriage was illegal? She sighed. So many problems. They never seemed to end. With Lottie chattering beside her, Bella walked home in a very sombre mood.

DS Unwin and PC Riggs sat on one side of the table, and Lloyd Massie sat on the other. It was a day after the suspect had been brought in and he had been kept in a cell overnight while the police waited for the report from the pathologist who had dealt with the exhumed body of Massie's father. The police were eager to re-bury the victim's remains as quickly as possible so the examination and subsequent report had been given priority and the findings now lay on the table between them. Douglas was pleased to see that Massie eyed the paperwork with obvious nervousness although the contents of the file had not yet been mentioned.

Douglas knew from the duty officer that Massie had spent a restless night and had awoken this morning in a slightly subdued mood. His suspect was unshaven and his eyes were bleary but he was making an effort to appear calm.

Douglas said, 'You may want to ask for a

solicitor.'

'I don't need one. I've done nothing wrong and you know it.' He leaned forward, clasping his hands – a sign that perhaps he was trembling and wanted to hide the fact.

PC Riggs scowled at him but said nothing. He was there to learn and not to interrupt but to provide the answers Douglas might require during the interrogation. If Douglas needed to leave the room for any reason, PC Riggs would remain with the prisoner.

Douglas leaned back in his chair. 'It's all there,' he remarked. His tone was conversational. 'The results of the examination of the body. Traces of opium. You told us your father was...' He reached for the file, opened it, turned a page and read aloud. '"My father was never in good health but he was never an addict. He did, however, suffer from depression ..."'

'That's right. He must have taken the opium as laudanum but I knew nothing about it.'

'You said something very similar about your wife, Dora.'

Massie shrugged.

'Isn't it a bit of a coincidence?'

'These things happen.'

'But only when there's money involved. Money that comes to you.'

'My father had been indisposed for some time. He kept to his bed. He saw himself as a semi-invalid.'

'So how did a semi-invalid get hold of laudanum?'

After a pause Massie said, 'I bought it for him to keep him quiet. I was tired of being pestered.'

'And how did he take it?'

'With wine.'

'Which you mixed?'

'Yes.'

DC Riggs glanced at Unwin.

'So if he took an overdose, you must have given it to him.'

'Prove it!'

PC Riggs gasped.

'You can't prove it,' Massie went on, with an arrogance that Douglas found infuriating. 'You can't prove anything. You may think what you like. You may dig up whoever you wish, but you have no real proof! Life is full of coincidences. Maybe my father and Dora died the same way but that doesn't mean I killed them.' He smiled thinly. 'You haven't got a leg to stand on, Detective Sergeant Unwin.'

'There's such a thing as circumstantial evidence, Mr Massie. It may interest you to know that the doctor at the asylum believed Lottie's story about the way you abducted her from her home—'

'Then the man's a fool! What kind of doctor believes the ramblings of an idiot?'

'—and abandoned her in the middle of the night in an area where a murderer was on the loose. How can you sleep at night, Massie?'

'I sleep very well.'

'But not last night, I hear.'

'No one could be expected to sleep in that flea-ridden cell.'

'Well, get used to it because we aim to keep you here for a while – until you confess to your crimes.'

'You have nothing to hold me on. I'm not even under arrest.'

'I believe bigamy is a crime, Massie. We know you were legally married to Dora, so you were *not* legally married to Bella. You also falsely assumed the right to commit Lottie to the asylum, claiming to be a relative by marriage...' He noted with satisfaction that the suspect was beginning to sweat a little. So he *was* getting rattled. About time! 'And you pretended to be the owner – by marriage – of Bella's house. A little rash, wasn't it? You've taken a good many risks, Massie. Did you think we wouldn't notice? Or did you think that we were so busy with Jack the Ripper that we'd forget about you?'

A fine sheen of sweat was beginning to show on Massie's forehead.

He continued. 'Maybe you've been just a little too clever, Massie. Fraud. Abduction. Bigamy. Not to mention a couple of murders. Oh yes! I think we can make something stick. Enough to hold you in our cells until the court case. A shame you didn't say goodbye to that pretty wife of yours ... but, of course, she isn't your wife, is she? So she could be called on to testify against you in court. Had you thought of that?'

The two policemen watched their prisoner trying to maintain his air of confidence, but they could see the cracks developing. A small muscle twitched in his jaw and a bead of sweat trickled down from his forehead. For a while he was silent, trying to ignore the triumphant smiles of his persecutors. No doubt, thought Douglas, his mind was working overtime trying to see a way out of the trouble he was in. He resisted the urge to cheer. This was the moment he'd waited for since the old man's death nearly two years ago.

Lloyd Massie wiped a trembling hand across his face. Then, without looking at either of the policemen, he said, 'I see that you are determined to ruin an innocent man. In that case I've changed my mind. I want someone to represent me.'

Douglas nodded to his constable. 'Lock him up again. I'll interview him again tomorrow.'

Bella was awoken early next morning by the sound of footsteps on the stairs from the flat above. The Schwartzes were never normally up that early and she wondered if one of them might be ill and went to find out. To her surprise, Mr Schwartz, looking anxious and distressed, was dragging a teachest down the stairs.

He rested for a moment on the landing and glanced up as Bella appeared at the bedroom door. He said, 'I am sorry if we disturb you, Mrs Massie. The carrier – he comes so early because of he is busy later.'

Bella stared at him. 'What carrier? I don't understand! What's happening?'

He paused in the middle of the stairs. 'But we leave today. Your husband is telling us to go. You, too, will be leaving soon, no?'

'Leaving? Not that I know of! Why are you leaving? Where are you going to live?'

At that moment Mrs Schwartz came down the stairs from their flat carrying a large suitcase. She, too, was grim-faced. Before Bella could speak to her, Lottie rushed out from her bedroom.

'Bella! Bella! There's a cart outside. I want to feed the horse. I want to give the horse a carrot. I really do!'

'Look in the kitchen, Lottie. There may be one.' Confused, Bella felt a moment's panic as she tried to make sense of what was happening. Was her entire world falling apart?

'I don't want you to leave, Mr Schwartz,' she said. 'Stop what you are doing and talk to me.'

He shrugged his thin shoulders. 'It all happen in such a hurry. "Go, go!" your husband tells us and we have so little time. Excuse me, please.' He made his way down to street level and his wife followed with her suitcase.

Bella watched her lodgers in dismay. Mrs Schwartz deposited the suitcase next to the teachest to await the carrier's attention. On her way up again, she said breathlessly, 'You do not know about this? But how is that possible? Do you not know the house is for sale?'

'For sale? Oh God! No!'

There was thunderous knock at the front door and a voice cried, 'Carrier! Look lively!'

Mr Schwartz opened the door which led on to the street. While Bella watched in shocked silence, the carrier made several trips up and down the stairs bringing down the few pieces of furniture the Schwartzes possessed. The bed, it seemed, had been dismantled. A small bundle of sheets and blankets followed.

Bella grabbed Mrs Schwartz by the arm. 'Where are you moving to? You don't have to go. I swear I know nothing of this.'

Lottie pushed past them, triumphantly carrying two carrots for the carrier's horse.

At last Bella managed to get a moment of Mr Schwartz's time.

He said, 'Mr Massie tells us to get out and we go. "What have we done?" I ask but he does not answer. We go to another flat. Just two rooms. It is all we can find. We were happy here. We paid our rent. We are quiet people. It isn't right for this to be happening.' He waved his arms around.

Mrs Schwartz came down stairs with an armful of faded cushions. She ignored Bella, her face set in resentful lines. Bella cursed Lloyd. But a larger worry was forming in her mind. Had the house been sold already?

Bella asked herself exactly what Lloyd had intended to do with her and Lottie? Were they all supposed to be leaving? Presumably he would have told them where they were going eventually, but now he was at the police station and might not be released.

The carrier took the cushions and Mrs Schwartz turned to go back upstairs but Bella caught her hand. 'I'm so terribly sorry,' she insisted. 'On my honour, I knew nothing about this. I never would have agreed. I don't want you to leave.'

'Too late! We go. It is arranged.' She fought back tears.

Struck silent, Bella followed them out into the street. Their pathetically few belongings were packed on the cart. The carrier helped the elderly couple up on to the rear of the cart where they clung to the raised tailboard looking very nervous. He then climbed up on to his seat at the front and, ignoring Lottie who was still feeding the horse, cracked his whip. She jumped back in a fright as the horse clattered forward and the cart rattled away. An uneaten carrot lay on the ground and for a moment both young women stared at it.

Lottie blinked. 'When are they coming back?'

'Never. Lloyd has sent them away. How I *hate* that man!' As she uttered the words, Bella realized with a deep sense of loss that it was true. Finally she had seen him for what he was and had let him go. The man she loved no longer existed. The bitter truth was that Lloyd Massie had made a fool of her. He had betrayed her – and he had broken her heart.

Lottie watched her face with growing apprehension. 'Is it very bad?' she asked, clasping her hands.

Bella nodded.

'Shall we tell Aunt Sadie?'

'She's dead, Lottie. Remember her funeral?'

Lottie's lips trembled. 'I think ... I think I'll go and do my jigsaw puzzle. I'm good at puzzles, aren't I Bella?'

'Yes you are, Lottie. Very good. You're very good at lots of things.' Bella forced a smile and slipped an arm round her cousin's waist. 'We'll have a biscuit and you can work on your puzzle while I decide what to do next.'

Bella was still pondering their next move when there was another knock at the door and she went downstairs to answer it. She rather hoped it would be DS Unwin and fervently hoped it was not Lloyd. Knowing what she did about him and feeling the way she did, she had no idea how she would greet him if, for any reason, he was released. Could she refuse to let him in? What was her legal position, she wondered uneasily.

Outside, a complete stranger waited on the doorstep. A heavy woman in her late thirties, Bella guessed. No smarter or less smart than anyone else in Whitechapel but she had the coarse features which spoke of the East End. She reminded Bella of Sadie.

'Mrs Massie? I'm Mrs Delloway, to see the house.' When Bella didn't answer, she elaborated. 'Your husband's expecting me, but I'm a bit earlier than what I said.'

Bella's stomach churned. More unwelcome news. 'I'm Mrs Massie, but I think there's been a mistake. I don't think the house is for sale. That is, I don't know what my husband told you but...'

'Oh yes it is!' The woman's smile faded. 'Don't muck me about. It *is* for sale. He told me so. He told me the price and the rents you get and when you're moving out. He said he'd get rid of the lodgers 'cos we need an extra bedroom, us being stuck with my

296

father-in-law and him being bedridden.' Bella tried to interrupt but the woman didn't give her the chance. 'My hubby's got a bit of a promotion, see, so we can move. About bloomin' time too, if you ask me, but his guvnor's a tight-fisted bastard. It wasn't 'til George threatened to leave that he come good on his promise and made him fore-man.'

'Mrs Delloway, I'm sorry but ... Well, there's been some trouble which I can't really explain but ... Mr Massie had no right to arrange to sell the house.'

'Why not? It's his house, isn't it? If it ain't then he lied to me.'

She was beginning to look annoyed and Bella sympathized with her. 'I'm sorry but ... the fact is we're not properly married and he doesn't own it.'

At last she had the woman's attention. 'Not properly married? What's that supposed to mean?'

Bella took a deep breath. 'The house is mine – *was* mine – and then we got married, so legally it was his, but now it seems ... Well, he was already married.'

'Already married? What – like bigamy? Jesus O'Riley!' Her tone changed. 'That's a bit of a facer, love. Gordon Bennett!'

'Yes. I've only just found out. So you see, he can't sell the house because it's still mine and I don't want to move. I'm sorry but...'

'You could find somewhere else, couldn't you? I mean, if he's pulled a fast one on me ... I mean, he must have known you wasn't really married.' Her eyes widened. 'Gawd! Suppose we'd give him the cash already? And it wasn't legal.' She shook her head, marvelling at the catastrophe that had narrowly been averted. 'My old man would have come round double quick and ripped his lights out!'

Bella, relieved that Mrs Delloway wasn't going to make more of a fuss, waited for her to go. She said, 'I hope you find another house you like.'

'Seems like I'll 'ave to, don't it? But my old man's gonna be 'opping mad!' After a short hesitation, she seemed to finally accept the situation and, with a sniff, turned and walked away.

Bella watched her until she had turned the corner and then went back indoors, shut the door and made her way upstairs. To Lottie she said, 'I have to see someone, Lottie. You'd best come with me. You can do your puzzle later on.'

Minutes later they set off for Philpot Street and Bella had her fingers crossed. Hopefully, Mrs Unwin would be able to help them.

Mrs Unwin was in and she welcomed them both and they were soon sharing the inevitable, but nonetheless acceptable, pot of tea. Lottie was stroking a thin, and somewhat wary, tabby cat.

'It turned up this morning from nowhere,' Mrs Unwin explained. 'It was lying on the back step and it looked so weary, poor thing. I gave it some milk and a few scraps. I do hate to see a stray cat. We had a funny old mongrel for years. Douglas will tell you. He rescued it from some horrid boys who were teasing it. They tied a tin can to its tail so that every time it moved it was frightened by the noise. I suppose it thought it was being chased by something.' She laughed. 'Douglas adored it. Benny, we called him.' She smiled at Lottie. 'Do you have any pets, dear?'

Lottie shook her head. 'We did once, a long time ago before Ma died. It was a mouse, but it got out one day and ran away. I like pets. I really do.'

'I'm sure you do, dear. Well, you can think of a name for this cat if you like. It's a tom cat. A boy. I've been racking my poor old brain but can't think of anything nice to call it. I'd be glad of some help, Lottie, and that's a fact.'

While Lottie sat with the cat, thinking hard, Bella explained to Mrs Unwin about the lodgers and the fact that the house might have been sold from under them.

'I know that at least one person was coming to look at it,' Bella told her. 'Goodness knows how many more there are. One might be knocking at the door at this very moment.'

'That wretched Mr Massie! What a lot of trouble and grief he's caused you. Poor Mrs Massie.'

Impulsively, Bella said, 'Please call me Bella.'

'Thank you, dear. I will.' She laid a comforting hand on Bella's arm. 'My son will help you sort it out, dear. He's very clever like that. He takes after his father, God bless him.'

Lottie said, 'We could call him Bonzo. That's a nice name.'

Bella smiled. 'I think Bonzo is a dog's name. Have another think, Lottie.'

Mrs Unwin lowered her voice. 'Your poor cousin. I said to my son, "How will she cope in the asylum?" It must have been an ordeal for her.'

Bella considered. 'The truth is, I'm not sure how much she understood about what was happening. Also, Dr Bannerman liked her and was very kind. She speaks about him sometimes. She also speaks more than she used to. What I mean is, she uses different words and longer sentences. I think talking to the doctor must have encouraged her. She doesn't seem any the worse for her stay there.'

'Then we should be very thankful. I was afraid – I said to my son – that there might be unpleasant people locked away there. Violent people. We were both worried about her but Douglas said she was at least safe from your husband. It seemed to be the lesser of two evils.'

'Your son's been very helpful, Mrs Unwin. I didn't want to believe what he said about Lloyd but ... he was right and I was wrong.'

'Well, you won't see him again, my dear, if Douglas has his way. He's determined to protect you. He thinks very highly of you and the way you've behaved. Many young women would have broken under the strain, but he says you've been wonderful.'

Flattered and cheered by this compliment, Bella relaxed. 'I don't know how I shall be in the witness box if I have to answer questions.'

'You leave that worry aside for now, dear. These things take time. By the time Mr Massie is taken to court you will be feeling much more confident.'

Lottie said, 'This cat likes me. He really does. Is Dobbin a nice name for a cat?'

Bella glanced at Mrs Unwin and grinned. 'It's really a name for a horse, Lottie,' she said firmly. 'But keep trying and I'm sure you'll think of a good name.'

She said, 'What about Bobbin? Is that a nice name for a cat?'

Mrs Unwin clapped her hands. 'Bobbin! Now that's a *very* good name. What do you think, Mrs – I mean Bella? Don't you think this cat *looks* like a Bobbin?'

Bella agreed and so it was settled. It was obvious, Bella thought, that Mrs Unwin had taken a shine to Lottie, which made Bella warm to her even more.

An hour passed very pleasantly but at last Mrs Unwin said, 'I have no idea when my son will come home. He might be very late. It depends on what he's working on. I'll pass on your information and no doubt he'll call on you this evening or else tomorrow. It's been so nice meeting you, Lottie, and talking with you both. I shall look forward to seeing you again.'

Bella and Lottie walked home, arm in arm, making a few calls on the way. They bought bread and eggs and jellied eels. It felt as though life was returning to normal and Bella felt a little more hopeful that everything might turn out for the best. She steeled herself not to think about Lloyd but to concentrate on more pressing matters. If anyone else came about the house, she would ask them how they knew the property was on the market and hopefully fend off further enquiries.

Twelve

Annie Unwin had fallen asleep over her knitting when the sound of the front door closing woke her up. She picked up her knitting from the floor where it had fallen and glanced up sleepily as her son rushed in to the room.

He cried, 'That bloo— Sorry, Ma. That wretch has gone. He's on the loose. That fool Riggs! Poor devil!'

'On the loose? Do you mean Mr Massie?' She looked at him anxiously.

Douglas threw himself into a chair without even removing his coat. 'Poor Riggs is in the hospital. Unconscious. Possibly in a coma.'

'Please, dear. Tell me this properly. What has happened?' She busied herself with the kettle as she waited for an explanation.

'I left Riggs alone with him while I spoke to the guvnor about whether to charge him with bigamy while we sort out the murder charge. The one thing I didn't want was to let him out on bail – or let him go for any reason at all. I suppose we were talking for about ten minutes, but when I went back

303

into the interview room there was my constable unconscious on the floor with blood running from his ear and mouth.'

'Oh my goodness! Poor man! Will he recover?'

'I wish I knew. The doctors wouldn't give much in the way of details. They never do. That basta— Oh, sorry, Ma. I'm so furious! I blame myself. I've always thought Riggs was a hopeless case. Never seemed to take things seriously. Always larking about. But I didn't expect Massie to try anything like that. He's never been vicious – not in a physical way, I mean.' He shook his head and sighed. 'I don't know what Massie used on him – maybe just his fists – but there was a huge gash on Riggs's forehead and a couple of his teeth were missing. Must have taken him by surprise because he's no weakling.'

Annie said, 'But what about Bella and Lottie? Are they safe?'

'Yes, Ma! They're safe. I've sent a constable round there to stand outside the house. One I can trust. PC Watts is due for promotion shortly. I've told him to search the flat as soon as he arrives, just to set their minds at ease. Not that I expect Massie to go back there. It would be the first place we'd look and Massie knows that. Whatever he is, he's no fool. He wouldn't dare set foot in the place. But where else would he go? If we've lost him after all I've done to catch him...'

He rubbed his eyes wearily. 'I can't believe we had him and let him go!'

'They were here today – the girls, I mean. Bella and Lottie. She's quite sweet, Lottie. Childlike but very sweet. Not at all how I imagined her to be. Not a bit mad. I don't know why they put her in the asylum. Anyway, she took a shine to the cat...' She pointed to a small box in the corner where Bobbin was sleeping.

Douglas, momentarily diverted, groaned. 'Not another stray, Ma!'

'Oh Douglas. Don't be like that, dear. I couldn't turn the poor thing away. And Lottie did love him so. She's named him Bobbin and...'

'What did they want?'

'It seems that Mr Massie was trying to sell the house they live in. He has turned out their tenants from the flat above and then a woman turned up to view the house. Said she'd arranged it with him. Bella was in a bit of a state but we talked about it and she calmed down. Now, take off your coat and drink your tea. Your tea's...'

Instead he jumped to his feet. 'Never mind my supper, Ma. I'll eat it when I get back. I think I should check with the constable that there's been no sign of Massie. I don't trust the wretch. And while I'm gone don't open the door to anyone who knocks. You hear me? No one!'

Annie shivered. 'You don't think ... I mean, why would he come here? Does he even know where we live?'

'I don't know, but I'm not taking any chances. If anyone comes to the door, open the window upstairs and if you think it's him – or you're at all suspicious – blow the whistle I gave you and the sound of it will be enough.'

'Right, dear. Let me see now ... I *don't* open the door and I look *down* from upstairs and *blow* the whistle?'

'Well done!' He gave her a hasty kiss and was gone. Annie locked the door behind him and slid home the bolt.

The church clock struck nine and Bella thought, *don't say it, Lottie! Please don't say it.*

Lottie said, 'Is he still out there? The policeman?'

Bella counted to ten. 'Go and see for yourself, Lottie! I've told you – he won't go away. DS Unwin told him to stay there and guard us.'

Lottie crossed to the window and looked out on to the street. 'He's still there,' she reported. 'He's got his hands behind his back. Do you think he's hungry?'

'I should hope not! We gave him half the bread and jellied eels! Before we go to bed you can take out a mug of tea.'

'I like him. I really do. Do you like him?'

'Yes I do! Now could we stop talking about him?'

'Can we talk about Bobbin? I like Bobbin. I really...'

Bella fought down her irritation, reminding herself how wonderful it was to have Lottie safely back home. 'Shall we play snakes and ladders?' she asked, her suggestion interrupting her cousin's chain of thought. Bella hated snakes and ladders but she couldn't face the jigsaw. Anything to take her mind off the awful thing Lloyd had done to poor PC Riggs. He was in the hospital and very poorly, according to PC Watts.

'I'll get it!' said Lottie. 'The snakes and ladders. It's in my bedroom.'

When she came back she said, 'Have Mr and Mrs Schwartz come back? I think I heard them.'

'No, Lottie. You imagined it. Sadly they are never coming back. Lloyd sent them away.' Bella sighed. 'It's no good hoping, Lottie. They won't come back because they've moved to another house.' She watched her cousin set up the board and pulled her chair closer to the table.'

'Will we have some new lodgers, Bella? I like lodgers.'

'Yes we will. As soon as this is all over.'

For a few moments they took turns to move their tokens around the board.

Lottie shouted, 'Whoops! I'm going down

the snake! Down, down, down...' She turned to Bella. 'Are you married now, Bella?'

'No. And Lloyd is never going to come back so you must stop worrying about him.'

'But if he did...?'

'Lottie! I don't want to think about him any more. It makes my head ache.'

'You could marry someone else,' Lottie suggested eagerly. 'You could have another party and some more mutton pies and another big cake.'

Bella laughed as she shook the dice. 'Five. Here I go up the ladder. Up, up, up! Now it's your turn.'

'Is the policeman going to search the flat again?'

'No. He searched once and that's enough because how could Lloyd get in? The policeman's standing right outside the front door, and the back door and all the windows are locked.'

'Did he look at all my dolls?'

'I shouldn't think so. Come on, Lottie. Shake the dice!'

The church clock struck the quarter and Lottie said, 'Is he still out there?'

Upstairs, in the empty flat, Lloyd sat on the bare floorboards with his elbows on his knees while he worked on his plan. He had come straight here after his escape from the police station because he had guessed it was the last place they would expect him to be. He had no idea, at that time, what he would do when he reached the house but he thought he could frighten Lottie and Bella into keeping his presence a secret. If he threatened them they would do what they were told. In fact, it hadn't been necessary to do anything so drastic. The house was empty and the upstairs flat offered the perfect hiding place. As long as he kept quiet he would be safe until it grew dark and he could leave. A bit of luck that the Schwartzes had already gone.

He hadn't bargained for the constable outside the front door but he intended to go out the back way so there was no problem. He had been amused by the perfunctory search the constable had made downstairs. One solitary policeman! Presumably the rest were still chasing Jack the Ripper. They were all idiots. That Riggs had been so easy to dupe. Halfway through his second interrogation Unwin had been called out, leaving the constable. Lloyd had simply groaned and fallen to the floor, clutching his stomach as if in agony. The poor fool had rushed to his assistance. When he bent over his prisoner, Lloyd had punched him hard in the face and knocked him backwards. Once the man was on the floor, a few hard kicks to his head had silenced him long enough for Lloyd to stroll out of the station past unconcerned officers who were still trying to catch the Ripper. It had been so easy. He laughed quietly now at the memory...

From his present hiding place Lloyd had heard DS Unwin checking on his escape. 'No sir. No sign of him,' the young sergeant had reported. 'I reckon he's miles away by now.'

How wrong can you be! He smiled. Time had passed slowly, the light had faded and much later he heard Bella and Lottie go to bed. Bella would sleep like a log, he knew, but Lottie might be restless. He would have to time his escape carefully. He would creep down the stairs and out of the back door where he could clearly see that there was no constable waiting for him. If by some stroke of bad luck one of the girls saw him, he would have to deal with her promptly, but that was not part of his plan. He would only silence them if it became necessary. Flight was his main object. Not that he had any soft feelings for either of them. Lottie had been a nuisance and, according to the detective, Bella had betrayed him. She was no longer his wife and would have testified against him in court.

'Rotten little slut!' he muttered bitterly. Women were all the same. Still, he would have gained financially if things had gone to plan. With Lottie in the asylum and Bella dead, he would have been sitting pretty with a large house which he would rent out, three to a room, to the many drabs who nightly trudged the streets looking for desperate men before they went in search of cheap lodgings. Now all that was gone, thanks to DS Unwin's persistence. How good it would feel to close his hands around *that* particular throat!

The clock struck three. Time to go. Carefully he stood up and eased his cramped limbs. No sounds came from below. He moved to the door and opened it slowly. There was a small click as the lock moved, but that was all. Lloyd had considered whether to remove his shoes but had decided against it in case he had to make a run for it. Stopping to put them on again might ruin his chances of escape. Having attacked a policeman meant that, if he were to be caught again, he would get some very rough retaliatory treatment from Riggs's colleagues. He slid through the partly-opened door and began his descent. Suddenly, behind him, the door swung to on its hinges – and creaked. He froze. Had anyone heard it? With his heart thumping, he waited. No sound from Bella but he fancied he heard movements in Lottie's room. Suppose she was on her way to wake Bella? He felt sweat break out all over his body. Nothing for it but to press on down the stairs.

Once on the landing, he hesitated, listening. Still no sound from Bella's room, but suddenly Lottie's door opened and she stood there in her nightdress, staring at him in shock, quickly replaced by terror. For a moment neither of them moved, each startled by the appearance of the other, but then Lottie began to close the door. Without a moment's thought, Lloyd sprang forward and thrust his arm into the gap. He winced with pain but then forced a foot into the gap as well and pushed with all his weight. The door opened. Lottie turned to run. Lloyd lunged forward and grabbed hold of her. He put a hand over her mouth to stifle her protests.

'Don't make a sound,' he whispered, his face close to her ear. 'Unless you want me to strangle you right here and now.' He was gradually forcing her back towards the bed. 'One sound out of you and I'll kill you. You know I will.' He had never been so close to any of his victims before. Poisoning had been a very easy method in which he could keep his distance and need not see or feel anything until the actual death had occurred. This was different, and Lloyd felt a frisson of exhilaration as he looked into Lottie's terrified eyes and felt her trembling. This was power.

She struggled half-heartedly, but she wasn't fighting for her life because she knew she was going to die and fear had all but paralyzed her. He pushed her down on the bed, his hands round her throat. Then, thinking better of it, he changed his mind. Strangulation would leave bruises and he had always believed that killers should leave no incriminating marks that might be used in evidence. What was he going to do with her if he didn't strangle her? He was anxiously aware that he was wasting precious time. If it hadn't been for Lottie he would be on his way by now. Free as a bird. He would disguise himself and go up north. Maybe to Lancashire. He would hide away for a few weeks and then look for another bride. With his good looks it would not take long.

He stared down at Lottie with distaste. Having her committed had been a brainwave. He had never expected her to be released – nor to have given credible evidence against him. He'd been unlucky there, he thought angrily. Dr Bannerman had been too clever. He rolled his eyes, angry with himself now for wasting so much time. He would smother her with the pillow. As soon as he withdrew his hands from her throat she screamed out. A high-pitched, piercing scream: one which would most definitely rouse Bella.

Lottie bit his hand and managed to turn her head. 'Bella!' she screamed.

'Now you're for it!' he muttered furiously. He slapped her hard across the face. She burst into loud sobs but was beginning at last to attempt some resistance. She tried to twist and turn in an effort to free herself.

Lloyd found holding her captive with one hand difficult, but he managed it somehow and began to tug the pillow from beneath her head. Guessing his intention Lottie let out another scream and tried to prevent him from gaining a grip on the pillow.

'No you don't!' he told her, enjoying the look of desperation on her face. 'Say good-bye, Lottie.'

He brought the pillow down on her face and threw his body on top of it. He could now hold her flailing arms, which grew weaker as the seconds passed – and then he heard a familiar voice.

'I'm coming, Lottie!'

She won't help you, Lloyd thought, amused at the idea of Bella struggling to pull him away from his victim. He'd finish Lottie off and then deal with Bella. Before he could do either something very hard and solid hit him on the back of the neck. For a second or two he was too shocked to move, waiting for the pain that would follow the blow. Below him, Lottie's struggles had ceased and he tried to lever himself up. Bella gave a scream of fright as she saw her cousin's weakly flailing hands fall limply by her side.

'You've killed her! You wicked...'

A second blow struck him, this time on the

side of his head and he slumped forward on top of Lottie. All sight and hearing faded into a silent blackness and he knew no more.

'Lottie! *Lottie!* Oh dear God, don't let her be dead. Lottie! Open your eyes. Speak to me.'

Bella dropped the poker. With a huge effort she heaved Lloyd's unwieldy form off the bed and on to the floor. She snatched up the pillow and threw it on top of him. At first Lottie lay there, pale and still, but suddenly she gave a frantic gasp as she drew in a lungful of air. Colour was already rushing back to her face.

'Oh, Lottie. Thank the Lord. I thought he'd killed you.'

Lottie was now red-faced and shaking violently but she continued to gasp and splutter, sucking air into her empty lungs.

'Sit up! Here, let me help you.' Bella supported her cousin, who was easing herself into a sitting position. As soon as she could breathe properly, Lottie looked for her tormentor and saw him lying on the floor beside the bed. She uttered a muffled cry and slid from the opposite side of the bed where Bella joined her. They clung together for a moment and then cautiously moved round the bed to look at Lloyd.

'Is he dead, Bella?'

Bella shook her head. 'I don't know but I don't want to get near him. He might be pretending.' Her heart was pounding with fright. Had she killed him? Had she hit him too hard? Did she hope he was dead? Stricken with doubt and guilt, Bella stared down at him. Lloyd's soft brown hair which she had once stroked so lovingly now flopped over his forehead and the grey eyes she had once admired stared blankly ahead. His face was very pale and she could see no movement. No rise and fall of his chest. The dreadful certainty crystallized within her. She had killed him. He was a murderer, but so was she!

Lottie held tightly to Bella's arm. 'Perhaps he's asleep.'

'His eyes are open.'

'I couldn't breathe, Bella. I didn't like it. I really didn't. I was frightened.'

'So was I – but I was angry too, Lottie. He was trying to kill you. Maybe I hit him too hard.' She put a hand to her head, trying desperately to decide what to do next.

'We must tell that constable,' she said. 'The one outside the front door. He'll get reinforcements.'

Bella took Lottie to the kitchen and left her while she ran downstairs. Pulling open the door, she found the constable half asleep on the doorstep in a pool of moonlight.

She shook him furiously. 'Come at once!' she told him. 'Your escaped prisoner is upstairs. I hit him with a poker because he was trying to smother my cousin.'

Snapping himself awake, the constable blew his whistle for support from his colleagues then dashed up the stairs behind Bella. Lottie, her head in her arms on the kitchen table, sobbed quietly to herself. Ignoring her for the moment, Bella led the way into Lottie's bedroom where Lloyd still lay on the floor where Bella had left him.

The constable glared down at him. 'Serve him damn well right,' he said. 'For what he did to poor old Riggs.'

'I hope ... That is, do you think he's dead?' Bella swallowed hard. 'I wasn't trying to kill him. I was trying to save Lottie.'

The constable knelt beside him and took hold of his wrist, feeling for a pulse. He shrugged. 'I hope he is dead. Prison would be too good for him. Why should we feed him out of our taxes?'

'But he isn't, is he?' Bella stared down at the man she had married just a few months earlier. Somehow she was clinging to the idea that Lloyd was simply stunned and would recover in hospital. 'There's no blood,' she said hopefully. Surely she hadn't killed the man she had loved so dearly. Lying on the floor with one arm thrown out, he reminded her of the way he had looked on her wedding night when she watched him adoringly as he slept. Tears gathered in her eyes.

Seeing them, the constable said hurriedly, 'What about a nice pot of tea, missus? Always a good thing in times of trouble. That's what my ma always says.'

'Will you stay here and watch him?' Bella had a horrible vision of Lloyd recovering and staggering away down the street.

The constable said, 'I shan't take my eyes off him.' His eyes strayed to the weapon Bella had used. 'Is that the poker?'

'Yes.' She regarded him nervously. 'What will happen to me? Am I a – a suspect? Am I a murderer? I mean, if he's dead.'

He shook his head firmly. 'How could you have murdered him? It was self-defence. Clear as a bell. Don't you fret, missus. No one is going to blame you. He was trying to kill your cousin and you were trying to save her. There'll be no argument about that.'

The tea was made and the constable drank his while he sat next to the deathly-still Lloyd. Secretly he believed that Lloyd was dead, but he might be wrong and even if he were right, he didn't want to be the one who broke the news to the 'wife'.

Three minutes later another constable joined them and soon after that a doctor arrived and sent for an ambulance. His verdict was 'Alive but only just'. He added that he didn't give much for the man's chances. Two heavy blows to his head had done considerable damage. The brain was certainly affected and the neck might be broken.

A wheeled cart, one that served as an ambulance, duly drew up at the door as the neighbours woke up to the drama in their street. Half-dressed figures appeared on the doorsteps and in the windows, to watch Lloyd Massie being carried outside, placed on the wooden platform and covered with a blanket. DS Unwin was fetched from his bed to attend and he quickly took charge of the scene. The injured man was quickly wheeled away to the nearest hospital.

Bella watched the proceedings with mixed feelings. She didn't care to think she had killed him with the poker but if he lived he might be hopelessly crippled for the rest of his life, which was not a pleasant prospect. But he did try to kill Lottie, she reminded herself, and he would have killed her, too, if she'd given him half a chance. She wondered who would write to his relatives in Australia and America. They would be shattered to be told that he was either dead or in hospital charged with murder. Poor souls ... Unless, of course, there were no such relatives. Had Lloyd Massie told her the truth about *anything*?

Now that Lloyd was no longer on the run, the constable's watch on the house was cancelled.

'Get off home,' DS Unwin told him, 'but

first thing in the morning I want a full report.'

Bella turned to him. 'Thank you for coming.'

'It was the least I could do,' Douglas answered. 'To think he was already in your house when the search was made. We should have caught him then. My constable should have searched upstairs as well.'

'It wasn't his fault. Who'd have thought Lloyd would have the cheek to head for home. You shouldn't blame the constable. He was told to search our flat and that's what he did. No one thought about the empty rooms overhead.'

Douglas shook his head. 'Too many loopholes. We should have done it better. *I* should have done it better.'

Bella smiled. He looked so downcast that she felt sorry for him. 'Live and learn,' she suggested. 'How's poor Riggs?'

'He's conscious, thank goodness. Came round late in the afternoon and asked for his pipe.' He laid a hand gently on her shoulder. 'Please go back to bed and rest easy. Sleep if you can. I'm going to follow Massie to the hospital. Can't afford any more mistakes. I'll see you tomorrow and will bring you whatever news there is ... and Bella – if I may call you that?' She nodded and he continued. 'You did well tonight. You were very brave, tackling him the way you did. You obviously saved Lottie's life. Don't have any regrets about Massie. If he dies we're well rid of him. Remember, he killed others deliberately. You killed him by mistake and in desperate circumstances.'

When he had gone Bella hugged Lottie, who was still shaken but slowly recovering from her ordeal. Bella saw her into her bedroom and waited until she was in bed. Then she tucked her up.

Lottie said, 'Where's the poker?'

Bella glanced round the room. 'I expect the policeman took it,' she said. 'It's a piece of evidence. I don't need it.'

'But your bedroom will be cold without a fire.'

'It's not that cold yet, Lottie. It's only October. Anyway, I can always buy another one. Now you go to sleep and don't worry about anything. Promise me.'

'I promise.'

'Goodnight, Lottie.'

'Goodnight ... Bella, when we can we go round to see Bobbin again? I really like Bobbin.'

'Maybe we'll go tomorrow. Would you like that?'

'Yes. Goodnight ... and thank you.'

Bella waited outside Lottie's room until she recognized the change in her cousin's breathing and knew she was sleeping. Then she stumbled back to her own bed and fell into an exhausted sleep. It had been a long and terrible day and one she hoped she could soon forget.

The news DS Unwin brought the following day filled Bella with a confusing mix of emotions. Lloyd Massie had died of his injuries and, unless the police could trace any relatives, he would be buried in a simple ceremony, and a cheap wooden cross would be all that marked his grave. Bella decided not to attend the service. Difficult though it may be, she wanted to get Lloyd Massie out of her life and the fewer reminders she had of their illegal marriage the better. She was seriously worried about the possibility of a child and was trying to get up her courage to speak to Mrs Unwin about the problem. If and when they spoke, she would insist that nothing should be repeated to her son.

Days passed and life at No 4, White Street began to return to normal. Bella and Lottie were invited to Sunday dinner with Douglas and his mother on the 6th of November which gave Lottie a chance to spend time with her beloved Bobbin.

While Lottie played with the cat, Bella spoke to Douglas. 'I know you might advise me against this,' she began. 'But the night when Lloyd took Lottie into the streets and left her, Lottie told me she was rescued by a woman called Mae Dunnley. I know she is … is not a respectable person but I'm sure she saved Lottie's life that night by finding her somewhere to sleep. I want to do something for her but I don't know what. If I give her money she may well spend it on drink or have it stolen from her. I wondered whether to let her live in one of the rooms that used to be let to the Schwartzes.' With her fingers crossed, she waited for his answer.

'That is so like you, Bella, if I may say so.' He hesitated, then his face brightened. 'I have an idea. Why not give a certain sum to the landlady where Mae regularly sleeps – I could find that out for you – and give her enough for, say, ten nights' lodgings. Then when Mae is unlucky and doesn't earn anything, she'll be allowed a bed.'

Bella smiled. 'I'll do what you suggest – and thank you.'

Bella was trying hard to begin a new life with Lottie. She found new lodgers for the upstairs flat – Mrs and Miss Mason, an elderly lady and her daughter who worked as a seamstress. She visited Mrs Levington, gave her a shilling and extracted a promise that she would honour their agreement with regard to Mae Dunnley, but could only hope that the woman was honest.

Douglas, his work on the Massie case finished, was once more fully involved with the Ripper investigation, which had seemingly stalled. There were still several conflicting lines of enquiry and there were suspicions that, higher up the chain of command, secrets were being kept for political reasons. On the ninth of November the Whitechapel murderer struck again.

Bella and Lottie were on their way to find a horse-bus to take them into the city to watch the Lord Mayor's Show. Bella felt they deserved 'a treat' after what they had both been through over the past months. Walking part of the way would save money for more exciting purchases.

'We'll buy some dinner from a pieman,' she told Lottie. 'And maybe we'll have ourselves a toffee apple. You'd like that, wouldn't you?'

Lottie nodded eagerly. 'Or we could have sausage and mash. I like sausage and mash. And barley sugar ... and licorice sticks. And jellied eels and...' A slight frown creased her face. 'Do you think Bobbin's all right? Do you think he'll miss me?'

'Mrs Unwin will take care of Bobbin, Lottie,' Bella said firmly. 'You know he will be all right. You can't keep going round to the Unwins.'

'But Aunt Annie said I...'

Bella stopped abruptly. 'Aunt Annie?'

'She said I could call her that. I told her about Aunt Sadie dying and she said she would be my aunt if I wanted. And I do.'

'Well! I'm astonished. That is kind of her.' As she spoke, two young urchins overtook them at speed, nearly knocking Bella over in the process. She shouted, 'Oi! You two! Watch where you're going.'

One of them turned back. 'There's been another murder. We're going to see the body.'

Bella stopped. 'Oh no! I thought he was done with killing. DS Unwin thinks...'

'He said you could call him Douglas. When we went for our dinner on Sunday. He said...'

'Yes, Lottie, I know what he said. It just seems ... a bit strange.'

'Aunt Annie says you're not strangers now. You are friends.'

'Aunt Annie says quite a lot!'

They walked on and as they entered Dorset Street they saw a crowd around the entrance to Miller's Court. She saw at least two reporters with notebooks in their hands and three constables trying to keep the crowd from entering the alley. Bella's first thought was that Mae Dunnley might be the victim but was quickly informed to the contrary. A young woman with two babies in a battered pram greeted them as they drew near.

'He's done for poor old Ginger!' she told them. 'She never done no one any harm but he's ripped her to bits. The man's a beast. He's a wild animal!'

An elderly man, his hands deep in his

pockets, his face unshaven, also turned to the newcomers. 'Poor Mary! She was a pretty little thing.' He caught sight of Bella. 'Hair like yours, Miss. He killed her in her own lodgings. She wasn't even walking the streets. Crikey! How'd that happen?' He jerked his head towards the little court that led off from Dorset Street. 'Number thirteen! That's where she lived. Unlucky number that. Unlucky for Mary Kelly, poor cow.'

Lottie clung to Bella's arm. 'Was she smothered with a pillow?'

'With a pillow? No! Like I said, he done her with the knife like always,' the man said. 'He's a monster. A ruddy fiend. That's what he is. I'd like to get hold of him. I'd give him cutting up defenceless women. I'd cut him up. I'd slit his throat and...'

Bella had heard enough. It was all too close to home and brought back memories she wanted to forget. 'We're off to see the Lord Mayor's Show,' she announced loudly. 'Come on, Lottie. I'm not waiting.' Hearing of the Ripper's cruelties would do Lottie no good. Bella was hoping that Lloyd's attempt to kill her cousin would fade from Lottie's mind but news of this latest atrocity was having the opposite effect.

A baker's cart had stopped and the driver leaned down from his perch behind the horse. 'If you ask me it's Satan's work. He's a satanist, this man.'

The woman with the pram said, 'How d'you figure that, then? You mean Satan's helping him? Satan's telling him what to do?'

The driver shook his head. 'Most likely give him the power. He might even *be* Satan. It'll need a clergyman to get Jack the Ripper. Someone with a cross and a prayer book.'

One of the babies in the pram began to cry and soon they were both howling their eyes out. The mother stuck a dummy into each mouth and said, 'I'm waiting for the policeman to come out. I'm going to give him a piece of my mind! All these months and they can't catch him. Useless, the lot of them.'

A large woman had joined the crowd. The two boys had pushed their way to the front and were now being dragged back again by a burly man who held each one by the ear. As they yelled in protest he told them, 'You hop it! These horrible doings are not for young brats like you to see. Get going before I clobber the pair of you.'

Lottie looked at Bella in dismay. 'Is Douglas useless? Is he?'

'Of course he isn't!' Bella flew to his defence. 'Don't listen to her, Lottie. The police are doing their best. Douglas is working very hard. Now come *on*, Lottie, or I shall go without you and you will have no toffee apples and no pies, neither.'

The large woman said, 'Couldn't catch a

flea in a jam jar, they couldn't. Who's he going to kill next? Could be me or you.'

Bella strode quickly away without a backward glance. As she went she called, 'Goodbye, Lottie!' and a few minutes later she heard Lottie hurrying after her.

'Bella! Wait for me!'

Bella strode on, still incensed by her cousin's question and the large woman's comments. How dare they say such things about Douglas? she thought resentfully. His image rose in her mind and she realized how much she liked what she saw. Smooth fair hair and those clear blue eyes – and such a nice voice. By the time Lottie caught up with her Bella was smiling.

Five minutes later, as they waited for the bus, a man nearby set up his street organ and began to play a jig. While the monkey chattered, Lottie and Bella, with eyes shining and their worries temporarily forgotten, were dancing to the music.

Three months later, Annie Unwin thought she had waited long enough and decided to broach the question directly. She waited until Lottie was in the back yard with Bobbin and her son was at work.

'Bella, dear,' she began. 'I want to ask you something but I don't want you to take offence. It's just that...' The words she had rehearsed slipped from her memory, leaving her floundering.

Bella glanced up from the petticoat she was mending. There was a tear close to the hem where she had caught her heel in it the day before. She often came round with her sewing or some knitting as, she had often explained, she hated to sit idly chatting.

Annie plunged on. Too late now to change her mind, she thought ruefully. 'It's been twelve weeks now since your ... since Lloyd died and it has worried me ... That is, for your sake, dear, if...' She swallowed but her throat was dry with nervousness. She had grown fond of the girl and was afraid of alienating her. 'I wondered if you had noticed anything strange ... or different, about what we might call, women's matters. Monthly matters.' She avoided Bella's face, dreading to see that tell-tale flush in her cheeks. Of course she would know what 'monthly matters' meant.

Bella bit off the thread she was using and stuck the needle into her petticoat. The petticoat was old and had lost its original whiteness and the lace edging was frayed. Bella seemed concerned to keep it as neat as possible. How many petticoats did she have? Annie wondered. Perhaps she could give each young woman a new petticoat as an Easter present. She had an old sheet she could sacrifice and could buy a few yards of lace when the pedlar called again with his tray of laces and ribbons.

Momentarily distracted, Annie returned to her question. 'The point is, dear, that a married woman, which you thought you were, might expect to ... to have a child and I was wondering...'

Bella rethreaded the needle. 'I wondered the self-same thing,' she confessed. 'And I waited for the signs and I didn't want a child by Lloyd but ... Well, I thought if the worst happened I would keep the child because it would be partly mine but ... Well, I couldn't blame the child, could I? I know it would have been a permanent reminder of him but suppose my mother had married a murderer and decided she didn't want me? It would have been so unfair.' She regarded Annie earnestly. 'I wanted to confide in you every single day but then I thought it wasn't fair to make you anxious on my behalf.'

Annie almost held her breath. What did Bella mean? Was she or wasn't she expecting the murderer's child? If she was, what on earth would Douglas do? She knew, without being told, that he was falling in love with Bella. Could she bear to see her son bring up another man's child – if that man had poisoned two people and tried to kill Lottie?

Bella bent over her sewing. 'But there are no signs that anything has changed.'

Annie let out a sigh of relief. Her fondness for the young woman was growing. What a burden for Bella to have borne so quietly all these weeks – and what a brave decision to have taken. Before she could reply, Bella went on. 'And you needn't worry about me and Douglas. I couldn't expect a policeman to marry the ex-wife of a murderer! It wouldn't be suitable.'

'Oh, but my dear! I think you would break his heart if you refused him. You cannot mean that.'

'I think he has more sense. It might spoil his chances of promotion and we wouldn't want that, would we?'

That night, after Bella and Lottie had left, Annie lay in bed and worried herself into a sick headache. It was her own fault, she thought miserably. She should have held her tongue. Bella was a grown woman and didn't need any help from a foolish old woman. Perhaps Bella was right. It might be best if the girl met someone else. Douglas would get over it and he, too, would meet someone else he could love.

'Yes,' she muttered into the darkness. Leave well alone, Annie. Whatever will be, will be.

Wide awake in her own bedroom, Bella tried to make sense of her feelings. She wished now that she hadn't said what she had about herself and Douglas. Suppose Mrs Unwin repeated it all to him? How would he take it?

Would he be offended? And how humiliating if the thought of actually marrying her had never entered his head. She groaned.

She had lain there for hours listening to the church clock sound the hours, quarter by quarter. She had just decided to put a few more coals on her fire when there was a thunderous knock at the street door. For a moment she was overcome by panic, but then she remembered that Lloyd was dead. So who was it? Hurrying to the window she pushed it up, shivering as the cold February air crept in over the sill.

She stared down in astonishment. 'Is that you, Douglas?'

'Are you expecting someone else?'

He sounded irritable and she shut the window and ran downstairs to open the door. Before she could speak he pushed his way in and shut the door behind him. Then he kissed her for the first time and held her close.

'I'm not asking you to marry me, Bella, I'm telling you,' he said. 'I've known from the first time I saw you that we were meant for each other. I was horrified that you were already married, but now you are free. I was terrified that Massie would kill you. I can't risk losing you, Bella.'

Bella tried to interrupt but he laid a finger against her mouth.

'Ma says you don't think you should marry

me but you're wrong, dearest girl. Say that you love me.'

'I do but...'

'Then we shall soon be man and wife and live happily ever after.'

The quiet wedding in August was a happy occasion. The radiant bride and smiling groom walked from the church amid cheers and rice and a flurry of petals. The small reception was held at the Unwins' house where Annie had prepared cold meats and salads, and after the toasts, Bella and Douglas cut the large cherry-cake which Annie had cooked. Lottie enjoyed it but was impatient for the celebration to end. She was longing to move into her new home with Annie and Bobbin. Annie adored her and saw her as the daughter she had always wanted. Bella and Douglas moved in to a house in the same street so that they could stay close as a family.

The Whitechapel murders seemed to have come to an end at last. Mary Kelly had been his last victim and that was nearly a year ago.

One morning, as Bella bit into her toast, she asked Douglas, 'Will he ever be caught?'

He shrugged. 'I doubt it. He may be dead. That's one theory. He may have fled abroad. He certainly seems to have left Whitechapel, thank the Lord. We've had our share of him.' He reached for his wife's hand. 'He cast a shadow over us all for a few months, but he's gone, Bella, and we can see the sun again. We have nothing but good things to look forward to.'

Bella smiled at him. Something very good was already happening, but it was early days and for the moment she was keeping it a secret.